Praise for *February Flowers*

"An exquisitely beautiful book about th~~
girlhood and womanhood, betwee
only too familiar to all women. Fan
—Sandra Cisneros, a

"*February Flowers* is a swift coming o.
writer and a promising new voice, anu ...ci cnaracters come alive in
this wonderful debut novel."
— Porter Shreve, author of *Drives Like a Dream* and
The Obituary Writer

"Characters, plot, and Chinoiserie combine in a debut novel that
shines . . . animated by unforgettable characters, and infused with
emotional honesty, Fan Wu's first novel is moving, sexy, and impossible to put down. Her style is deceptively simple, her prose confident,
clear and precise . . . a brilliant debut."
— *The Bulletin* (Australia)

"A fresh, original work that strikes a fine balance between intimacy
and restraint, and shatters several stereotypes along the way. . . . The
author's control of her subject matter is impressive, capturing perfectly
the claustrophobia and obsessive passion that youthful friendships can
assume, without ever rendering Ming's concerns as self-absorption. . . .
The novel's ultimate appeal, however, lies in the universality of its
themes—the pain and pleasure of growing up, and the discovery of
sex and the accompanying wonder and fear; few will not recall their
own adolescent pangs while reading *February Flowers.*"
— *The Asian Review of Books*

"An original and unforgettable story. Just like the flowers referred to
in the title, Fan Wu's novel is brimming with passion, vitality, and
hope. The girls in this book are the daughters and granddaughters of
The Good Women of China, and are products of the society both modern, expansive, and communistically introvert."
— Xinran, author of *The Good Women of China*

"Fresh and original."

"Gently paced . . . an elegant book."

"Fan Wu's debut novel captures the chasm between both the old and the modern of her motherland."

"A finely wrought first novel . . . deeply compelling."

"Wu has created a story full of emotional honesty that has engaging, complex characters who must negotiate challenging and uncertain situations."

"A winning debut . . . engrossing, beautifully written . . . sophisticated blend of lyricism, humour, sexual titillation and earnest exploration of being and becoming."

"First-time author Fan Wu's elegant pacing and tidy, vivid prose captures China on the cusp of its economic boom, with the characters caught in the social eddies that curl around it. . . . However universal coming of age stories may be, few capture a country's zeitgeist, as Wu's work does."

"Engaging . . . strong and intransigent."

february
FLOWERS

A Novel

Fan Wu

WASHINGTON SQUARE PRESS
New York   London   Toronto   Sydney

Washington Square Press
A Division of Simon & Schuster, Inc.
1230 Avenue of the Americas
New York, NY 10020

First Washington Square Press trade paperback edition August 2007

WASHINGTON SQUARE PRESS and colophon are registered trademarks of Simon & Schuster, Inc.

For information about special discounts for bulk purchases, please contact Simon & Schuster Special Sales at 1-800-456-6798 or business@simonandschuster.com

Designed by Davina Mock-Maniscalco

Manufactured in the United States of America

10   9   8   7   6   5   4   3

Library of Congress Cataloging-in-Publication Data

Wu, Fan, 1973–
    February flowers : a novel / by Fan Wu.—1st Washington Square Press trade pbk. ed.
    p.   cm.
    1. Female friendship—China—Fiction.   2. China—Social life and customs—Fiction.   I. Title.

PR9619.4.W8F43 2007
823'.92—dc22   2007005987

ISBN-13: 978-1-4165-4943-7

This book is dedicated to my parents and Xiang, Ye, Tong, Bo, my four brothers.

山行

杜牧（八〇三—八五二）

远上寒山石径斜，

白云生处有人家。

停车坐爱枫林晚，

霜叶红于二月花。

Far into the cold mountain a stone trail winds aslant,
Where white clouds rise a house appears,
Stopping my carriage, I sit to admire the late maple forest,
The frosted leaves are redder than February flowers.

Du Mu (Tang Dynasty, 803–852)

After my marriage ends I move to a one-bedroom apartment five blocks from the university where I studied twelve years ago. The grayish building, stuccoed, slanting slightly to the right, is a conversion from a single-family house owned by a grocery store proprietor—now the landlord—and has six units. Mine is on the top but the view is blocked by a forest of half-built commercial high-rises. The landlord wants me to sign a one-year lease, but I have agreed only to a six-month term. I know her apartment building, like other shabby two- to three-story buildings in the neighborhood, will be torn down and replaced by another high-rise in less than a year.

I could have lived in the more modern Tianhe District like most of my friends but I like the narrow cobblestone alley in front of the building, where old people gather in the late afternoons under a spreading banyan tree to play mahjong or sing Cantonese opera. Across the alley is another identical apartment block. All its balconies are covered with laundry and flowers such as roses, chrysanthemums, lilies, and hibiscus—Cantonese people like flowers and arrange them well, often in window boxes that decorate the streets and houses, bringing a little gentle beauty to the cityscape. Sometimes a middle-aged woman appears on a balcony, yelling in Cantonese at someone in her family to return for dinner.

I wake up every morning to the sounds of my landlord chopping meat bones in her apartment across from mine. She has lived in Guangzhou from birth. She loves to cook and has taught me how to make salt-baked chicken, beef stew clay pot, and shrimp wonton noodle soup. On warm days she will prepare cold herb tea and save a cup for me. After trying many different cuisines from many different regions, I have acquired a taste for Cantonese food with its mild flavor and freshness.

On weekends I sometimes go to Shamian Island to read on the beach of the Pearl River. There, all the historical Western-style mansions are well maintained, with their white stone walls, wrought-iron banisters on the balconies shaded by banyan trees, and ornate wooden doors. The sight of them makes me think of the history in the nineteenth century when the Qing Dynasty government allowed European and American businesses to set up a trading zone here. High-rises stretch along both sides of the river. The five-star White Swan Hotel is busier than ever—now a hub for foreigners adopting Chinese orphans. I often encounter white parents on the beach, holding a Chinese baby girl they are planning to take home. Once a couple from Sweden approached me and asked if I could suggest a good Chinese name for their newly adopted baby.

After living in Guangzhou for over ten years, I have begun to fall in love with this city, not just for its amiable weather, but also for the relaxation, generosity, and down-to-earth nature of its people, which wasn't how I felt when I first came here as a student. A decade has changed the city, and has also changed me in subtle ways that reflect my age and experience. I drawl involuntarily at the end of a sentence when speaking Mandarin—my mother tongue—as a Cantonese would; I start my Sunday mornings with dim sum and cup after cup of tea at a teahouse; I buy an orange tree for New Year and hang red envelopes on its branches to be blessed with good fortune, in accordance with the old local custom. I realize that I am becoming a citizen of my adopted city, adapting and assimilating.

I am an editor at a reference and textbook publisher. The job pays well but to me it is just a job. I go to work at eight, leave at five and never stay late. After work I often stroll to Tianhe Book City next to my office to check out the latest arrivals in the literature section. Some nights I go to a bar or coffee house with my coworkers or old college friends. We talk about work, fashion, politics, the economy, or other subjects that matter or don't matter to us. Single again, I appreciate their companionship and enjoy spending time with them. But sometimes, when I hear them talking, my mind will stray to completely unrelated thoughts, often too random and brief to be significant—perhaps about a book, a childhood incident, or a unique-looking person I just saw on the street. If I let my mind wander, I always end up thinking of Miao Yan, a college friend of mine. I have not seen her for more than ten years. Though for about eleven months we were extremely close—at least I would like to think so—I now feel I know little about her and her life.

One Saturday morning, my mother calls from my hometown, a city in another province.

3

"So what do you plan to do?" she says, after asking about the weather and the cost of living in Guangzhou.

"I have a good job and a lot of friends."

"You aren't a little girl anymore. You're almost thirty. A woman your age should be settling down by now."

"Ma, I did," I say. "At least I tried."

"You didn't even tell your father and me until after it happened. If you had just told us and listened—"

"You just said I'm not a little girl anymore." I smile. We have had this conversation a score of times. I know she will never understand no matter how often I try to explain it.

Silence on the other end. Then, "A friend of your father's called him yesterday. His son was just relocated from Beijing to Guangzhou. He's thirty-four, also divorced. No children. He's an engineer." My mother clears her throat and her voice becomes soft. "I think you should meet him."

"Don't worry about me."

"I don't understand—"

"I'm fine. I can take care of myself. Tell Baba not to worry. Nowadays, no one cares if you're divorced or not." I sit down on the bed and look at myself in the full-size mirror—sleeveless black turtleneck sweater in the latest fashion, whitish low-cut jeans with yellow seams on the sides, dark brown ponytail which is shining in the sunlight from the window, and two big silver earrings dangling above delicate but well-shaped shoulders. I am startled by how much I look like Miao Yan, except for the ponytail.

"China isn't America," my mother finally says.

"How's Baba?" I ask.

•   •   •

Next day I spend the whole morning cleaning my apartment. Like other big cities, Guangzhou has too many cars and too few trees. If I don't wipe my desk for two days, a thin film of dust accumulates. While organizing my books, I put on the phonograph an old recording of Paganini I bought at an antique store a year ago. I used to play the violin but haven't done so since I graduated from college. Among the books is a collection of poems from university students, a few of mine included. Even after all these years I still remember some of the poems I wrote then. They tend to have a melancholy tone, obviously written by a much younger woman.

The biggest task is tidying my wardrobe. Even if I changed my clothes twice a day for a month, it would still leave a lot unworn. I got into the habit of shopping in my senior year at university, at first purely for job interviews, but over time it became an indulgence, resulting in my overstocked walk-in wardrobe.

The white box is lying in the corner like an ice cube. It contains a black dress with straps made of shiny material, and a flower-patterned silk blouse. They used to belong to Miao Yan but are mine now. I dust the box and put it back.

In the afternoon I visit the university's Alumni Administration Office. I am applying for graduate school in the U.S. and need transcripts for my application. As I wait in the lobby for the documents to be signed and sealed, a woman in her early thirties joins me. She is wearing a crimson pantsuit with a pearl necklace, looking as though she has come straight from an interview. She says she needs her transcripts to get to Canada, where she is emigrating with her husband and five-year-old daughter.

"I've been taking cooking classes," she says, shrugging like a Westerner. "I hear chefs make more money than librarians. Who'd hire me as a librarian in Canada anyway?"

"Did you study library and information science?"

"Yes, from eighty-nine to ninety-three."

"I was a first-year student in ninety-one," I say, thinking about how different the university was back then. Now it is like the center of the city. The buses to downtown run round the clock and every week a seafood restaurant opens nearby. Students ride their bikes while talking on their cell phones.

The woman walks elegantly to a long table, pours water from a glass jug into a small paper cup, and sips it.

When she sits, I ask, "Do you know Miao Yan?" My heart is pounding suddenly.

"Sounds familiar."

"You were classmates."

"Oh, that tall girl! She's from Sichuan, isn't she?"

"No. Yunnan."

"Maybe you're right." She looks at me with curiosity. "How did you know her?"

"Just coincidence. Have you seen her? Do you know where she is?"

"Not really. We were never close. She was always on her own. I doubt she was friends with any of her other classmates."

The administrator calls her name. She stands up, smoothing her jacket and pants. Before going inside she turns abruptly at the door. "Now I remember. She moved to the U.S. a few years ago. I don't know how she did that. Anyway, someone said she met her at a boutique store in San Francisco's Chinatown last year. Believe it or not, she owned the store."

I thank her and wish her good luck with the emigration.

That night I can't sleep. The past fills me with deep emotion. I recall the evening Miao Yan and I first talked. The details return with such vividness that it seems as if I am watching a video of it—the low-hanging moon, the whitish cement ground, Miao Yan's glittering eyes, her fluttering blouse, the way she lit her cigarette and exhaled the smoke. It is all imprinted on my memory and can never be removed.

After allowing these memories to consume me for a time I can't measure accurately, I get up and take the white box from the closet. I put on the black dress in the bathroom—it still fits perfectly. There in the mirror, I stare at myself for the longest time. In the mirror, in my eyes, I see Miao Yan and more and more of myself at seventeen.

⌒

"Noodles. Chef Kang brand. Fifty fen a bag."

One Sunday afternoon a girl knocked on the open door of my room with a broad smile, a white cardboard box between her legs, a thick stack of money in her other hand. A few streaks of sweat anchored her splayed long hair to her rose-colored cheeks.

"Are you from the Student Association?" my roommate Pingping asked, her eyes narrowed with skepticism.

"No, but they sell Chef Kang for sixty fen a bag. You do the arithmetic." The girl flipped her hair behind her back and crossed her arms.

"Who knows if your noodles really are Chef Kang?" Donghua, another roommate of mine, poked her head out of her mosquito net—she had been knitting a sweater on her bed since noon. A week ago, she had bought a few bags of knock-off Kang noodles from a street vendor and had diarrhea for three days.

"I don't carry around this box for nothing. Forget it." The

girl bent over, picked up the box, placed it on her lifted right knee, and pushed it up to her chest. The metal-tipped spikes on the high heels of her black leather shoes glittered in the sunlight.

Before she walked to the next room, I put down the book I was reading and said, "Give me ten bags."

The noodles turned out to be authentic but I found out later that the Student Association sold them for forty fen a bag.

That was how I met Miao Yan for the first time, in the autumn of 1991. I was a sixteen-year-old first-year student at a university in Guangzhou, one of the most prosperous cities in south China. Of course, I didn't know her name then.

I saw her again a month later. That evening I was having dinner with a few classmates in a restaurant on campus and our table was next to hers. Apparently half drunk, she was playing a finger-guessing drinking game with two men who could barely raise their heads from their chests. Two bottles of Wu Liang Ye and a dozen Qing Dao beers stood on the table. She lost badly in the game and as the agreed-upon punishment had to dance. While laughing aloud, she took the bottles, one by one, from the table. She stepped up on her chair and from there onto the wooden table, which shook a little under her weight. In a long-sleeved white dress, her hair pinned into a chignon at the back of her head, she looked like a goddess in the dim light.

"What are you looking at?" She pointed at some men at a corner table. "If you've never seen a woman before, go home and take a look at your mama."

Her words drew loud laughter. She didn't seem to care. She turned to the two men at her table. "I'm going to dance now. Be sure to get an eyeful—next time you won't be so lucky."

8

She started to spin and almost fell trying to execute a swift turn. When the restaurant owner came and attempted to pull her down from the table, she yelled at him, "Don't touch my dress with your dirty paws!" She jumped down herself, twisting her left ankle when her pink high-heeled shoes hit the floor. She took off her shoes, cursing in Cantonese, and stumbled out of the restaurant barefoot with the two men, one of whom threw a crumpled hundred-yuan bill on the floor on his way out.

Another three months passed before I finally learned this girl's name. It was a Saturday night in spring, two months after my seventeenth birthday. We met on the rooftop of West Five, the eight-story all-female dormitory where I lived. The rooftop was an empty expanse of white cement, half the size of a soccer field, with ventilation ducts and large pipes along the walls. It was known among the girls as a filthy place where the janitors went to fix water or heater problems, though it was quite clean. Few girls would visit it because of its emptiness and the possibility of running into rats on the way there.

I had discovered the rooftop by accident not long after I moved into the dorm. On that day, a few of my classmates and I, as delegates of the Literature Department, visited a model room on the eighth floor—the winner of that year's university-wide competition called "Year's Cleanest." When the other students rushed into the bright room that smelled of flower-scented air freshener, I noticed a passage a few meters away at the northern corner. At the time I was looking for a quiet place to play my violin in the evenings so I ventured there after visiting the model room and thus discovered the rooftop.

I often went up there to play my violin—the open space made the sound travel farther and more clearly. I played the violin in the orchestra in middle school and high school, but since coming to university, I played merely to entertain myself. It seemed a good diversion from studying. I played the same études that I had been playing for years, as well as *Butterfly Lovers,* a Chinese violin classic

Somehow, the rooftop reminded me of the attic in my parents' house, which served as a storage space. I liked to go up there when I was a kid, playing with my toys or fantasizing about the fairy tales I had read. At that time my parents still lived on a farm, where they had been sent from Nanchang City for "re-education" during the Cultural Revolution— they were considered intellectuals. By the time I was born, the Cultural Revolution was ending. Later, my parents told me that they had used the attic to store their books that weren't approved by the Party; they were hidden carefully underneath old clothes, blankets, and broken furniture. Since middle school, I had begun to read some of the books, which included Laozi's *Classic of the Way and Virtue,* Ba Jin's trilogy *Family, Spring, Autumn,* and Byron's and Shelley's poems. I couldn't understand these books fully but found them fascinating.

An old wooden ladder led to the attic. Though dark and stuffy, it was my favorite place in the house. When my parents weren't watching I would take a torch and my toys up there and be perfectly happy. I read children's picture books, played with my toys, hummed the Russian songs my mother had taught me. When I was tired I napped beside my toys and books. My parents didn't return to Nanchang until I was eleven. The city had a revolutionary history and a long river called the Gan. I hated Nanchang, especially its gloomy houses, overcrowded streets, and querulous people. Even after

I had lived there for a few years I still dreamed of the farm now and then.

That evening, the third time I saw Miao Yan, I had taken my violin in its black leather case, climbed the stairs to the eighth floor two steps at a time, then raced through a long, narrow hallway that ended at the northern corner of the building. A flight of stairs, almost hidden, led to the roof. The handrail shook and squeaked at my every grip. After eleven steps, which I had counted many times, the stairway turned ninety degrees before continuing upward to a paint-chipped wooden door with a handle so rusted it seemed like it was coated with sand. The door was usually closed. That day, though, it was ajar, like a half-opened envelope.

From the south corner of the roof I could see the student canteen where a party was going on. The canteen was always transformed into a dance hall on weekends, decorated with twinkling lights inside and out. The music was the Carpenters' *Rainy Days and Mondays,* played often for slow dancing. The students liked their melodious and emotional songs. In front of the canteen was a long queue of people waiting to get in, shaped like a big *S,* all the way to the main road. The *S* kept changing form, sometimes lengthening, sometimes shortening, sometimes shifting into a *Z.*

When I began to play *Butterfly Lovers,* the clock on the Bell Tower had just struck eleven. Though I had played it often, each time I felt it more touching and powerful. As soon as my bow hit the strings, the tragic love story of Liang Shanbo and Zhu Yingtai filled me; I could see them turning into butterflies after they died. At the climax, I held my breath and my

11

fingers jumped rapidly between the strings. After I put down my bow, I had to close my eyes for a moment to calm down.

Since my roommates were playing poker in our room, I decided to stay on the roof a little longer. I strolled to the other side and looked down. Facing the dorm was a brick wall and a row of sparsely leafed palm trees; a little farther away stood the white, five-story building of the History Department and a big unpaved area bordered by a few brightly lit dorms for graduate students. Behind those dorms I could vaguely make out the main entrance of the university— grand, solemn, ancient-looking—with the name of the university inscribed on a plaque on top of it.

I didn't see her until I turned back. There she was, sitting in a corner, her knees drawn together tightly. That night a thin layer of clouds, black and dark green, gathered low in the sky. The moonlight shone on her plump face. She seemed to be asleep. Her head was tilted against the wall, her long black hair streaming over her left shoulder and settling on her chest. She wore dark flared pants, hiked to reveal her long, slim calves. Her blouse was near-transparent silk, with palm-sized red flowers set against a black background. When a breeze came, the blouse fluttered on her body and those flowers bobbed up and down like fire on a black sea.

I didn't recognize her right away but as I approached I knew who she was. A few steps away I stopped. I wondered why she was here. A girl like her should have been dancing at the canteen. I had met other visitors on the roof only once before: three girls. When they saw me, they smiled, a surprised look on their faces. They walked around the roof with curiosity but soon got bored and left. I heard one of the girls complaining about the roof being too empty and cold. "There are no benches, no plants or flowers, or any other decoration," she said.

I was going to walk past this girl. I was sure she would have left by the time I had circled the rooftop. But just then she woke up; or somehow I felt she hadn't been sleeping but perhaps had been observing me through her narrowed eyes.

"Bravo," she said, clapping slowly and rhythmically. "What a performance! Do you live in this dorm?"

I nodded, then said, "I've seen you before."

"I'm not surprised. Everybody knows me." She squinted her eyes to get a better look at me, then laughed. "Now I remember you. You bought ten bags of instant noodles from me. My biggest sale that day. I bet they tasted pretty good. It was a good business, but I don't sell them anymore. Too many people did the arithmetic." She didn't look guilty at all.

"Are you here by yourself?" I looked around to see if someone else was hiding in the darkness.

"I was, but I have you here with me now." She winked. "It's boring here, isn't it? It's nice to have someone to talk to."

"This place suits me. I only come here to play my violin."

"I heard your playing. It was pretty good. It's something, you know, knowing how to play a musical instrument. I always admire people who can do that. It must take forever to reach your level. I've never had that kind of patience. By the way, you don't play for money, do you? If you do I can hook you up with some fine bars. I know them all in the city. A good way to pay your tuition. But of course, you wouldn't play classical stuff at a bar. Listen." She obviously detected impatience in my silence and stared at me. "I want to help you because I liked your playing and you bought noodles from me. I usually don't play the role of fairy godmother."

"Thanks, but I get scholarships to pay my tuition," I said. I was pleased with her praise but annoyed by her suggestion of playing in a bar.

"A scholarship girl." She nodded mockingly. She tilted her head back, stroking her chin with her left hand. "Do you mind chatting for a while?" she asked.

It didn't sound like a bad idea, and in any case I wouldn't have been able to read in my noisy room right then. "What do you want to chat about?" I asked.

"Sit down first, would you? You're standing like a soldier. Aren't you tired? My legs would get sore in no time if I was in that position." She moved her body away from the wall, gesturing that I sit in the gap between her and the corner.

I frowned at the smallness of the space and the heap of cigarette butts beside her feet.

"How about now?" She moved a little farther away from the corner and laughed. "What are you afraid of? I won't eat you. You're a girl. I'm a girl, too. I just thought you wouldn't mind keeping me warm. You know, you're wearing jeans and a sweater. I only have—Aachoo!" She couldn't hold her sneeze anymore. "It's goddamn cold."

I was amused by her loud sneeze and cursing, and laughed.

I sat down where she had suggested. Though I was careful when I sat, my left arm still brushed against her. Her body radiated warmth, and a pleasant light perfume that seemed to blend into her own smell. I never used perfume and didn't have a nose for it, but hers suggested a mix of honey and rose petals. Sometimes girls in my class would put on perfume before going dancing but theirs was often too heavy and stifling.

She looked pleased with my obedience. "My mood's always good on weekends. No school, fewer people bothering me. Really, no one should feel sad on weekends."

"Do you come here often?" I asked, trying to find something to talk about.

"Yes, quite a bit. But it's the first time I've come in the evening. It's not a bad place to sunbathe."

"Sunbathe?" I noticed her face was glowing with a healthy tan.

"I sometimes come here to take a nap after lunch. I just put a mat on the ground and sleep on it. Once I scared a janitor. She thought I had sunstroke. She pushed me and even slapped my face, trying to wake me up. You should have seen her expression when I sat up and told her what I was doing. She must have thought I was crazy. It was . . . hmm . . . last summer. How about you? Do you come here often?"

"I only come here to play my violin in the evenings."

She narrowed her eyes. "You're quite a character. Don't you hang out with your girlfriends on weekend nights?"

"I don't have many girlfriends. I like being by myself." I regretted saying this instantly. It seemed silly to reveal so much about myself to a stranger. But at the same time I felt obliged to answer her questions and keep the conversation going. After all, we were the only ones on the roof and we were sitting close to each other.

"Is that so? I don't like girls much, either. They're too nosy, you know? They always want to get into your business. And they're tricky. God knows what's on their minds. I don't like having to figure them out," she said, as if she wasn't a girl herself. She then switched the subject. "Where are you from?"

"Nanchang City."

"Never heard of it." She frowned, lines forming between her eyebrows.

"Really?" Now it was my turn to frown. "But it's the capital of Jiangxi Province."

"Aha, now I know, it's an old revolutionary district. Aren't people there called Jiangxi Lao Biao?" She laughed.

"Don't call me 'Lao Biao.' No one uses that term anymore." I stared at her sternly, not appreciating her joke. She must have known that was how Chairman Mao referred to the people from the countryside during the revolutionary era.

She was still laughing. "Anyway, that's what I know about Jiangxi. I don't remember who told me that. I always remember useless stuff. So what's interesting about Nanchang?"

"There's Teng Wang Pavilion Tower there. It's one of the most famous—" I saw her shaking her head, so I said, "Wang Bo, the Tang Dynasty Poet, wrote about it in his most renowned poem. 'Essence of the earth, precious gift given by the gods, inspired scholars, enchanting—' "

"I don't read poems."

"But we learned that poem in high school."

"Not me," she said with coldness both in her eyes and in her voice. "No one taught me anything." She picked up a cigarette butt and began to tear the paper wrap to pieces.

"Did you grow up in Nanchang?" she asked after a brief silence.

"Not really."

"Where, then?"

"A small farm. My parents were exiled there during the Cultural Revolution."

"A farm?" She raised her eyebrows and sized me up with new interest. "What do your parents do nowadays?"

"They're teachers."

"No wonder."

"No wonder what?"

"Nothing. You look like a good kid. That's all. I bet you

write letters to them every week." She smirked, then asked suddenly, "Why didn't you go to the party?"

"I don't know how to dance. Why didn't you go yourself?"

"Nice try. Guess you don't have a boyfriend." She nodded at me meaningfully, as if saying, "You can't fool me. Admit the fact."

"None of your business!" I said. Her half-joking remark annoyed me more than I expected.

"You've got a bit of a temper, haven't you? Really, I don't care if you have a boyfriend or not. Knowing that doesn't do me any good. Sooner or later you'll have one anyway."

"I don't care."

"I can totally see through girls like you. You always dream about a handsome prince. Well, there aren't many princes in this world, you know. Even if there were, you don't want to trust them. If you ask me, a woman's fatal weakness is to trust a man." She looked straight into my eyes, wearing a serious expression, like a professor lecturing her student.

I was becoming a little tired of this conversation. Her talking about men and women didn't interest me. The night had grown darker and no more music came from the canteen. I stretched my legs and took a deep breath, getting ready to leave. If my roommates were still playing poker I would just read in the hallway. The light there was dim but I could use a torch. I only had a few chapters to go before I finished Faulkner's *The Sound and the Fury*. I had read about it in a journal. When I got it from the library it was covered with dust. In the beginning, I had a hard time following all the flashbacks recounted by one of the main characters, an idiot, but soon I began to like that kind of stream-of-consciousness style, which I hadn't read in Chinese literature.

She seemed to have sensed what was on my mind. "I know

17

you're here to play the violin. Don't you want to know why I'm here?" she said. Without waiting for a reply, she went on, "Well, my boyfriend and I just broke up tonight. I don't know how I ended up here. As I said, I don't normally come here in the evenings." She began to play with a lock of hair hanging over her shoulder, her fingers long and thin. "He dumped me."

"Sorry to hear that," I said after hesitating—she didn't look upset.

She gave me an appreciative smile. "You were the first to say that."

Now it was hard for me to say goodbye to her right away. I decided to stay a little longer to keep her company so I wouldn't appear too unsympathetic.

"Actually it's no big deal. Men are everywhere, like dust." She stopped playing with her hair and patted her arm instead, as if she was dusting the sleeve. "If I want I can meet another guy tomorrow. I can get you a date, too."

She yawned and took a pack of cigarettes from her right pocket. The white box was printed with fancy calligraphy that read "Salem." I didn't smoke but knew this American brand was popular among trendy girls. She popped open the lid of the pack with her thumb, shook out a cigarette, and put it in the corner of her mouth. She had sensual lips, a little dry but fleshy. She lit the cigarette with a transparent lighter. The small flame from the lighter lit up the center of her face and formed a bright circle around her nose and lips. She drew long and deep on the cigarette, then holding it between her fingers, she extracted it before slowly opening her mouth to emit a plume of smoke. As she exhaled, she closed her eyes, dropped her arms to her sides, and extended her legs forward. Her face was filled with satisfaction.

"Why are you staring at me like that? You've never seen a woman smoke? You never smoked?"

"Of course I have."

"Then smoke with me."

"I don't want to smoke tonight." I fanned away the smoke spreading in my direction.

"What are you afraid of, little sister? Your ma and ba aren't around. Let me tell you, smoking isn't bad at all. Countless artists depend on cigarettes for inspiration. So many things in the world are more harmful than smoking."

I didn't like her tone—she seemed to be trying to belittle me.

"Mind your own business. If I said I don't want to smoke, then I don't." I stood up. "I really have to go now."

"Come on, you're not going to leave me like that! I thought we were having a good conversation. Look at you! Just look at you! You can't be more than a second-year student. Preoccupied, pretentious, righteous. You must major in Chinese literature."

"Look at yourself! Cynical, worldly, a chain smoker. You must be in your final year. How's job-hunting? It can't be too much fun."

She burst out laughing, clapping her hands together. "How do you know so much about me? Are we connected in previous lives or what? By the way, my name is Miao Yan. Not the 'Yan' as in 'colorful' or 'swallow,' but the 'Yan' as in 'wild goose.' Twenty-four years old. Perhaps the oldest undergraduate in the university. I started school late, you know? How about you?"

"Chen Ming. Chen as in 'morning' and Ming as in 'bright.' I'm seventeen." Hesitantly, I extended my hand to meet hers.

"Seventeen? What a lovely age! You must have started school really early then." She laughed again. Clear and unrestrained, her laughter pealed out and echoed in the darkness. I could never imagine my laughter as hearty and bright as hers.

Then she leaped to her feet. She was tall, at least five foot nine. "Time to go," she said. "Thanks for the company." She walked away in her high-heeled shoes, keeping a distance of eight inches or so between her moving feet and maintaining a straight line all the way to the door. The sound of her heels clicking on the rooftop cement lingered in the air even after she had disappeared.

When I got back from morning classes the next day, I was surprised to see her waiting for me in the hallway outside my room. Wearing jeans and a white cardigan, hands in the back pockets of her jeans, she looked cheerful.

"I just read your poem in the university paper," she said. "*'Childhood, a dried snail shell, shivers on golden grass.'* I love it! My goodness, you're a poet! Let's have lunch. My treat."

"Hmm . . ." I didn't know what to say.

"Aren't we friends? Didn't we shake hands last night?"

"It's just too early to eat. Can't you wait another half an hour?"

"Please, please, please, I'm hungry!" she exclaimed like a little girl.

I had to give in—there was something in her that I couldn't resist.

"Aren't you going to change? You're wearing the same clothes you wore last night." She crossed her arms over her chest, sizing me up. "Also, you know, jeans this year should be low-cut and flared, and turtleneck sweaters aren't in fashion.

You're a poet and violinist, you know. Artists should be snappy dressers."

"Who cares? We're still students."

"I care. Girls should be pretty. Anyway, let's go eat."

The only road from West Five to the student canteen was sandwiched between two male dorms where the second- and third-years lived. It was half-paved, full of bumps and pot-holes. Around the peak time between twelve and twelve thirty, male students would lean on the windowsills of their dorm rooms to watch passing female students. Whenever they saw a pretty girl or a girl wearing sexy clothes, they would whistle or bang on their desks or stomp their feet. I knew some girls liked being watched and would smile at these males to encourage them. My roommate Pingping was one. She would actually rush back to our dorm to put on makeup be-fore going to the canteen. I, however, hated being watched and believed these male students must be commenting on girls in unflattering terms. I once overheard one of them call a girl "a fat sow."

Whenever I walked that road, I always looked straight ahead and pretended to be deaf to the noise. I wished I could become a superhero and cover the whole distance from the canteen to West Five in one giant stride. Unless I really had to, I would usually not go to the canteen until after one o'clock when there were fewer people on the road and these male students had stopped watching.

But I had no choice today. Miao Yan took my arm and marched me toward the canteen.

"Hello, Yan! How are you?" As soon as we appeared on the road, a shout came from one of the windows on the right, fol-lowed by a roar of laughter from both dorms.

"Do you know these people?" I quickened my steps.

"Of course not. But they know my name." She sounded proud, then pulled my arm. "Slow down! Are we late for a plane flight or something? I can't walk fast in my heels."

"I don't like them."

"Who?"

"Them." I motioned with my chin to one of the dorms.

"They're just immature. All boys like girls."

"It's obnoxious."

"It's hormones. They're not real men yet. Maybe they don't have a girlfriend. That's why they're so interested in girls. I see nothing wrong with it. Don't you like their attention?"

"No."

"Wow, you're arrogant. I've never seen a girl quite like you."

"They act like they're picking meat in a supermarket."

"Hmm, picking meat in a supermarket." She glanced at me. "Now I know why you don't go dancing in the canteen."

"Why?"

"You don't want to be a piece of meat!" She laughed.

"Whatever you say."

"But you don't have to be like that. You can make them the meat instead. When I go dancing, I never wait for them to invite me. If I spot a handsome guy, I just go up to him and ask him to dance with me."

Another shout from one of the dorms, "Hey, my little sister, you walk ahead bravely." It was a line from a popular movie. Other voices followed, with more laughter. "Bravely, bravely."

I frowned and walked faster.

"If you want, I'll tell them to stop." Miao Yan pulled my arm again.

"They won't stop. They do this every day." I snorted.

"They will. At least for a short while," she said. Before I knew what she was going to do, she cupped her hands over her mouth and yelled at the top of her lungs up at the dorm on the right, "Shut up! My friend hates it!"

Suddenly it was dead quiet. No more noise came from either dorm and everybody on the road stopped to look at Miao Yan and me. I felt like jumping into a hole.

"What are you doing?" I murmured. "You nut!"

"You told me to do it," she said, her cheeks ballooning from holding in her laughter. She ran toward the canteen, despite her heels, dragging me with her.

Behind us, a huge burst of laughter exploded like firecrackers.

⌒

The university sat alongside the Pearl River—a big campus, separated from the outside by a high brick wall. The main entrance looked over a long, wide road lined with tall palm trees. Between the trees, flowers blossomed all year round. At the end of the road was one of the university's oldest buildings. It had a multilevel green tile roof, brick walls, and a copper-studded double door. It was now used as an auditorium, where admission and graduation ceremonies were held. These kinds of old buildings could be seen everywhere on campus, some hidden by luxuriant trees. Most of them were office buildings, like the one occupied by the Admissions Bureau behind the Bell Tower. When I first arrived, I brought a campus map with me to check out the historical buildings. It took almost a full day to see all of them.

The heart of the university was a pavilion surrounded by

lawn. A tiled walkway divided the lawn into halves at the pavilion. The lawn extended at least fifty meters on each side of the walkway, connected with a pond on the north side, where weeping willows grew along the gray stone edges. After sunset, if the weather was nice, the lawn would be crowded with students. It was once voted the most beautiful feature on campus. The Central Library and most of the department buildings and classrooms were situated around the lawn. Between the library and the Mathematics Department building stood a long wooden poster board used to display daily newspapers and notices of university events. On normal days readers were scarce but when there was big news or a popular event, a crowd would gather there.

Most of the undergraduates lived in the eastern part of the campus. Tennis courts, basketball courts, and a huge stadium were nearby. Donated by a rich alumna, the stadium included a high-ceilinged gym and a track field. Inside the oval-shaped track was a soccer field, where games were always going on. Around four thirty every weekday afternoon a loudspeaker inside the field would broadcast recorded exercise music for ten minutes, even when it was raining and no one was there.

The shabbiest buildings on campus were the undergraduate dorms. Most of them were white, rectangular, made of cement blocks. On each floor long, external hallways went straight from one end to the other with nothing in between. All the rooms were identical—a square open space with one double door and one window. The door and window trims were brownish and looked like they hadn't been painted in years. In the middle of each floor was an eight-sink washroom and a bathroom with cold water only, so students had to go to the public bathhouse next to the canteen for a hot-water shower. The toilets were the squatting kind and some of the doors were missing. There was nothing interesting about these dorms, let alone romantic. They were said to be styled after Russian steelworkers' accommodations of the fifties. It was probably a joke but I had no desire to investigate further.

West Five was one of these buildings. It didn't become all female until 1989—two years before I came to university. From that time on male students were no longer allowed to enter the dorm and a high brick wall surrounded the whole building. The only entrance was through an iron gate that had a duty room built on one side of it. Two women in their sixties, both called Dama—meaning "old auntie"—took turns managing the duty room and the only phone in the building. The phone was connected to a speaker installed right above the doorframe of each dorm room. If someone asked for one of the girls, the Dama on duty would dial that girl's room number and pass on the message.

Every day before dinner a crowd of guys would wait outside the duty room and keep the Dama busy dialing room numbers and passing on messages. The girls who were called would meet their boyfriends outside the duty room and disappear with them beyond the brick wall. Then, a few minutes before the gate was locked at 11 pm every evening, another crowd would gather. After saying goodbye to their male escorts, the girls would go back to the dorm. The crowd would reach its peak on Friday and Saturday nights, when the queue extended well beyond the iron gate. Some of the guys clutched bunches of flowers, stuffed animals, or gift boxes. Dama's voice would become hoarse and impatient, yelling room numbers and names in a never-ending stream. West Five would be transformed into a huge dressing room, with dolled-up girls swinging down the stairs, the air filled with a heady mix of perfume, lotions, and nail polish.

25

In the beginning I was shocked by the long line at the gate. It wasn't until a few months later that I became indifferent to what was happening around the duty room; its existence actually made me more aware that I was inside a university, not a high school where the only thing students did was study. After all, this crowd had nothing to do with me—I had promised my parents I would focus on my work and wouldn't date until after graduation. Even if I hadn't made the promise, I wouldn't have wanted to date anyway—I simply couldn't imagine dating any of the guys in the line. Never having dated anyone, I saw love as something sacred, almost religious, like a monument. I read about that kind of love in books, like the love between Catherine and Heathcliff in *Wuthering Heights,* which had made me tremble with admiration and awe. Compared with such passionate love, everything I saw around West Five seemed naive and meaningless.

As far as university life was concerned, I was content with my world of books, my violin, and what felt like plenty of freedom compared with the rigid schedule and endless homework of high school.

I shared Room 301 with three roommates—Pingping, Donghua, and Yishu. The room, about eight square meters, was shabbily furnished with two-drawer desks, wooden chairs, and bunk beds. There was no cabinet, bookshelf, or wall mirror, or even a towel rack. The only storage space consisted of six square holes, each about one meter deep and one meter high, in the walls beside the door. We each had our own hole to store our suitcases and other belongings.

On the back of the door was the College Student Brochure, secured by four rusty iron drawing pins. The sentence "College students shoulder the historical mission of building a modern socialist China" was both highlighted and underlined. Next to it was an ink sketch of a girl dozing off at her desk, probably done by one of the room's previous occupants.

Our room was absurdly plain compared with those occupied by other girls in our class, where the walls were covered with posters or magazine pictures of movie stars and singers. One girl had at least twenty pictures of Paul Newman on the wall over her bed. Another girl had placed a life-size cardboard image of Leslie Chuang, a Hong Kong singer, beside her desk. Every few days there would be an argument between supporters of different stars. Stuffed animals were popular, too. It was a little strange to see *The Book of Odes* next to a pink rabbit, or a white bear astride *Hamlet* or *Three Hundred Tang Poems*. Some girls claimed that they couldn't fall asleep without having their favorite animals next to them.

Although our room reminded me of an army barrack, I was excited to be leading a new life at a university. The first thing I did when I arrived was get a tall bookshelf to hold my collections. The room had two sets of bunk beds, one near the window, the other near the door. Through lottery, my roommates and I decided on where to sleep. I slept near the door, above Yishu, who was the only Guangzhou native in our room. She rarely slept at the dorm but went downtown to her parents' house most nights. When she did stay she went to bed early, even before curfew. By the time I got up in the morning she would be sitting at her desk reading, her silk-covered pillow on top of her neatly folded mosquito net and blanket. Occasionally girls from other rooms would visit our room just to take a look at Yishu's bed. Though they made fun of her tidiness—even her shoes were arranged by color and type—

they took a picture of her bed and sent it to their parents, pretending it was theirs. Girls who didn't want to lie to their parents took two pictures: one of their own bed, the other of Donghua's. Any bed would have looked clean compared with Donghua's. We had a saying among the girls: "We're lucky to have Donghua."

Donghua came from a small village in Sichuan Province. She had a dark complexion as a result of working in the open air from a young age. In the beginning she blushed often, even when she spoke to me. I would never have thought a shy girl like her could be so messy if I hadn't lived with her. The corner she occupied was like a garbage dump: tea mug and lunch box on the floor, clothes piled up on her bed, books inside her washing basin. Once I saw three muddy shoes on her desk. Since Donghua never washed her mosquito net, it was becoming grayish. I wouldn't have been surprised if the net had turned black by the time we graduated. Pingping even predicted that it would have "dissolved into dust" by that time.

Then there was her hair. At barely five feet, she had thick, waist-length hair, which she said was a sign of longevity. "My great-grandma's hair reached her thighs and she lived to be over a hundred," she once told me. She used to comb her hair while walking around the room until Pingping and I protested—we had found her hair inside our thermoses!

Every month, the day before the Student Association from our department came to inspect the condition of the dorm rooms, Pingping and I would have to help Donghua hide her stuff in every possible place. We would also light incense to cover the smell of her socks, which she would wear for days without changing. But as soon as the inspectors left she went back to her messiness. "I'll get better, okay?" she would say, sincerely, whenever Pingping and I complained. But often she simply moved things around—they were still in the wrong place. After a while Pingping and I had to give up—we decided that was the price we had to pay to live in a dorm.

Another amazing thing about Donghua was her knitting. She was so skilled that I could barely see her fingers moving. Once I asked her whom she knitted for.

"For my ba, ma, brothers, sisters, uncles, aunts . . ." She smiled shyly. "Too many people."

"They all need sweaters?"

She nodded seriously. "They work year-round and don't have time to knit. Also, it's expensive to buy a sweater. My sisters wear the sweaters I wore in middle school. Though I'm far away from my family, I want to be useful."

She had one older brother and four younger sisters. It was the first time I had met someone around my age with so many siblings. Her parents must have wanted to have more sons. It was a wonder how they had got around the government's birth control policy.

Our room would have been uncomfortably quiet if not for Pingping. Wherever she went, the air seemed to vibrate. If she was talking in our room, you could hear her on the first floor. Her nickname was "Little Pepper." She was from Harbin, a city in the northeastern corner of China, two days by train from Guangzhou. "When I was applying for university, I told my parents I wanted to go to a place where there's no snow, and where there are green vegetables all year long. Now here I am." That was how she introduced herself when we met for the first time. She spoke with her tongue rolled to make the "er" sound—what's called Standard Mandarin—and often corrected Donghua's and my pronunciation. "You pronounce *h* and *f, sh* and *s* the same," she said to me. "As for you"—she turned to Donghua—"you're doomed. Your tongue is like a dead fish."

Pingping liked eating snacks. She had a few cans to hold snacks like melon seeds, roasted peanuts, egg rolls, chocolates, or biscuits. Even after she had gone to bed, she still couldn't help sticking out a hand from inside her mosquito net to reach for one of her cans. Oddly, the more she ate, the thinner she became. By the end of our first semester she reminded me of a malnourished child. At first I suspected that she took medicine to make herself vomit after eating—quite a few girls did that to keep themselves slim. But later I found out she actually wanted to gain weight. "My grandparents and parents are all very thin." She sighed. She didn't change her eating habits even after being bitten on the nose by a rat—she had fallen asleep with half a biscuit hanging out of her mouth.

Yes, there were rats. The second week in West Five I saw a rat the size of a small kitten in the hallway. It didn't leave right away but stared at me for a moment with its teeth exposed, then turned and ran through the gutter. All the dorms had rats and they weren't afraid of people. They disappeared during the breaks and returned as soon as a new semester started. In West Five, rats were frequently seen in the washroom on each floor, where there was an uncovered plastic bucket for food scraps. Though most girls in my class were slim, they wanted to be even thinner. It didn't take a day to fill the bucket on our floor. Donghua would sigh whenever she saw it. "What a waste! I wish the pigs back home could have that food." In the evenings, I often heard screams of "A rat! A rat!" from the washroom. Once in a while the university would send someone to poison or trap rats in West Five, but none of the efforts at wiping them out seemed to make much difference.

Perhaps because Yishu and I preferred to be alone, Pingping and Donghua quickly became best friends and were always seen together, whether they were going to a class or a movie. Sometimes they even waited for each other to go to the bathroom. Though I was mostly in my own world, I observed my fellow students and the things happening in the dorm with curiosity—they made my life more interesting. I was amazed to see how different people were from one another.

When I think of myself at seventeen, I see: short hair to the earlobes with a fringe above the eyebrows, round face with a curved jaw, high forehead, thoughtful eyes often narrowed slightly. My bag was always stuffed full and I sometimes had to hold extra books in my arms. When not in a hurry, I liked to walk and knew exactly how long it would take me to get to certain destinations: eighteen minutes from West Five to the Central Library, seven minutes from the Central Library to the building of the Chinese Language and Literature Department, twenty-two minutes from West Five to Classroom Ten, where I normally had my classes. I walked fast, often looking at the sky or the ground with a preoccupied expression on my face. I wasn't really seeing either of them; I was dreaming about my future. The question of what would become of me was stuck in my head. As much as I took pride in myself for being a university student, I felt anxious about the uncertainties of the future.

I had tried to make friends when I first came to university. I watched a movie or explored the city with classmates every weekend. Most of us had left our parents for the first time to live in a city far from home. Though Guangzhou, the capital of Guangdong Province, was just as polluted and crowded as where we had come from, it was a dazzling metropolis with soaring skyscrapers, air-conditioned buses, and gorgeously decorated department stores that sold brands I had never heard of before. As the richest and most liberal province in China, Guangdong was one of the most desirable places to live for the Chinese. A popular saying was, "East, West, South, North, and the Middle, no matter where you go, the money is in Guangdong." Guangzhou, as its capital, of course, was even more appealing. While businesses usually closed at eight in my hometown, the nightlife here lasted until dawn. Once my classmates and I went to the evening fair on Up and Down Nine Street, downtown, and saw thousands of makeshift stands selling everything from clothes, accessories, and handicrafts to electronics and flowers. Sometimes, if we wanted to be outdoors, we would climb White Cloud Mountain or row a boat at Flowing Flower Lake Park. How thrilled we were by our newly acquired freedom!

My effort at making friends didn't last long though. I quickly realized that I couldn't be close to any of my classmates. Many of them spent their free time playing poker, shopping downtown, or working part-time to make money. Apparently getting into a prestigious college had been their ultimate goal after studying hard for twelve years. From then on, to them it was party time. It was common knowledge that once you got into a university you would have no trouble getting a diploma.

As for those classmates who studied hard, they mainly read what our professors told us to and weren't keen on going beyond that. But I had read most of the prescribed texts before entering university, thanks to my father's book collection, so with time on my hands I could delve into foreign literature that I had been interested in since middle school. I remember being so absorbed in Marquez's *One Hundred Years of Solitude* that I skipped meals. Whenever I discovered a good book, I was excited for days.

As my reading list expanded I began to spend less and less time with my classmates. Since we all came from different provinces and knew nothing about one another's past, it somehow felt fine to be a little aloof. In any case, because I played music and had published a few poems in the university's newspaper, I had earned the reputation of being one of the most intelligent students in the class and that helped justify my aloofness.

⌒2⌒

Whenever I told Miao Yan about the girls in my class, she would reply with a snort. "A bunch of little girls," she would say. By this time, I had learned some basics about her: she lived on the eighth floor and was a third-year library and information science student. Most interestingly, she was a Miao, a minority group mainly from southwestern China.

But she didn't seem interested in discussing her background. "All the people in my town have been assimilated by you Han people," she said, her face blank. "We wear Han clothes, we eat Han food, we go to Han schools, we speak your Mandarin." But she did tell me at some point that her original surname wasn't "Miao"—her father changed it for her when she went to primary school to make her remember her ancestors.

She didn't like to talk about her hometown, either. She was

from Yunnan, a western border province famous for its to-bacco industry and textiles. "I like Guangzhou much better," she said. "And my favorite city is Shenzhen."

"What's Shenzhen like?" I asked. I knew it was the first special economic zone in China and right next to Hong Kong, but had never been there.

"It's like Manhattan in the United States," she said curtly, as if everyone should know what Manhattan was like.

The first month after I met her had passed like a quick sum-mer shower. Every few days she would visit me—we had din-ner together, we went for walks, we had long conversations during which I was usually the listener. She knew all the small paths on campus and often took me to places I had never been. She also seemed to know everything about Guangzhou. Two more disco halls had opened on Beijing Road, an eighty-story skyscraper would be built in Tianhe District, two robberies had just taken place near the train station, a British rock band was going to arrive in a few days—she always knew what was going on.

Once she took me to Qingping Market near Shamian Is-land in the old part of Guangzhou to show me that Cantonese people can eat just about anything. As I frowned at the stands selling dried bear claws, guinea pigs, live turtles, snakes, and ar-madillos, she reached over to pick up a live scorpion with chopsticks and asked the vendor to fry it on the spot. The scorpion struggled wildly when it landed in the boiling wok.

"Yuk!" I turned away from this gross scene.

"That's nothing." She looked smug, gobbling down her cooked scorpion. "I once ate them raw. I drowned them in strong alcohol and ate them. They're nutritious and good for your skin."

"Aren't scorpions poisonous?"

She laughed. "Don't you know I'm more poisonous than scorpions?"

In the beginning, I went out with her merely because I didn't know how to say no. I figured she must have been lonely after breaking up with her boyfriend and needed someone to talk to. As soon as she got over it, she wouldn't come to visit me anymore. But she seemed to like being with me. In fact, ending her relationship with her boyfriend didn't appear to bother her at all.

I soon found myself sitting in my room awaiting her impatiently. I wondered where she would take me this time and was eager to know about all the new things happening in Guangzhou. To my surprise, I felt much happier since I had come to know Miao Yan. I was more talkative in the dorm and would hum songs while eating. Even Pingping noticed this change in me. "Did you receive a love letter or something?" she asked me more than once.

Every time we walked together Miao Yan held my arm tightly, leaning her head against my shoulder. She did this without any pretension and seemed to enjoy the intimacy between us. It was not uncommon for girls to walk hand in hand or even to put their arms around each other's waist to show their friendship, but growing up as an only child I had never been so close to another girl. This intimacy scared me as much as it excited me. The harder I tried to push her away, the closer she stood next to me and the more she mocked my resistance.

"What's there to be afraid of? I won't eat you. You're a girl. I'm a girl, too," she would say.

I remember the first few days she stood close to me, the strong scent of her perfume made my heart pound. Her soft breath never failed to make my legs stiff. The two of us must have made a real contrast—me: stiff, face red, eyes lowered; her: body swinging, smiling brightly, flirtatious. But in less than a month I found myself at ease with the intimacy and it even occurred to me that it was how girls should act in a close friendship: Pingping and Donghua always held hands while walking and girls in my class sometimes shared one bed when they had visitors staying over.

But I never liked her flirting with guys. I could hear myself saying to her: "Don't be such a superficial girl." Sometimes, if a group of guys passed us, she would laugh loudly for no reason and even throw seductive glances at them. She would poke me in the side and laugh even louder when those guys turned their heads to watch us. Once, a young man on a bike collided with a big tree because he couldn't avert his eyes from us. Another time, a bespectacled, baby-faced male student followed us for more than half an hour, insisting on walking with us. He didn't leave until we threatened to report him to the Security Department.

Miao Yan said it was me they were looking at.

"Don't try to fool me," I said.

"Actually you're good-looking," she said, "like a white daisy." As she said this she stopped to look at me, then fumbled out a round mirror from her pants pocket and studied herself in it. "We'd be twins if your face was a little thinner, your eyes a little bigger, and your nose a little higher."

"If we could be twins, then you could be twins with any other girl in the world." I laughed. "You could even say the same thing about a black girl—if your skin is a little fairer, your lips a little thinner, and your hair a little straighter . . ."

She put the mirror back into her pocket and shrugged. "You don't know what you'll be like in the future, but I know what I was like before."

～

One Thursday evening after dinner I sat down at my desk to write to my parents. As a ritual, every Wednesday or Thursday I would receive a letter from them; every Thursday night I would write to them. Their letters were almost formulaic— first they would say they were doing well and tell me of their daily life, then ask about the weather and living expenses in Guangzhou, then my university life and what books and authors I had read. At the end, they would stress the importance of focusing on study. My mother would typically write the first half of the letter and my father the second half. In quite a few letters my father warned me not to be distracted by what he called "unhealthy ideologies among college students," which included smoking, drinking alcohol, and dating.

Their letters bored me. Sometimes, when my father wrote too much "don't do this and that," I would get irritated and want to rebel just for the sake of it. I wasn't a kid and they should have trusted me. I had never disappointed them. Ever since primary school I had been the top student in my class. I even skipped two grades in middle school. Whenever the result of finals came out at the end of a school year, I would bring home an award, a trophy, or some kind of scholarship. "Your daughter will grow up to be a professor, a scholar," every teacher in the school said to them. Though my parents always replied modestly, I knew they were proud of me.

37

Whenever they talked to me, they would only ask about school, nothing else.

Sometimes I had felt that becoming successful was not just about me, it was about fulfilling their own unrealized dreams, especially my father's. My mother once told me that when she met my father he was about to publish two books on ancient Chinese literature. But in the mid sixties, when the Cultural Revolution started, the book deals were quashed and my father was condemned for his "feudalist" research and confined to the farm. For a few years he lived with pigs and ducks. These days, he only wrote student lectures. Once I overheard him telling my mother that he had lost his passion for academic writing.

As for my mother, she was a biologist before she was sent to the farm. After the Cultural Revolution, when my father was offered a teaching job in Nanchang on the condition that my mother also taught in the same school, she gave up her beloved biology and became a math teacher.

As I wrote to them this particular Thursday, Pingping and Donghua were hanging up their laundry on the clothesline outside in the hallway. Donghua's big-legged flowery underpants swayed on the hangers next to Pingping's bikini-shaped underpants.

"Did your ma make those underpants for you?" Pingping asked.

"I made them myself."

"You'd better throw them away before I do it for you."

"I can't wear the small underwear you city people wear. It hurts."

"You just have to get used to it."

"I like mine better than yours. No one sees them anyway."

"Look at that guy! Over there, the one holding a bunch of

pink roses. I love pink roses." It was Pingping's loud, squeaky voice.

"They must have cost a fortune. Isn't one rose five yuan? That's two meals."

"Look! See the tall guy who's speaking with Dama right now? Isn't he handsome? I like guys with broad shoulders and muscular legs."

"Why don't you go down and talk to him? If you stare any harder, your eyes will fall out of your head."

"None of the boys in our class has muscles like that. Lucky us, there are only ten of them. They probably think they're pretty charming. The other day, Qi Wen asked me out to see a movie or something. Who wants to go out with him? Just look at his freckled face and bowlegs. His arms are even thinner than mine."

"Only gloomy boys study literature. They never exercise."

"Check out that girl! She must be his girlfriend. Don't you think it's too cold for her to wear that miniskirt?"

"I don't think she's a first-year." Donghua hesitated. "If I dressed like her my parents wouldn't let me into their house. They'd kill me if I dated. They said I'd get bad grades if I dated. They had to sell a few pigs to pay my tuition. I'm the only one in my village who has ever gone to university."

"They don't know. They're too far away," Pingping snorted contemptuously.

I put on the headphones and turned on the music. "Dear Ma and Ba," I wrote, but couldn't continue—I hadn't read much during these past few weeks since I met Miao Yan. Sometimes I was amazed and a little puzzled by how quickly I had been drawn into this friendship. Though I didn't wish to be like her, her boldness, rebelliousness, and wildness attracted me. She was so different from me, from the rest of the people

39

I knew, like a strange species from another planet. The more I was with her, the more I wanted to know about her. Perhaps I should have mentioned her to my parents. But then they would have asked a lot of questions—where she was from, what her parents did for a living, what we did when we were together. Almost certainly, they would have asked what she wanted to become after graduation, to which I had no answer.

I stood up and paced. On Yishu's desk was a small bunch of carnations in a vase—though she didn't usually stay overnight she stopped by at least once a week to put flowers in the vase. I smelled the carnations before settling back at my desk. No, I wouldn't mention Miao Yan to my parents. I would keep her a secret, even if only for the sake of disproving my parents' illusion that I was a perfect kid. "I've been reading Lu Xun," I wrote, as I always did.

My father often said that one could never claim to have mastered Lu Xun because his writing is so profound and elusive, thus often difficult to interpret. He especially liked Lu Xun's essays and short stories, which occupied two full shelves of his biggest bookcase. Though he typically didn't write notes inside a book—he had a box of notebooks—he filled the pages of Lu Xun's books with highlights and notes.

Once a few of his students visited him at home and I heard him talking about Lu Xun's revolutionary spirit and thorough criticism of feudalism and reality. My father's voice was passionate, almost quivering, as he analyzed the Crazy Man, Kong Yiji, and Ar Q, as though he wasn't talking about characters in a book but people he knew intimately. I liked reading Lu Xun, too, but I preferred his poetic prose, like *Wild Grass*. The book I had was printed in the early eighties, the pages yellowish with age and half-transparent. I learned some of the prose in middle school. Though the teachers, just like my father, focused on Lu Xun's political views, I was mesmerized by his innovative language and metaphors. Smiling pink flowers, snow with spirit, fire that committed suicide, and sad dreams. Whenever I read his prose, I would be transported to a different world.

"301, Chen Ming," the speaker blared with Dama's voice. I was so startled that I almost dropped my pen. Who wanted to see me?

"Come down, sweetheart," Miao Yan yelled through the speaker, mimicking a man's voice. "It's ferry cruise time!"

I laughed, then my eyes sparkled—she had remembered me telling her I wanted to go for a cruise on the Pearl River.

We took the ferry at the northern gate of the university. Since it was a weekday, few people were on the boat. We leaned against the railing shoulder to shoulder at the bow. Not far from us an old couple chatted intimately. The woman, petite-looking, with silver hair, sat in a wheelchair, her lap and legs covered with a checked blanket. The man, also silver-haired, sat on a bench beside her, his hand on her shoulder. They often smiled at each other as they talked.

"What a nice couple!" I said, noticing Miao Yan was watching them as well.

She turned away from them. "Do you believe there's true love in the world?"

"Of course. Don't you?"

"I guess you have to get lucky."

"I think both of us will get lucky."

She smiled faintly, combing her hair with her fingers. "Perhaps."

We spoke a little more but mostly were quiet, listening to the rhythmic humming of the engine resonating above the

Pearl River, watching the whitish moonlight chasing the endless dark ripples. The reflections of lights from hotels, restaurants, and newly built residential high-rises twinkled in the river.

"Want to hum the song *Let's Row Our Oars?*" she suggested.

It was a song I had learned in primary school. So we hummed and in our synchronized low-pitched humming my mind drifted back to my childhood, to those carefree days on the farm. I turned to look at Miao Yan. She was looking straight ahead, statuelike, her chin resting on her folded arms, her hair waving. She looked ten years older when she wasn't smiling.

"What are you thinking about?" I asked.

She didn't hear me until I asked again.

"Oh, nothing special," she replied, assuming a lively expression almost instantly. "What were you thinking about?"

"About the farm I grew up on. Though my parents suffered there, it was like paradise to me."

"What did you like about it?"

I told her about the attic where I liked to read or play with my toys.

"That's unusual. Weren't you afraid of the darkness?"

"Guess not. We had power failures all the time so I was used to darkness. Actually it was more exciting to be in the dark. You can imagine things more freely. Once, during spring sowing time when my parents were helping the local peasants prepare seeds one evening, I sneaked out of the house to find them. I was probably nine at the time. Halfway there I dropped my torch in a ditch filled with water as I was trying to catch a grasshopper. Not wanting to turn round, I decided to keep walking. The road ran between two big cotton fields and it was so dark that I could barely see my hand in front of my face. To keep myself company I began to talk to myself. I told myself the sky was a piece of light blue paper, stained by a naughty angel. I also told myself the cotton fields were blossoming with big pink flowers now and the only reason I couldn't see them was because they were sleeping under black blankets. The more I talked to myself, the more I believed that at that moment the sky was actually blue and the fields pink. It was such a wonderful experience. Next day I even visited the cotton fields again to see if there really were pink flowers there."

"I wish I had that kind of imagination." She held the railing with both hands and leaned backward. "I don't like darkness. Big city, bright lights, busy streets, that's my kind of life. That's probably why you can write poems while I can only file documents." The stern look on her face made me uneasy, but before I could say something to cheer her up, she smiled. "Maybe someday you can write a poem for me. I'd like that."

"Certainly. I'll write more than one for you."

"Really?" She smiled broadly. "Just be sure to make me young and pretty in your poems. I can't stand the idea of being ugly or old."

"You bet!" I said, still a little confused by her sudden shift in mood.

We walked to the stern of the boat, hand in hand. Her hand was cold but when I asked her if she wanted to go inside the cabin she said no. Most passengers had gathered on the stern because it was less windy there—a young couple with a baby, some students talking about a soccer game, and a few tourists sharing their plans for the coming days. The old couple we had seen earlier had gone inside and were visible through a big window. The woman had fallen asleep, her head tilted. The man was reading the *Guangzhou Daily*, his hand slowly stroking his wife's head.

"What was your childhood like?" I asked Miao Yan when we walked back to the bow. "Did you grow up in a Miao village? I heard Miaos are good singers. Do you know how to sing a Miao song?"

"It was so long ago, I don't remember now." To make her reply more believable, she added, "I don't have a good memory like you."

From her tone and expression I could tell she didn't want to talk about it.

During our return trip, we spoke little. She sank into a trance once more—this time her eyes were closed. From time to time she bit her lower lip for a long moment, as people do when they are trying to control their emotions. How I longed to know what was on her mind!

It was nearly one o'clock when we got off the ferry. On the way to West Five she was back to her normal self—telling jokes and laughing for no particular reason. I was happy, too, till I saw the locked iron gate of West Five.

"Let's see if anybody is in the duty room," she said.

We clung to the windowsill and looked into the room. The light was on but nobody was there. We knocked on the window a few times. No response.

"Maybe we can squeeze in between the bars of the gate," I said. But there wasn't enough room. Moreover, the squealing from the iron chain lock was particularly piercing in the quiet evening.

"We should have come back before curfew." My heart sank.

"We can always climb." She looked quite at ease.

I pointed at the sign—"climbing prohibited"—written in

alarming red paint on the brick wall above the window of the duty room. But she began to climb even though the gate was at least five meters high. Despite her high-heeled shoes, she climbed over in no time and waved at me from the other side.

"How did you do that?" I said with admiration.

"Practice. Your turn."

Under her guidance, I began to climb. I stayed as close to the wall as possible. I gripped the iron bars tightly, pushing my weight forward until the door opened up to the maximum extent the chain lock permitted, so I wouldn't make a lot of noise.

She held the door for me. "Trust me," she said. "You won't fall."

Once I almost lost my balance. The door swung under my weight, which caused the chain lock to rattle. Luckily nobody jumped out from one of the rooms. As I swung my left leg across the top, my right foot slipped and I almost fell. After regaining my balance, I climbed down. When both my feet touched the ground I could feel the muscles in my thighs trembling. But I had made it! The spirit of adventure and camaraderie filled my heart in a way I had never experienced before.

2

During our frequent walks over the next few weeks, Miao Yan began to share with me the rumors about her class and department, along with many of her love stories.

"I can tell he's a womanizer just from his eyes, you know. Those eyes like a wolf's in the darkness," she said to me one day. She was talking about her class counselor, a married man with two kids. "He always finds all kinds of excuses to inspect the sanitary conditions in the female dorms and manages to stay as long as he can to flirt with the girls."

"Does he bother you?"

"What do you think? I'm the prettiest in the class."

"You don't flirt with him, do you?"

"Not him. He doesn't have power. And he's ugly. He has double chins and a bald head and the lines on his forehead are as deep as ditches."

"If he had power—"

"Don't try to trick me."

We were sitting on a stone bench in the woods near the Violin Lake, which had acquired its name from its shape and was the most beautiful lake on campus. It was a starry evening and we could hear crickets chirping in the grass.

"The Big Dipper!" I said, pointing at the sky.

"Where?"

"There! See the Milky Way? The Big Dipper is on the right. One, two, three . . . see the seven stars?"

"Who taught you about stars?"

"My ba. There wasn't much to do on the farm in the evenings. When it was warm, people would move their bamboo beds outside and sleep there. My ba would let me lie next to him, telling me the stories from Hans Christian Andersen's fairy tales. He was often too tired and would fall asleep halfway through telling a story. If I wasn't sleepy, I'd count stars. Sometimes the sky was so black that you could see even the faintest ones. I remember one night I counted to more than five hundred. I'd also connect some stars in my mind to draw all kinds of animals. Once I got an elephant. The eyes, the legs, the body were all there."

"You've got a nice dad." Miao Yan raised her fingers to check the red lacquer on her nails.

"He wasn't always like that. Most of the time he talked little and looked preoccupied. Farm life was very depressing to him. Nowadays, we don't talk much, other than about study or books."

"Do your parents love each other?"

"Of course." I stared at her, a little irritated by her question. "They went through a tough time together. They suffered so much during the Cultural Revolution."

"Did you ever see them hugging and kissing?"

"Don't be so obscene." I opened my eyes wide. "Did you see your parents hugging and kissing?"

"I like teasing you." She laughed, then asked, "Now tell me what kind of boys interest you?"

"I don't know yet." I felt uneasy. It was the first time I had been asked such a question.

"You must know something about it. You've read so many books."

So after some pondering I told her. "Intelligent, athletic, doesn't wear glasses, a little shy and nerdy. We'd go to the library together every day after dinner and we'd talk about books and writers."

"Good luck, little sister. Athletic guys don't hang out at the library every day; you'll be lucky if they read at all. Likewise, brainy guys usually wear thick glasses and the only exercise they're interested in is mental." Miao Yan mocked me. "Tell me more about this superman."

I ignored her sarcasm and continued—it seemed that the image of my soul mate had been stored somewhere in my brain for a long time. "His hair isn't too long, but not too short, either. Mature, good-humored, but not foolish. His eyes are bright, thoughtful, yet a little pensive. His forehead is broad, indicating his generosity and endless wisdom—"

Miao Yan erupted with a raucous belly laugh. "Are you talking about a boy or Confucius?"

I refused to acknowledge her interruption. "He doesn't need to study literature but he likes reading and he writes when he's inspired. He doesn't need to dress like a movie star but his clothes always fit him perfectly, with style. He doesn't talk much but when he does he says something brilliant, something that makes other people listen attentively. He's understanding and . . ." I blushed as I was rushing into a long list of seemingly conflicting characteristics.

"You've got it all figured out, haven't you?" Miao Yan kept laughing. "Now I know why you don't have a boyfriend. He doesn't sound like anybody I know. But if you run into a guy like that, do tell me. Maybe we can share him. He goes to the library with you and goes dancing with me."

"Well, I'm not in a hurry. I can wait."

"I bet you have to wait for a long time," Miao Yan said, drawling the word "long."

We sat quietly, both looking up at the sky. Then I heard Miao Yan say, "Want to hear a story about me?"

"What about?"

"About me ruining a man's life." She pulled a hangnail from her finger.

"Did he die?"

"Close."

"Tell me."

"Promise you won't tell anybody else."

She wouldn't tell me until I swore with my hand on my heart that I would keep it to myself.

"It was in middle school. You know, many years ago," she said. "I was only thirteen. He taught math, my weakest subject. I was afraid that I wouldn't pass an important exam, so one day I went to his office after class, late in the afternoon when the other teachers had gone home for the day. I knew he was a workaholic and always stayed late in his office. I also heard his wife was an unattractive countrywoman a few years older than he was—"

"You seduced him!"

"I didn't! Don't use that word." Miao Yan stood up and walked along the brick road, her unusually high heels making a rhythmic sound—dense and forceful. I followed her.

"Sorry," I said.

"Maybe you're right," she said. "Anyway, before going to his office, I changed into a blue miniskirt and a tight, short-sleeved white blouse. Instead of wearing a tank top like I normally wore underneath the blouse, I wore a thin pink bra that I borrowed from one of my cousins, who was ten years older than me. She was also the one who taught me how to dress. You should have seen the way the teacher looked at me when I walked into his office. He had to pretend to pick up a piece of broken chalk to cover his nervousness. He agreed to let me pass the exam as soon as I asked him. Before I walked out he asked me if he could kiss me. He looked so funny, trembling, sweating, breathing heavily, and all that. I let him kiss my forehead. That was it. He didn't even know how to kiss. After leaving his office, I had to scrub my forehead really hard to get rid of the saliva he'd left there. I never knew he'd be so serious about a kiss. The same night he told his wife he was in love with me and asked her for a divorce."

"How ridiculous!"

"I agree. Maybe he thought kissing somebody was the same

as proposing to them. Next day I became the most famous person in the small town I lived in. His wife came to my parents' house and called me a whore. I still remember how badly my ba beat me when he found out about the whole thing."

"If I did something like that, my ba would—" I stopped. I simply couldn't imagine what my father would do in such a situation.

She snapped a handful of leaves from an evergreen bush with so much force that the whole bush rocked. "He ordered me to take off all of my clothes before beating me. Of course he was drunk, but . . . I don't know why I'm telling you this story. He also called me a whore when he swung his belt at me like a madman. I didn't duck or cry. It was like the belt was falling on someone else. I was just confused about who I was. And when I heard the word 'whore' from his mouth, I knew the answer.

"From that moment on I wasn't a girl anymore. I became a woman. A thirteen-year-old woman. Also, from that moment on I could no longer love my ba but feared and distrusted him. The weird thing was that I got my first period the night I was beaten. It must have been part of the punishment. When I saw the blood on my panties I thought it was because of internal injuries the beating had caused. I thought I was going to die. I lay on my bed silently, waiting for death to fall upon me, till my ma saw my bloody panties in the morning and rushed to a store nearby to buy me some sanitary pads. When she showed me how to put on a pad she looked so ashamed, like I'd been raped or something. Maybe she thought I was too young to have a period, or maybe she just felt I was dirty. Funny, isn't it?"

"My ma didn't tell me either until it came," I said, wanting to make her feel better.

"Believe it or not, the kiss I got from the teacher was the first kiss I'd ever received. It wasn't a great experience and it had a haunting effect on me. You don't know how I hated being kissed for the longest time after that. From that day on, I knew I'd never be serious with men in my whole life."

"What happened to your teacher?"

"His wife divorced him and he lost his job. No school would hire him, so he had to sell boiled eggs on the street to make a living. I once saw him riding a bike with a basket of eggs behind him. He had a beard and wore a dirty shirt. I called out to him but he pretended not to hear. He once tried to commit suicide but was saved. After that, he left our town and no one knew where he went."

I sighed, not sure how to comment on such a sad story.

"Do you despise me now? Do you think I'm a bad girl? Do you still want to be my friend?" She put her hands on my shoulders and spoke eagerly, her eyes dark and fathomless.

"Of course I'll be your friend," I assured her. I was suddenly overwhelmed with protectiveness, guilt, and intimacy toward her. Protectiveness because I felt she needed me. Guilt because I wished I had been there to console her when she was suffering. Intimacy because nobody had confessed such a private experience to me before.

Miao Yan grinned and immediately started to tell a joke about one of her roommates who often ate only fruit to keep slim. I could tell that she was disturbed by her confession and wanted to shake the memory from her mind. But I could no longer concentrate on what she was saying as she went on with her banter. I was too preoccupied with my own mixed feelings for her.

Then I started thinking about her teacher. To him, kissing Miao Yan must have been an unfaithful act, adultery; other-

51

wise he wouldn't have been so silly as to propose a divorce to his wife. Living in a remote small town almost all his life, he might never have kissed a woman other than his wife. Or maybe he had never even kissed his wife—it was possible that his marriage had been arranged and that he had never loved her.

As for myself, I had never kissed any boys, nor had I dared to wear a bra but instead wore thick tank tops as underwear until I came to university. There were twenty girls in my high-school class and only three wore a bra under their thin tops in the summer. They were secretly mocked by the other students and called "women" behind their backs—for us girls at that age, nothing was a bigger insult than being called a woman. It seemed that being called a woman was a mark of shame, as though to say we were no longer cute or pretty, or our purity and innocence were somehow in doubt. As if cursed by this label, none of the three girls went to college and one got pregnant right after high school.

I shall never forget the next day, which engraved itself on my mind as it unfolded like a Chinese ink-brush painting. At six in the morning I heard a gentle knock on my door. Pingping and Donghua were still asleep and I could hear their soft, even breathing. They had played poker until two in the morning.

"It's me. May I come in?" Miao Yan whispered outside the door.

I hesitated, but said, "Come in." I kicked away the blanket and sat up on the edge of the bed with my bare legs hanging in the air.

She pushed open the unlocked door, scanned the room quickly, and tiptoed up to my bunk.

"Like my new clothes? I bought them a few days ago. Thought I'd show you first," she whispered.

She wore a grass-green blouse and white bell-bottom pants that reached all the way to her pointed leather shoes— also in grass-green. Her long, braided hair, bound by a green elastic band, hung over one shoulder and the hair below the band was loose. Her forehead was half hidden under a narrow-brimmed straw hat with a palm-size golden yellow sunflower decorating one side.

"Very nice," I said under my breath.

She quickly glanced at Pingping's and Donghua's beds and shushed me, then took off her shoes and hat and put them in the doorway.

"I'm a good dancer," she said, slowly raising her hands above her head. "All Miao girls are good dancers. I was once picked to dance at a national spring festival show in Beijing."

"What do you dance?"

She didn't answer. Then she started to whirl round and round, up toward me, then away, the wide legs of her pants fluttering as she moved.

It was the early morning of a hot spring day. The reddish morning light poured in through the half-opened door and there she was, whirling against it. She looked so angelic, so delicate, the most beautiful thing I had ever seen. I sat on the edge of my bed and watched her, my heart jumping, speechless.

Then, with the suddenness of a door slammed shut, she stopped swirling; she bowed her head and curtsied, holding on to her pants legs, as though she was responding to a curtain call. Her glittering smile contained no trace of shyness or restraint, as if she was confident of a standing ovation. Before I could say a word she put on her shoes and hat, all the while smiling dazzlingly at me, then backed out of the door and closed it without a sound.

I wanted to follow her but instead I fell back onto my bed—a strange dizziness struck me in a kind of ecstasy. I felt my blood pumping through my veins and crushing my organs. A strong current of warmth permeated my heart. I had difficulty breathing. Never before in my life had I been so paralyzed by an unspeakable emotion and so incapable of expressing my thoughts.

In later years, whenever my friends talked to me about their first love, I would think of this moment when I saw Miao Yan dancing in the morning light. At seventeen, I was both frustrated and thrilled by the intimacy I shared with her. I couldn't ignore it, nor did I dare face it.

I remember writing a poem for her on that day she danced in my room.

> *I saw you, in the morning glow*
> *Pondering, eyes cast low*
> *On tiptoes, I passed by you*
> *Not wanting to disturb the grass*
> *And the sleeping dew*

For some reason I never showed it to her. Perhaps I felt it read too much like a love poem.

From that day on I began to view her as a sister, as someone superior, dominant, sexy, and mature—all the things that, as a teenager, I wasn't. Reassured by this conclusion, I allowed myself to be drawn even more closely to her. Whenever she needed my company I was available; wherever she wanted to meet, I was there. I played truant, avoided social activities, minimized my time in the library. I did what I could to be with her. I didn't know how to hold back; I just let my passion and will run their full course without worrying about where I would end up. Later, I questioned my friendship with Miao Yan and the value of spending so much time with her. But early on I didn't think about it any more deeply—or my mind simply refused to do so.

A few days after she surprised me with her dancing, Miao Yan suddenly disappeared. I waited for her during lunch, went up to the roof in the evening to find her, even visited her department hoping to bump into her. She was nowhere to be seen. Finally I decided to go to her dorm room—I should have gone there first but somehow I felt that if she had been there, she would have visited me.

I could tell just from the clothes on the clothesline that the eighth floor was occupied by more senior students. There were dressy pants, frilly skirts, pantyhose, and other fancy clothes. I even saw a few men's shirts—their girlfriends must have done laundry for them. Against the wall, two pairs of silk high-heeled shoes stood side by side, one with thin blue ankle straps. A little farther, a stuffed garbage bin was next to the gutter, a bunch of dried flowers sticking out from under the lid.

I didn't know her room number so I asked the first girl I saw in the hallway of the eighth floor—she was picking up a sweater from a basin near her feet and was going to hang it up. The water was dripping onto the floor, forming rivulets. I jumped back as they threatened to come my way.

"Miao Yan?" She didn't look at me. "The other side."

"Which room?"

"I don't know." She bent and picked up a blouse from the basin.

There was no one in the hallway on the other side. All the doors were closed. I decided to wait—Miao Yan might be sleeping right now. She once told me that she sometimes slept in the daytime.

Two girls strolled toward me but before I could question them they went into the second room near the stairway, leaving the door open. I walked over to the room and heard them chatting. I didn't want to appear rude by interrupting their conversation so I stayed in the hallway, out of sight, thinking I would knock on the door when they stopped.

"Did she go to Shenzhen again?" one girl said.

"I guess so. She always has an entry permit ready. But what's the point of her looking for a job right now? She isn't even a senior yet," the other girl said. "Also, there are only two openings in Shenzhen right now. Everybody wants them. There's no way that she can compete against us senior students."

"I think she's desperate. Perhaps she's just trying to build connections."

"For God's sake, she's a C student, you know. I heard from her classmates that she cheats on almost all the tests."

"I'm not surprised. She got into university under a special policy. I bet she had failed in the university entrance exam many times before finally getting lucky. That's why she's so much older than us."

"She thinks her pretty face will get her a job."

Both laughed. The girl who had just spoken repeated "her pretty face" in a mocking voice.

"Someone told me that she sent a lot of gifts to Counselor Liu," the other girl said.

"Must be more than that. She might even have slept with the old dog."

"I don't think he could help her much even if she was a senior. Job arrangement has to be transparent."

"Hmm, you don't want to be too trusting. You just never know."

"So . . . you think we should buy him some gifts, too?"

"I don't know. But it wouldn't hurt."

"I don't want to get into trouble for bribery."

"Come on, don't be so naive."

Then there was a pause. I walked to the door and was going to knock on it—I could see both girls lying on their beds. Just then the girl on the bed near the window said, "But isn't she a Miao? I thought minority people had to go back where they came from."

I kept quiet but the girl near the door saw me. She sat up. "Yes?"

"Oh, I think I've got the wrong room," I managed to say, flustered.

"Who are you looking for?" The girl near the window sat up, too.

"Hmm," I said, "Pingping."

"No such person here," the girl near the window said impatiently.

"Check the list in the duty room," the other girl said.

"Thank you. Sorry for the trouble." I ran off as fast as I could.

Miao Yan returned a week later. She said she had gone to Shenzhen to visit a sick relative. I wanted to tell her what the two girls on her floor had said about her—though I didn't believe what they had said, I couldn't forget it. But when I saw how tired she looked, I decided not to say anything. I assumed that the two girls were jealous of her beauty and diligence in looking for a job.

That Friday, for the first time, Miao Yan invited me to her dorm room. It was the fifth from the stairway. A square mirror with blue ribbons taped around it took up a good part of the door. Her room was the same size and shape as mine but she had five roommates. Like my bed, hers was close to the door and on the upper level. Despite the crowding, Miao Yan had many places to store her clothes. Besides her standard assigned space in the wall, filled to capacity with one suitcase and half a dozen shopping bags, a lot of suits hung on a row of nails hammered into the wall above her bed. I did a quick count: nine suits. All were of solid colors, spanning the entire spectrum—red, orange, yellow, green, blue, violet—stacked on top of each other and covering half the wall, which at first sight looked like a huge abstract painting. On subsequent occasions when I was there, a few nails failed under the weight and fell out. I would help Miao Yan gather the clothes on the bed or floor and find new places on the wall to hammer those nails back in. It was not easy—the wall was already dotted with nail holes.

"How come they're all solid colors?" I asked.

"You never read fashion magazines, do you?"

"But you were wearing a floral-patterned blouse when we first met on the roof."

"Your memory is terrible!" She laughed. "I have no such blouse."

"You do!" I could recall it perfectly.

"I don't. Only country girls wear that type of blouse. Country girls, you know, they're everywhere in Guangzhou. Janitors, street sweepers, garbage collectors, waitresses."

"Without them, the city would be a mess. They—"

"Drop the subject, will you? We're not in a Party meeting." She kicked a fallen hanger under a bed.

"Where did you get the money to buy them?" I asked.

"I have a part-time job."

"What kind of job?"

"I'll tell you later." She picked a banana from a bamboo basket on her desk, peeled it, and took a big bite. With her mouth full, she muttered, "I'm hungry. Do you want something to eat?"

"I'm okay," I said, still thinking about her many suits. "But why do you need so many clothes? It's a big waste."

She finished the banana in another two bites and wiped her mouth with the back of her hand. Standing where she was, she threw the skin into a wastepaper basket near the window. "I like looking at them. They make me feel good. And I lend them to my roommates so I won't need to clean the room and fetch hot water. The better they treat me, the prettier the clothes I'll lend to them. The world is all about people using each other."

I was going to ask if she was also trying to use me, but since I didn't see how I could possibly be used, I said instead, "I never see you wearing them on campus." I stood closer to examine those expensive-looking suits.

"They're for my interviews, you silly girl."

"Don't call me silly."

"You silly woman!" she laughed.

"Don't call me a woman!"

59

"I can call you whatever I want: little birdie, dearest kitten, sweet cookie, fresh cabbage, sad poet, pretentious philosopher, silly—"

"You crazy woman!" I covered her mouth with both hands, but she shook me off and jumped aside, laughing so hard that she had to hold her stomach and squat.

Her laughter was contagious; I couldn't help but laugh with her.

"If you want, you can call me chameleon," she said after we stopped laughing.

It was perfect—a chameleon changes its body color depending on the environment, as Miao Yan changed her outfit depending on her mood.

I noticed a two-piece blue bikini on her bed. I picked up the bottom with two fingers—it was small enough to fit into a matchbox. "Do you actually wear it?"

"Of course, I'm no country girl. I've even watched porn videos. Don't stare at me like that. I'm twenty-four. I haven't told you even one-tenth of what I've experienced. Want to know? I'll tell you when you're eighteen." She laughed again.

"It's only a few months away. Why not tell me now?"

"Well, you'll be a woman when you're eighteen. I'd feel better telling you everything about me if you're a woman like me. At least your parents couldn't blame me for making you a bad girl then," she said, half jokingly. "I don't want them to chase me all over the world, asking me to return their innocent daughter." She put a cigarette between her lips and lit it. When the ash was about to fall, she walked to the window and tapped it off outside.

A woman like her? That would never happen, whether I was eighteen or thirty, I thought.

That night I remember counting the days until my eighteenth birthday. Though I liked to imagine that something magical would happen when the day arrived, I knew in reality it would be just another day, a normal day on the calendar. It wouldn't be any different from my sixteenth or seventeenth birthdays. But being eighteen did sound different from being seventeen. Somehow I felt I would be reborn on that day, like a new person. There was uncertainty attached to that age, a transition from being an adolescent to the world of adulthood. I wondered how people would see me as an eighteen-year-old. Would they treat me like an adult or would they just get impatient with me for not knowing more than I did when I was seventeen? Would my parents stop lecturing me after I turned eighteen? Would I suddenly want to date, even if I couldn't find the perfect man?

Just as showing off her wardrobe pleased her, criticizing my clothes was also something Miao Yan truly enjoyed.

"You've got to show off your curves," she said. "Curves! You hear me? You can wear these T-shirts and jeans when you're eighty."

"Come on, they're not as ugly as you say," I argued. "Other girls in my class also wear these kind of clothes. If I wore clothes like you—" I was going to say, "everyone would laugh at me," but changed it to "I would no longer be myself."

"Not being yourself might be a good thing. I hate to see girls in baggy clothes."

My biggest mistake, Miao Yan pointed out, was not having a pair of high-heeled shoes. "Every other woman in the world owns a pair of high-heeled shoes!"

"Why does it matter? I'm not a woman yet," I said.

"Girls can also be sexy! Being sexy is about how to make the world do things for you."

"Well, I don't want to be sexy."

"What do you want?"

"I want to become a professor."

"Geek! You don't even know what sexy is."

"You sound like you do."

Obviously my answer frustrated her. She became silent and started to walk up and down in my room. Then she asked when my roommates would be back. I said they would be out for at least another two or three hours. Before I could finish my sentence, she darted out of the room and fifteen minutes later returned in a knee-length beige coat and a pair of red shoes.

"Lesson number one for today," she announced while closing the door behind her, "is what being sexy is all about." I laughed and thought she was really funny. It was late April already—way too warm to wear a coat.

She didn't look at me or laugh with me. Instead she started unbuttoning the coat. Underneath she was wearing a deep red bikini! She threw the coat onto my desk and smiled at me.

My first instinct was to leave the room. I was angry—I wasn't interested in seeing her in a bikini, or in knowing what "sexy" was. It crossed my mind that she might ask me to try on the bikini, which panicked me even more. But a few minutes later my curiosity overpowered my anger and I calmed down. I assured myself that it was perfectly fine for a girl to see another girl in a bikini. I still felt nervous and trapped but I stared at her, wondering what she would do next.

She had tanned skin and long legs—so long that they seemed twice the length of her torso. Her thighs were firm, though a little thin. There was a light birthmark the size of a pea on her right thigh. She didn't have much of a bosom, which she carefully covered with her long hair falling forward over her shoulders. Her belly was flat, like a boy's. A tiny silver ring glistened in her navel.

"You have a belly ring!" I couldn't believe my eyes.

"I got it last week." She seemed proud. "Now look at me closely," she said. She retied the straps of her bikini to make them tighter on her shoulders and stretched the bottom to make it wrap her hips more snugly and a little higher up. She did these things slowly and carefully.

"Walk like this, okay?" She twisted her body to adjust her weight on the fingerlike high heels of the red shoes, and started to pose—craning her neck, sticking out her chest, rolling her waist, swinging her hips, strutting exaggeratedly back and forth as if on a catwalk at a fashion show. The room was small and every few steps she had to turn around. It was almost comical to watch her, so gorgeous in a shabby dorm room filled with worn-out furniture, faded mosquito nets, and ugly bunk beds. She glanced at me often to make sure I was looking at her.

"This is sexy," she said at the end of the show.

Though I had been a little daunted by her seriousness earlier, I was now amused and started to laugh.

She didn't laugh with me. "That's my dream. I want to be a model, just as you want to be a professor. You've heard of *Playboy*, right? Those cover girls make tons of money."

"*Playboy*?" I stopped laughing. "You can't be serious." I had read about it and knew it was an American porn magazine.

"They wouldn't pick me anyway. I don't have a big chest. But . . ." She walked to her coat and fumbled out a rolled-up magazine from one of the coat pockets and handed it to me. "Here you go!" She beamed.

The cover of the magazine showed a photograph of a woman in a two-piece black swimming suit. The picture was a little blurry.

"So?" I said.

"It's me. The model is me."

I rubbed my eyes really hard. It was her, though I would never have guessed. In the picture she wore heavy makeup and stood barefoot on a wave-worn rock on a beach, one hand holding a white scarf that fluttered in the wind. I had seen such pictures on magazines sold by street vendors on Zhong Shan Fifth Road for three yuan an issue, or ten yuan for five issues. Most of them were copies of low-quality entertainment magazines from Hong Kong and Taiwan.

"When did you have this photo taken?" Dumbfounded, I managed to stammer the question.

"A while back." She put on her coat. "So I guess you don't like it."

"How did you find out about this magazine?"

"A secret."

"Did you get paid?"

"Of course."

"How much was that?"

"You don't want to know."

"It's not a good magazine."

"What do you mean by 'good'? Even *Reader* uses pretty girls on its cover."

"But you wore so little—"

"At least it's not see-through."

"I don't like your makeup. It's so heavy. You look like an old woman."

"Don't call me an old woman!"

"A bad girl then."

"What's wrong with being a bad girl? How can you tell a good girl from a bad girl just from a picture? Just because you're covered up in ugly clothes, does that mean you're a better girl than I am?"

"I don't want to argue with you. Your parents sent you here to get the best education. There are so many decent jobs in the world for a person like you with college education. Why do you want to become a model?"

"First of all, they didn't send me here, I did it on my own. Secondly, I am who I am and I do what I want to do."

"Like wearing a bikini?"

"I thought you were open-minded."

"I am. But—"

"I'm telling you that I'll become a model."

"Only uneducated shallow girls want to become models."

"Too bad. You'd better accept the fact that your best friend is an uneducated shallow girl who wants to become a model!" She stormed out of my room, waving the magazine.

I suspected that she took private lessons to learn how to become a model. Once I saw a model-training studio business card on her desk.

This was our first real fight. I quickly learned to ignore her dream of becoming a model, just as she ignored my opinion of it.

⌒

One Sunday morning I was awakened by the radio— Pingping was mimicking the speakers on a Cantonese program. She was quite diligent in learning Cantonese, which she had laughed at as "a language for birds" when she first

arrived at university. She complained that it was more difficult to learn Cantonese than to learn English. "It has nine
tones. That drives me nuts! Five tones more than Mandarin!
My tongue and teeth keep fighting each other. I heard that
Cantonese ancestors are snake-eating barbarian natives. How
could such a backward place have developed such a complicated dialect?"When she was in a good mood she would sing
a popular Cantonese song from a recent Hong Kong movie.
Her Cantonese was so terrible that the Cantonese girls in the
dorm would cover their ears and beg her to stop.

"If you want to find a job here, you'd better learn Cantonese," I had heard her lecture Donghua the other day.

Miao Yan had said the same thing to me more than once
but I never took her seriously—if I had time, I'd rather read a
book. Of course, I could see why knowing how to speak Cantonese was important. For many non–Cantonese students, the
ultimate goal after graduation was to obtain permanent residence in Guangdong, especially in Guangzhou, its capital. The
most ambitious students would want to work in Shenzhen
and Zhuhai, where salaries were the highest in China.

"Ming, get up! Time for the election." Pingping's high-
pitched voice penetrated the room.

I opened my eyes and saw her standing next to her bed,
wearing a tight red T-shirt and holding a duster, her bony legs
spread apart.

"Which election?"

"Class leaders. Don't you remember? Counselor Wang
asked us to pick candidates two weeks ago."

"Oh, I was reading a novel." I smacked my forehead with
my palm, remembering that meeting. "I guess I forgot to turn
in my list."

Counselor Wang had recently been assigned to my class to

take charge of students' ideological education. Every other week he would call for a meeting to discuss the latest Party documents or things related to ideology. If he ran out of things to say he would ask us to read aloud the handouts, one paragraph per person. Since his meetings were mandatory I had to attend them, but I always sat in the back row, reading my own books. For the last meeting, he asked us to suggest a student leader in each field—general studies, arts and entertainment, sports, and political studies.

"Didn't you see the result? Both you and Pingping were nominated, Pingping for the leader of general studies, you for head of political studies," Donghua chimed in, a half-knitted black scarf in her hands.

"Political studies?" I almost jumped up from my bed. "I never like reading Party documents."

"It's a good position. You'll have a chance to talk with Counselor Wang every week. You only need to write a report once a month." Pingping threw the duster behind the door and grabbed her bag. "Donghua, we need to go now."

"It's perfect for you. You spend more of your time reading and writing than anyone else in the class." Donghua winked at me before she left.

A little while later, I got on my green bike, which I had bought for fifty yuan from a final-year student when I first arrived, and headed to the department. Though I would rather have sat in the library reading, cycling on such a sunny spring day was enjoyable. Moreover, I had something to look forward to—Miao Yan and I planned to eat dim sum for lunch at a newly opened restaurant. She knew I loved dim sum and could never get enough of it.

Once away from the dormitory complex for undergraduates, past the History Department, the unpaved area where seven or eight people were playing soccer, and a high-rise building for male graduate students, I hit a wide, straight road. A short distance ahead, next to the Violin Lake, stood the three-story building for female graduate students; its glazed tile roof and green-painted poles never failed to remind me of the university's long history. This building was nicknamed the "Moon Palace," which conjured up the female graduate students' arrogance and lack of understanding of the real world.

I took a short detour onto a less traveled road lined with silk cotton trees and eucalyptus. The moment I reached the shade, a soothing breeze embraced me. I felt I was flying. I looked up at the sky between the branches and the leaves—it was serene, clear, and appeared closer than ever before. I let go of the handlebars and raised my hands, imagining how it would feel to hold it, to possess the sky.

When I left the woods, a typical campus scene rolled out before me. It was late spring, the best time of the year. Students strolled on the paths with their headphones on. On the stairs to the library, two girls in white blouses were chatting, eating apples, a stack of books at their feet. In front of an ivy-covered brick building, a young woman in a long blue skirt was telling a group of primary school students about its history. The lawn at the center of the campus was thick, green, and perfectly trimmed. Strung between two banyan trees, a white banner with red characters read: "Welcome delegates from universities in Australia and New Zealand." Several students sat at a stone table playing chess under one of the trees. The sight of the peaceful campus always filled my heart with happiness and pride.

When I parked my bike and stepped onto the squeaky wooden stairs of the Chinese Language and Literature Department building—a building more than one hundred years old—I was sweaty from the ride.

There were about thirty people in the conference room. Counselor Wang stood in front of the podium, his hands behind his back. He was in his early fifties, short, and skinny. While talking, he liked to move his hands abruptly to emphasize his points. Sometimes he would stop in the middle of a sentence and look at us to see if we were listening.

I saw Pingping and Donghua sitting together in the front row. There was an empty seat next to Yishu in the back row. Like me, she wasn't very sociable. Though we talked little, I felt she was especially friendly to me. Whenever she saw me she would smile. Occasionally, when she was wiping the frame of our bunk beds, she cleaned the upper part for me as well. I would have liked to talk more with her but she spent so little time in the dorm that I seldom saw her other than in class.

"Hey," I said, and sat down next to her.

She raised her head from the book on her lap and smiled at me. Pingping didn't like Yishu and insisted that she was so silent because she was pretentious and snobbish. In Pingping's eyes all Cantonese were snobbish and they all looked down on northerners.

"You were nominated," Yishu said.

"I don't know who nominated me but I hate reading Party documents."

"I nominated you." She smiled again. "It might help you in the future. At least that's what I heard."

At ten thirty, Counselor Wang announced the election. He passed around a stack of paper with the names of candidates written in black ink. Under the category of "Head of Political Studies" I saw my name and two other names.

After a lot of whispering and suppressed laughter, we turned in our ballots. Then Counselor Wang counted the votes and began to read the results.

To Pingping's disappointment, she didn't get the position as head of general studies. When the winner was accepting a round of applause, she didn't clap.

I was becoming agitated with the slow pace of the meeting. The clock on the wall pointed to ten minutes past twelve. Miao Yan must have been wondering where I was. Perhaps I should pretend to go to the bathroom and slip out?

"The last one, head of political studies," Counselor Wang finally said. "Zhou Tao, eighteen, Wang Meili, nine votes, Chen Ming, eighteen." He used his hand to cover his mouth and cleared his throat. "There's a tie here. Let's have another vote."

There was a roar of impatience.

I don't know what got into me but I stood up. "I think Zhou Tao is more qualified than I am. She reads more Party newspapers and political works." I glanced at Zhou Tao and saw a big smile spreading across her face.

My suggestion was accepted. As soon as the class was dismissed, I ran outside the building, grabbed my bike, and rode back to West Five.

"What? You gave up the position?" Miao Yan didn't laugh as I had expected.

"Why not? It's a silly position. You know me. I never read political stuff."

"Did you vote for yourself?"

"Of course not. Why would I do that?"

"I'm sure she voted for herself. You'd have outvoted her if you had voted for yourself as well, and then you'd have the position."

70

"But I'd hate it. It's boring to write reports like that and have to meet the counselor every week."

"You're crazy." She shook her head hard.

"You'd never have taken it if you were me."

"Oh, yes. I'd have taken it. My problem is that I would never get nominated. Everyone in my class hates me."

"I thought you didn't care about titles like these."

"When will you grow up? You can't be a kid forever." She walked to the window, pulled a blouse down from the wire used for hanging wet clothes, and turned to me abruptly. "Students who've held those kinds of positions have much better opportunities to stay in the best cities in Guangdong. Don't you get it? You're competing with your classmates for a handful of opportunities. You have to go through the university's job-assignment office to get permanent residence here. Without it, you can't stay in Guangdong. The government and the big companies simply won't hire you. Even if you could stay in Guangdong, you want to stay in Guangzhou, Zhuhai, and Shenzhen, not the less developed areas. Listen, the last thing you want to do is return to your poor hometown. You'll have no future in Jiangxi and people will laugh at you for being a loser. There's no way I'm going back. I'm not going back even if my classmates bitch about me every day, even if everybody wants to kick me out of Guangdong."

"I don't want you to leave," I said, taken aback by her sudden outburst. "I thought you got a few interviews in Shenzhen."

"I'm trying." Miao Yan suddenly looked exhausted.

We didn't go to the dim sum restaurant. She was in a grumpy mood and I was angry at her for being tough on me. Though Guangdong was wealthy, I never felt that I had to stay here after graduation. There were so many other places I

71

had yet to explore, like Beijing and Shanghai. Also, some Cantonese seemed too arrogant to me. They either didn't speak Mandarin, the official language of China, or chose not to. They often looked down on people from the other provinces. Some were openly hostile to outsiders, complaining that they took jobs from the locals and made the traffic horrendous. Almost every day I could hear the Cantonese referring to outsiders as "northern bumpkins"—they thought or liked to think they were all backward country folk with savage ways. It frustrated me to see Miao Yan so determined to stay in a place where outsiders weren't welcomed.

On the other hand, I felt that her outburst was more than just a reaction to my not taking that position. She seemed to have hidden something about herself from me, something beyond her wanting to stay in Guangdong. Although at the beginning of our friendship I saw her as a happy person, after being with her for a while I had begun to think that was not true.

Next day, when I visited her to make sure she was okay, she looked more alive than ever, as though nothing had happened the day before.

⌒

When summer arrived three weeks after the election, everything seemed brighter. In Guangzhou, summer dominates and seems eternal. Even after living here for more than a decade and having seen all the seasons, what I remember most is the blinding summer sunlight and how the sweat pours off my skin.

That summer was especially hot. In the dry, scorching heat the wild grass behind West Five turned yellow in a week. The water levels in the ponds shrank to their lowest, and stainlike moss could be seen on their darkened walls. When the sun was at its zenith, the campus looked empty—everyone was either in her dorm napping or in one of the libraries where the ceiling fans rotated at full speed. Our dorm had no air-conditioning and was like a sauna when the temperature hit a record thirty-eight degrees Celsius for a few consecutive days. Although I had an upper bed and the window was open all night, there was little breeze.

Then there were the mosquitoes to worry about. The ones in Guangzhou were unusually big. Cantonese people said that three mosquitoes could make a meal. Of course they were exaggerating, but I had never seen mosquitoes as big as they were here. Their bodies were gray and their legs extremely thin and long. If I didn't close my mosquito net tightly, or if I accidentally kicked it open while sleeping, I would be stung all over by the time I awoke; the mosquitoes would be so well fed with my blood that they couldn't even fly. Once I was stung on both my eyelids and they were swollen for days. I tried all kinds of pesticides and repellents but they didn't help—these mosquitoes seemed to be immune.

If you ask me what I like least about Guangzhou, I would say it is the summers. But summer was Miao Yan's season. She loved to wear revealing clothes. Unlike most other girls, who preferred a pale complexion, she was never afraid of getting tanned. Though she was busy looking for a job, every few days she would stop by my room to show me the new outfits she had purchased. One top was transparent except around the chest, and another was strapless, in a slim-fitting, bodice style.

Whenever I asked her where she had gotten the money to buy these clothes, she would say, "I have a part-time job." But she never told me what that job was.

One day at about five in the afternoon, just as I had laid down my schoolbag to go to the canteen to buy dinner, Miao Yan rushed into my room. Without saying a word, she dragged me up the stairs into her room. Panting, she double-locked the door from the inside. As always, none of her roommates was home—somehow, whenever Miao Yan was home during the day, all her roommates would stay away.

She walked to the window, poked her head out, looked both ways, and closed the window, then she took down a big pink shopping bag from her bed and shook out a black dress.

"See what I bought today! Try it on! You must try it on!"

Her eyes were gleaming, her cheeks red with excitement. Holding the dress with both hands, she looked at me with a hopeful and encouraging expression on her face.

Almost before I knew it her fingers were at my waist, unbuckling my belt. I pushed her away and insisted on changing inside her mosquito net. She frowned and looked at me mockingly, but agreed.

"Do you have to close the net? I promise I won't look at you."

"No way."

"What's the big deal? I don't mind you watching me change clothes."

"I mind."

"You incurable country girl!"

"I'm doing you a favor," I said. "Otherwise I wouldn't even look at the dress."

This stopped her. She left me alone and started to pace the room. Then she sat down on a chair, rocking left and right, her gaze focused on the bed. By the time I took off my jeans and T-shirt she had lost patience. "Hurry up!" she cried.

I sat on her bed in my underwear, holding the dress. It took me more than a minute to work out how it was supposed to be worn. As soon as I figured it out I changed my mind.

"Who made this stupid dress with so little material? It's impossible to wear!" I said.

"Oh, my little sister, you're going to wear it." Miao Yan snatched up my jeans by one of the legs that was hanging outside the net and immediately hid them behind her back. "I'll only return the jeans if you put on the dress," she said firmly.

I had to put on the dress.

"What are you doing up there? Climb down!" She pulled open the net. "I want to see you in the dress!"

"Give me back my jeans."

"Climb down first."

She gripped my hand, her other hand holding a big mirror. There was an uncomfortable silence when I climbed down the ladder. I assumed she must have thought the dress looked really ugly on me. If she hadn't been gripping my hand I might have gone back up the ladder to put my own clothes on again.

"Now you can look in the mirror," she said.

I looked at her instead—I had never seen her so serious. Her eyebrows knotted, then spread like the wings of an eagle. "Shoes!" she said.

She leaned the mirror against a wall and got down on her stomach, her cheek almost pressing against the dusty cement floor, scanning underneath all the beds and desks. When she finally found a pair of black leather shoes my size, she used a piece of tissue to wipe them, then ordered me to sit on a chair while she put the shoes on for me. "They're cheap shoes but they should fit," she said.

"Slow down, be gentle, you're killing me." I couldn't stand the pain. The shoes were the pointy-toed type.

"Just one second, my sweetie. Now you can stand up."

"I don't think I can." I almost lost my balance the moment I put all my weight on the high heels.

"Don't hold my arm. Just open your legs a little wider. Yes, just like that."

I tugged the dress upward, downward, then sideways, before I dared to look at myself in the mirror. The dress clung to my body like a surgical glove, revealing every curve. In the mirror I looked slim and tall. My neck, upper chest, arms and legs were pale in contrast to the black dress.

"Stick out your chest. Don't look at your shoes. Stand up straight. Don't shake your legs," she demanded, sizing me up, then murmured, "Something isn't right."

She walked to her desk and came back with a comb.

She held my chin up with one hand and used the other to play with my hair. She looked very serious. I closed my eyes and decided to yield to her ministrations.

She combed through my chin-length hair a few times, redid the part to make it sit a little more to the left, plucked a few strands from behind my right ear onto my cheek, and flipped the fringe carefully so that one side covered part of my eye. She applied hair spray all over my head for the finishing touch.

"Done!" she pronounced.

I opened my eyes and at that instant the comb dropped from her hand, hitting my right breast, almost catching on the clingy material before landing on the floor.

"Damn it!" Miao Yan said, reaching out immediately to examine the dress where the comb had struck. Though she was only checking the fabric I was panicked by the sudden brush of her hands on my chest.

"Don't step back. I can't see properly." She frowned.

"Let me do it myself." I stepped even farther away from her.

"I won't touch you. I'm only checking the fabric."

"I can do it."

"You don't know where the comb hit." She moved closer.

"It's fine. It didn't hit hard. It didn't hurt," I said.

"That's not what I'm worried about. This dress is expensive," she said, still motioning toward my chest.

"I see," I said, a little disappointed. "So it's about your dress."

"It didn't do any damage." She quickly raised her head and beamed a relieved smile, her hands now by her sides.

I straightened my back and sucked in my tummy, as I had been told. Even if I hadn't been told, I might have done it anyway, since the dress was so tight.

I carefully examined my reflection in the mirror. The dress was suspended from my neck by two spaghetti straps covered with shiny silver sequins. A choker held the straps together behind my neck, the ends swinging over my naked back. The neckline of the dress plunged to just above my nipples. My breasts pushed the dress forward to form an arched bridge on my chest, my nipples hardening from the caress of the fabric. The dress fit me perfectly at the waist; below the waist, it wrapped around my hips in a pear shape and stopped halfway between my hips and my knees. Most of my thighs were exposed, the skin delicate and firm. The rear zipper started a little below my waist and extended to the bottom of the hem. My back was completely bare, save for the two hanging straps.

Speechless and motionless, I felt my heart pounding against my ribs. I was exultant, curious, bewildered, puzzled, all at the same time. I couldn't believe I was the person in the mirror. The sudden change made me feel that I was completely naked and I wanted to cover myself with a blanket.

Miao Yan stood a step behind me in her beige silk skirt, her long hair hanging over her cheeks making her face look really small. She stared at me—or more precisely, stared at my reflection in the mirror—like a painter impressed by her own masterpiece. "At least 36B. So beautiful. This dress was made for you. Sexy . . . this is what's called sexy."

I often recall that afternoon, the instant when I stared at my reflection in the mirror with such wonder and bewilderment. It was at that moment I realized I could be somebody completely unknown to myself—a woman. I could become a woman. This discovery was both frustrating and devastating since all my confidence in controlling my destiny as a carefree young girl was abruptly challenged and shaken. A simple black dress could convert me into a woman, which seemed so strange. That very same evening, after I tried on the dress, for the first time I found myself pondering what "becoming a woman" meant.

It was a hot summer night in June, exactly three months after I had met Miao Yan. The room was quiet and dark. Pingping and Donghua were deeply asleep, Pingping snoring lightly. These days she seemed to be out a lot at night, not returning to the dorm until a few minutes before curfew.

As I lay awake I recalled the moment when I noticed that boys could pee standing, while I had to squat. I was a little girl at that time, but even then I knew I was different from boys, other than having longer hair. When boys stole looks at me in middle school, I panicked and was a bit disgusted—they must have been bad students. Good boys and girls studied hard and went to university while bad girls and boys ended up in factories doing menial work. That was what my teachers and parents had told me. They didn't tell me anything about menstrual cycles and budding breasts. I had to learn about all those things for myself.

When I got my first period I thought it was shameful but accepted the fact that all girls had to go through the process to grow up. I wished I was a boy so I could be rid of this troublesome monthly thing. I don't know when it started but I wanted to keep a distance from the boys. A few students had become couples in school, but they were disliked and condemned by the teachers and laughed at by their classmates. It was considered "dirty" to have a boyfriend or a girlfriend at that age. I didn't want to be one of those "bad students." Actually, I didn't think about boys at all; I only wanted to get in to the university of my dreams.

This attitude continued even when I reached university. I wanted a simple student life, to focus on study. But now Miao Yan had led me to a door with a sign on it that invited me to "become a woman." That was when I got lost. Nobody had taught me anything about it. I thought it had something to do with sex, which was even more unfamiliar. Then I learned that might have been true but psychologically it was really about how I viewed myself—when Miao Yan said that she had become a woman at thirteen, I believed her. Every time she said she was a woman she seemed proud of herself and the way she spoke the word "girl" it was as though she was referring to something small and weak.

"Women . . . girls . . . girls . . . women . . ." I whispered repeatedly. When I finally drifted off I dreamed that I was flying a kite, half asleep, eyes half closed. I was standing on the flat roof. I could see only the empty gray sky; there were no trees around. The roof was soft as well-chewed gum. I saw holes here and there—some as big and deep as a well—and they forced me to jump around like a frog. I didn't have the spool in my hand but the kite was following my steps in the sky. Sometimes I would stop and look at the kite and it would stop as well. Obscured by fog, the kite had no shape or color. It started to rain, the raindrops fast and dense. My clothes were getting so wet and heavy that I couldn't jump anymore; I had to move inch by inch in the space between the holes. The rain followed me wherever I went but there was no trace of water on the roof. I looked up at the sky. It was not raining. The raindrops that fell on me were the kite's tears.

I asked in the dream, "Kite, why are you crying?" The kite didn't answer. It was melting, dissolved by its own tears. When I looked up again, the kite had completely disappeared into the sky.

It was four in the morning when I awoke. As soon as I opened my eyes I discovered to my shame that my hands were somehow on my chest and positioned like an extra bra. I always slept with my bra on, something Miao Yan had laughed about when I told her. I quickly removed my hands and touched my forehead, where a layer of cold sweat had formed. Wide awake, the whole dream filling my mind, I began to wonder if the kite was Miao Yan. I asked myself why she cried and why she didn't answer. For a moment I was so worried that I was tempted to get up and go knock on her door. It seemed like a sad dream but I could make no sense of it. The more I tried to analyze it the more confused I got.

Then I heard stirring from Donghua's bed. She was not sleeping but was rearranging the bottom of her mosquito net to press it under the mat. In the moonlight I saw her hand sticking out from the opening of the net. I wondered if she was going to get up to knit but she softly closed the net with a pin. Then she lay down and began to touch herself. Even through the net I could see her hands move over her chest and down to her lower body. Then I heard her panting softly, on and off, for a few minutes. At last she released a long satisfied sigh. Then she was quiet, as if she was exhausted from touching herself.

◌◜◝◌

I like to think that Miao Yan and I were always together during that summer of '92. I clearly remember her tanned skin and a lot of her sexy outfits at that time. But in fact I barely saw her during those three months. Firstly there was a two-month summer break, then she had a one-month internship in Shenzhen—she was now in her last year.

Right before the summer break she had asked me to write her dissertation for her. When I walked into my room that day I saw her reading at my desk. Pingping and Donghua must have gone to the canteen to buy lunch. Miao Yan visited me so often that both Pingping and Donghua knew she was my best friend and would let her in if I wasn't at home. Miao Yan

81

never bothered to introduce herself to them, nor did she let me introduce her. "Having one girlfriend is more than enough," she once said. Whenever she mentioned my room-mates she would say, for instance, "I went to your room this morning, but you weren't in. The skinny girl said you went to the library." She always referred to Pingping as "the skinny girl" and Donghua as "the black knitting girl." But she used "that mysterious woman" to describe Yishu, though she only saw a picture of her. I asked her why Pingping and Donghua were "girls" while Yishu was a "woman."

"I like the way she smiles. A seductive smile. She's a woman like me," she answered.

Occasionally, as I lay on my bed, I held my palm-size mir-ror and examined myself, mimicking Yishu's smiles. It was a difficult exercise. I never quite understood what kind of smiles were "seductive."

I put down my bag and stood beside Miao Yan. She didn't notice me. She looked completely absorbed, her head bowed so low that it almost touched the book in her lap. She was myopic but rarely wore glasses because, as she said, they didn't look good on her. When she went to classes or watched a movie, she wore contact lenses, but at other times she was too lazy to put them in.

I was surprised to see Miao Yan engrossed in reading. She didn't read books unless she had to. She abhorred textbooks, calling them nonsense, and wouldn't open them except when she had to pass exams. Whenever she came to the library to find me she would complain about its strict environment and said she couldn't stand seeing several hundred people in a room quiet as a morgue. In fact, most of her textbooks looked almost new. They were piling up, overflowing on her desk because she had no bookshelf. When she went to bookstores she would buy music tapes, postcards, but never books. Ironically, she liked to know what I was reading and was always interested in my book collection. She would hover before my bookshelf, which almost hit the ceiling, and check out my latest purchases. If I was busy, she would sit down, select several books, and leaf through them quickly without stopping at any page for more than a few seconds, as though she was just checking to see if any pages might have defects or marks.

"What are you reading?" I extended my hand toward the book.

"Qian Zhongshu's *Fortress Besieged*. Quite interesting." She raised her head alertly, putting the book behind her back.

My face turned pale. I had written a lot of comments and notes in the book's margins. It was almost like my diary.

"What do you mean by 'there is an invisible wall between people, which prevents them from—' "

"Don't read my notes!"

"You know what? One of my friends just said the exact same thing. He told me about this book. I thought you were bound to have it, so I came over."

I wondered who the "he" was. She had never mentioned any of her male friends to me—at least not anyone who would read this kind of serious book.

"Who's this friend?" I asked.

"Don't assume I only have shallow friends."

"I didn't. But who is he?"

"You'll meet him someday."

"When?"

"I don't know. Someday, as I said." She shrugged.

Desperately wanting to get my book back, I said, "You won't be interested in such books. If you really want to read it, you can get a copy from the library."

"I couldn't find my library card. Also, the old man guarding the door doesn't like the sound my high-heeled shoes make on the floor. He once asked me to take off my shoes."

"I can get you a copy."

"But I only like your copy." She laughed, pulling away from me, holding the book behind her back.

"You can borrow other books." I took a book by Taiwanese writer San Mao from the bookshelf and handed it to her. I knew she liked San Mao and had always wanted to travel around the world like her.

"No. I only want this book. I won't return it unless . . ." She picked up her bag from the floor and, like a magician, took out a stack of books, a box of ballpoint pens, and a pad of white paper, ". . . unless you agree to write my dissertation for me."

I agreed, both because I wanted my book back and because I figured that if I didn't help her she wouldn't be able to write the dissertation herself.

"I knew you'd say yes." She jumped up.

"How did you know?"

"I can tell just by looking at you." Then she patted my shoulder, grinning. "Don't work too hard. No need to be creative. Just copy an idea from one of those reference books. Any idea is fine. No one will read my dissertation anyway. It's just part of the stupid graduation requirement."

Before I had a chance to say anything she tucked my *Fortress Besieged* under her arm and ran out the door. I could hear her bell-like laughter echoing in the hallway.

She kept her promise and returned the book a few days later. It was now dog-eared with a wrinkled cover. But I was glad to have it back.

"You aren't *reading* books, you're *eating* them." I tried to flatten the curled page corners. "I'll never lend you books again."

"Cheer up! You should feel happy that I liked your book. Now you can talk about books with me. I liked your notes too, but they seemed . . . hmm . . . too abstract. See, I don't remember any of them now. Were you really thinking that way when you read the book?"

"I don't know. It's good that you don't remember them."

She studied my face for a minute. "You're a bookworm, the biggest dreamer I've seen." She suddenly burst out laughing.

I knew she was referring to my notes. I crossed my arms, pretending to be angry.

"Okay, I won't tease you anymore." She put on a serious face. "You know what? After reading the book I began to think that I'm living in a besieged fortress."

"Everyone lives in a besieged fortress, more or less," I replied.

"I live inside and you live outside. Or the other way around. We can never live on the same side." She sighed deeply, as though she had discovered the most profound truth on earth.

❧

Summer break arrived in early July and after a few days' cleaning and packing, Donghua and Pingping had gone back to their hometowns and wouldn't return for the next semester until late August. Between the day finals ended and the day she was due to leave, Donghua knitted day and night to catch up with her assignment—one sweater for her brother and one scarf for her aunt. Whenever I saw her during that one week, she was either sitting on her bed knitting with her mosquito net up or sleeping with the mosquito net down. When she was up she would lean against two or three stacked pillows and remain in the same position for hours, a solemn look on her face, knitting.

I didn't return to my hometown to visit my parents over the summer break as I had planned. I wrote and told them I was participating in a research project in my department and had to stay on campus to help out. That was a lie. In fact I found a summer job teaching English to a middle-school student three times a week for three hours each session. The pay was ten yuan an hour. If I didn't miss any classes, I would make five hundred and forty yuan—enough to fund my trip to Miao Yan's hometown during the winter break, my secret plan. I was happy whenever I thought about what a surprise it would be to her.

Miao Yan never told me much about Yunnan and the Miao people. Whenever I asked she would say that the Miaos in her area were just like the Hans. "Don't you see me eating rice and speaking Mandarin every day?" she would say. After a while I stopped asking her and did my own research instead. Once I read in a travel book that Miaos had a custom of "kidnapping brides" and one of their festivals was called "Stepping Over Flower Mountains."

Another reason I decided to stay on campus was that I had to write Miao Yan's dissertation. Though I regretted that I had agreed to the minimum 100-page project without hesitation, I felt obliged to help her—without the dissertation she simply wouldn't be able to graduate.

She left the university the week after she returned my book. When I asked her what she would do during the summer break, she said she would stay off campus. I asked where she would be living but she wouldn't tell me. "I do what I need to do and I stay where I should stay," she said, smirking.

Then she said she had to run for an appointment. Before I could respond, she was gone.

It was the first time I had stayed in the dorm during a break. Most students had gone home and those who had stayed were either working or preparing for some kind of test. I was the only one on my floor but there were quite a few girls on other floors—I could tell how many rooms were occupied by the laundry hanging on the clotheslines in the hallways. The canteen opened for only half an hour, with two windows serving takeout food. The chefs looked sleepy and yawned often. Spiderwebs had grown in the corners of the cafeteria's locked door. Through the dusty windows, I could see chairs stacked upside down on the tables.

Along with most of the students, the rats were gone. Mosquitoes seemed much fewer and some nights I didn't even need to hang up my mosquito net.

There was no laundry on the clothesline outside Miao Yan's room. I once went there to see if she had left her contact information on the door. She hadn't.

Since my tutoring wouldn't start until a week later I set up a schedule to keep myself busy. My time was divided between violin practice, writing Miao Yan's dissertation, reading, writing poems or book reviews, and jogging around the campus—I began to like jogging. It felt good to have time under my control. Sometimes, when I was jogging through the quiet woods, I had a strange feeling that time had stopped and that I was jogging on the same spot, at the same speed.

The sky, the winding roads, the bees and snails, the pine needles on the ground, the leaves rustling under my feet seemed to be part of a huge, still picture. It wasn't until I emerged from the woods and heard people talking that the feeling began to fade, and then the world came back to me.

One day I saw a small sign on the poster board, an advertisement from a newly opened bookstore downtown, claiming to have a wide collection of fiction. After lunch I took the bus there. A traffic jam due to a multiple-car accident caused the bus to stop often. The driver, obviously new, operated the bus with abrupt movements. I had to hold the sides of the seat in front of me tightly to avoid falling. By the time I got off I felt sick.

The bookstore was close to the bus station, in the middle of a long brick bungalow. Outside, a bunch of balloons was tied to a stack of books on a desk. The owner was in his forties and wore a white shirt and a tie. He greeted me at the threshold with a five-yuan coupon. "I just opened the store, please buy your books here," he said in Mandarin, bowing deeply.

The bookstore had one room, slightly bigger than my dorm room. Two rickety bookshelves displayed the so-called wide collection of fiction, more than half of which consisted of Kung Fu novels. The rest of the bookshelves held magazines, comic strips, or popular books about Qi Gong or investments. Two seven- or eight-year-old boys were reading comic strips. A young man in a black T-shirt stood in front of the magazine section, humming *I Have Nothing*, the biggest rock hit that year. An old man held a Qi Gong book, his eyes narrowed.

Not wanting to disappoint the owner, I bought Lao Se's *Rickshaw Boy*, which I had read before. I was thinking I would give it to Miao Yan—she might like this humorous yet tragic novel. Since she had read *Fortress Besieged,* she had asked me to recommend other books to her. I suspected that this change in her had something to do with the male friend she had mentioned. If this person had read a book like *Fortress Besieged* he must have been very different from the other men Miao Yan went out with. A thought suddenly crossed my mind: he might be Miao Yan's new boyfriend. Perhaps she was with him right now. I felt a little jealous and sad but decided not to be bothered by my speculation.

I didn't go back to the university right away but walked about the neighborhood to get over my travel sickness. As I passed by a house with an open door I saw an old man in traditional clothes performing Cantonese opera inside. He moved his arms and legs slowly yet with a lot of strength. People— perhaps a dozen of them—sat on stools watching him and applauded when the old man finished an extremely long recitation. I had heard about this local art, which was said to be disappearing because few young people were interested in it.

I had been watching only a short time when a tall woman in the audience waved me in. I sat on a stool near the door and looked around—I was the only young person in the room.

Though I spoke little Cantonese, I could understand quite a bit. After watching for five minutes it was clear to me that the story was based on Mu Lan, a heroine who, dressed as a man, substituted for her father to fight in a war. It was boring to watch it since there was no music and the old man was extremely slow—he could stay in the same position more than a minute. Fortunately, he soon took a break and the woman who had waved me in earlier went to the center of the room and began to talk about nutrition for old people. She said pig-lung soup could prevent cancers and fish-head soup could help the eyesight. At this point I left.

I kept walking and quickly arrived at a busy street. It had been a long while since I had walked downtown by myself. When I walked with Miao Yan I seldom paid attention to my surroundings; I just let her take me where she wanted to go.

The street was filled with people. They passed by me—pretty, ugly, fat, thin, freckled, scarred, powdered, happy, weary—like a river. Each face was unique but I knew I wouldn't remember them. I suddenly had the odd thought that if I saw Miao Yan's face among all these others, I wouldn't be able to recognize it.

I followed the crowd across the street toward the bus station. A black sedan with an army license plate ignored the traffic light and divided the crowd, almost knocking down a pedestrian. The moment I stepped onto the footpath I heard a roar from the cars as they got a green light.

Under a tree by the roadside an old woman was selling used books on a piece of soiled plastic cloth. She wore a straw hat with a broken rim, her thin, tanned legs crossed underneath her. She stared intently at the pedestrians as if her eyes could somehow lure them to come to her shabby stand. I picked up a few books—they were all pirate copies of the most popular romance novels on the market.

While waiting for the bus I noticed a job fair going on inside a high school a little distance ahead. With the slight hope that I might come across Miao Yan there, I went in. A few companies, having failed to get space inside, had set up their stands at the entrance. Wherever I looked I saw job seekers, standing, squatting, or sitting, with a briefcase or folder in hand. Most were speaking Mandarin. Two uniformed security guards, both holding night sticks, pushed their way into the crowd, one yelling, "Stand in line!" the other, "Beware of pickpockets!" I almost felt relieved not to find Miao Yan in the mess.

When I returned to the university I was genuinely happy to see the familiar scenes on campus: the glittering greenery, the stately historical buildings, and the strolling people on the wide roads.

When I walked into my room the next morning, I saw Yishu lying on her bed, reading Zhang Ailing's *Red Rose and White Rose*. Though I didn't read Zhang Ailing, I knew she was most famous in the 1940s for her complicated love stories.

"You're here!" I said, surprised to see her. I had just returned from the library where I had been doing some research for Miao Yan's dissertation—I had decided to write about the library system's reform after the Cultural Revolution. It was boring to read those reference books but I was glad to be making good progress.

Yishu nodded, almost apologetically. "I'm waiting for a friend," she said, then went back to reading. She maintained a poker face when she was reading and I could never tell if she was interested, excited, moved, or saddened.

Yishu was an old-fashioned beauty. Her eyes were almond-shaped—the traditionally preferred shape for a beauty. They were bright and calm with two neatly plucked dark eyebrows arching above them. The tip of her nose was slightly upturned, giving her a Western look, even adding a touch of mischievousness to her oval face. She had long legs, not bony like Pingping's but well proportioned, with lean muscles. She said her muscular legs came from ballet practice in primary school. She was about Donghua's height but looked at least a few inches taller.

I sat at my desk and began to organize my drawers and bookshelf. When I took a textbook from the bookshelf, a photo slipped out and landed faceup on the floor. I picked it up. It was a picture of Miao Yan in traditional Miao costume. She must have been no more than seven years old when the picture was taken. She was dancing with a group of kids her age in front of a bamboo house, arms waving above her head, one leg kicking high in the air. Her round and smiling face was half covered by a tall and oversized black hat decorated with colorful embroidery. Around her neck was a shining neck ring on top of two elaborately embroidered silk ribbons tucked like a V into her belt. This picture was the only one in her album with her wearing Miao costume. But she disliked it and often said she would destroy it. I had stolen it from her in case she decided to throw it away one day.

"Who's the girl?" Yishu had obviously noticed the picture when it fell out of the book.

"My best friend. She's Miao and her name is Miao Yan, which means 'wild goose.' Her family lives in Yunnan. She's a library and information science student." I was surprised that I was willing to disclose so much to Yishu. Maybe I had been wanting to talk with her, since she was quite different from the other girls in my class. Or maybe I felt lonely being in the dorm alone.

"I didn't know she was a minority. I thought she was a Han like us. I've seen her a couple of times in West Five. She's pretty."

"She is," I said. "But she doesn't like this picture of her in Miao costume."

"She looks really cute in that picture."

"I think so, too. But she thinks she looks like a country girl. She likes to wear sexy clothes."

"Just like a good friend of mine then. She knows she has a good body and always wants to show it."

"I've never seen her."

"She's not a student here." Yishu sat up and put the book in her lap. "How do you know that Miao girl?"

"Oh," I hesitated, not feeling like telling her about the rooftop. "We met through a mutual friend. How did you meet your friend?"

"Same. Through a mutual friend," she replied quickly.

Silence set in. We both felt ill at ease. Yishu looked back at her book. She flipped over a few pages, closed the book, then opened it again.

I noticed there was another book on Yishu's bed. It looked brand-new.

"Did you go to a bookstore?" I pointed to the book.

"Oh, that one." Yishu picked up the book and handed it to me. "It's Marguerite Duras's *The Lover*. I got it from a friend as a birthday gift last week. She said I can read this kind of book now that I'm nineteen." She laughed.

I read the cover blurb and thumbed through the pages: a love affair between a Chinese man and a fifteen-year-old French girl in Vietnam.

"I just finished reading it for the second time. It's a beautiful book. You'll fall in love with it as soon as you open the pages," she said, then asked, "Do you think this kind of love is possible? I mean, for a man to love such a young girl?" She stared at me with her glimmering eyes.

I didn't know how to reply. "I guess so. I've never read anything like this," I said, thinking it was a stupid answer. Yishu must have expected me to say something more intelligent. I gave the book back to her.

"Love is mysterious, isn't it?" She took the book and stroked its cover gently.

I recalled Yishu once claiming that she believed in true romance, which she defined as knowing about each other, understanding each other, and entertaining each other. This definition sounded to me more like a description of bosom friends than a romance.

Pingping had told me that Yishu had a boyfriend and they had been together for years, but neither Pingping nor I had met her boyfriend or seen a picture of him. There was only one five- by seven-inch picture on her desk, secured in a crystal frame beside her glass vase. There were two girls in the picture. One was Yishu and the other, according to her, was her best friend since kindergarten. The picture had been taken in the Eastern Entertainment Park in Guangzhou just before she entered university. They were sitting on the edge of a pool back to back, holding hands. Both were wearing patterned swimsuits and were smiling broadly. The other girl had short-cropped, almost boyish hair, prominent dimples, and an elegant neck.

I felt the urge to ask Yishu about her definition of romance. I moved my chair a little closer to her bed but at this moment the speaker blared—someone was waiting for her downstairs. We exchanged a quick smile and Yishu left.

I ran into the girl in the photo on Yishu's desk a few days later. She looked pretty much the same as she did in the photo, though her face was a little thinner and her hair was now well below her shoulders. I had skipped my noon nap to run errands on campus. As I passed by the stadium I saw her strolling with Yishu on the main road outside the stadium. The girl, much taller than Yishu, was wearing a short white skirt and a bright yellow tank top, a big red handbag hanging from her right shoulder. A black crystal necklace, in the shape of a cross, glittered against her white neck. I wouldn't have noticed them if not for the girl's eye-catching outfit.

Yishu didn't see me until the girl nudged her in my

direction—I was waving at them. When Yishu saw me she smiled softly. I said hello and the girl greeted me with a light nod. Yishu didn't introduce us. The two of them immediately walked away, passing the white statue near the stadium, across a green lawn, and disappearing into a small wooded area. They weren't standing as close to each other as they had been earlier. Before bushes and trees blocked my view, the girl looked back over her shoulder. Our eyes met. Both of us turned away at the same time. I was too far away to see her expression clearly.

∽2∽

My student lived in an old neighborhood in Yue Xue District. Since the bus there only ran till 10 pm, I had no choice but to take my bike. Though I had never bicycled outside the university campus, I didn't think it would be difficult. Miao Yan once told me that in her first year she biked downtown every day to work as a waitress. "I was riding in high-heeled shoes and a tight skirt," she had said proudly.

My first class was on a Thursday evening. The streets around the university were wide with a separate bike lane, but downtown the bike lanes disappeared and I had to swerve around buses, cars, scooters, and pedestrians. Scooters were the worst. They came from nowhere and never obeyed the traffic lights. I often had to look over my shoulder to avoid them when making turns. At the intersection of Yue Xiu South Road and another small street, a scooter carrying three passengers—one in front, two behind—whizzed by from the rear and almost hit me. On the really busy roads, when riding was just too dangerous, I had to get off the bike and walk.

When I arrived at the neighborhood where my student lived I got lost. The alleys were dark and narrow. Though it hadn't rained for days the ground was slippery—people living here dumped their dirty dishwater in the street. All the apartment buildings looked run-down and many had no street number, just like the typical neighborhood in my hometown. I never thought there would be this kind of place in Guangzhou. I had to keep reminding myself that I needed money to visit Yunnan, otherwise I would have found a phone and called off my appointment.

After a lot of asking around, I finally found my student's apartment—a brown-brick, six-story building. I locked my bike and walked up the stairs to the fifth floor. Apartment 504 was in the middle of a narrow hallway and had two doors—outside a green security one, inside a wooden one with a peephole at head height. I pressed the buzzer next to the doorframe and listened for sounds from the inside.

The wooden door opened a few inches and a middle-aged, short-haired woman in pajamas appeared. "Are you Chen Ming?" she asked, a suspicious look on her thin face. I said yes but still had to show her my student identity card through the security door before she would let me in. I took off my shoes and sat where she asked me to—on a faded, saggy black leather sofa without much support either underneath or behind. There were two big windows in the living room, both covered with dark linen curtains that fell halfway between the windowsills and the floor. It was a hot evening. The air conditioner was running like an old motor that might break down at any time.

The woman asked me to call her Aunt Li and, while pouring iced water for me, yelled in Cantonese, "Ar Yu, come out to see your teacher!" Three doors led off the living room. The door on the left cracked open immediately and a man's half-bald head appeared through the crack. He introduced himself as Ar Yu's father, said he was busy, and asked his wife to make me feel at home. With a polite smile, he closed the door.

A few minutes later the door on the right opened and out came my student: medium-sized, wearing thick-framed glasses, a polo shirt, and khaki shorts. He greeted me with "Hello, Teacher Chen" in a lazy voice, hands folded on top of his head. His mother asked him to sit down next to me and proceeded to tell me how smart he was and how he wanted to get into the best university and how she and his father expected me to improve his English grade from a C to an A. I listened, observing my student from the corner of my eye—he was looking at the ceiling, his feet tapping lightly.

When the clock struck eight—the scheduled starting time for the class—the boy's mother abruptly stopped talking and let Ar Yu and me start the lesson in his room, which was small and cramped with a single-size bed, a plastic four-drawer dresser, a desk, a floor fan, and two chairs—the leather one for him and the wooden one for me.

As soon as his mother left the room and closed the door behind her, Ar Yu turned the floor fan to the highest setting. A loud humming immediately filled the room. "Now it's safe to talk," he said. He jumped onto the bed, crossed his legs, and took off his glasses. "Do you study literature?" he asked.

I nodded.

"Girls in your class must be romantic."

"I don't know about that. Let's start the lesson."

"Absolutely, Teacher Chen." He raised his hand and gave me an army salute.

I suppressed a laugh. "So, what do you want to learn?"

He swung his leg up and down. "I don't really need an

English teacher. If I wanted I could become an A student to-morrow."

"Well, your parents pay me ten yuan an hour to teach you."

"I asked them to find me an English teacher. A *female* English teacher. They have a lot of money. Ten yuan an hour is nothing."

"You're not paying out of your own pocket," I said. He looked like a spoiled kid to me.

"You speak like my ma. She's a phony. My ba is an even bigger phony. Look at this room. Nothing! They thought I'd be a good student if I didn't have girls' pictures on my walls."

I looked around. The only decoration was a map of the world occupying half the space above his bed. I laughed.

"How old are you?" he asked.

I told him.

He winked at me. "You're only two years older than I am. You must have skipped grades. Actually, you look younger than me. You have a baby face."

"You're the one with a baby face!"

"Don't be mad. I think you look cute. Haha, your face is red! You're shy!"

I reached for his English textbook on the desk, pretending to be serious. "No more joking. Let's start the class."

"Do you have a boyfriend?" He flipped over on his stomach, fists propping up his chin, legs kicking in the air.

I shook my head.

"I thought every college girl had a boyfriend."

"I don't have time for that."

"Which male movie star do you like the most?"

"I don't like any."

"Not even Jackie Chan?"

"Let's start the class." I opened his textbook, thinking his parents would fire me if they overheard our conversation.

"Just one more question."

I sighed and put down the book. "Okay, the last one. Make it quick."

"Do you think I'm handsome? Some girls in my class say I look like Jackie Chan." He combed his hair sideways with his fingers in a pretentious gesture. He had a broad forehead, big eyes, straight nose, and full lips.

"You're a handsome little kid," I said.

A knock sounded on the door. Ar Yu leaped from the bed, jumped into the leather chair at the desk, grabbed a book, and opened it. "Teacher," he said aloud, "what did you just say about this verb?" He was pointing to a random page in the book.

His mother walked in. She seemed happy with what she saw. "Teacher Chen, how's everything?"

"He's smart. I'm sure he'll do well in English," I said, pretending that I was going to write something on the sheet of white paper Ar Yu was handing me.

She touched her son's head, said something to him in Cantonese, and shut the door.

"She checks on me all the time." Ar Yu jumped back onto the bed and lay down.

"Did you have many teachers before me?" I put down the paper and the pen.

"Oh, yeah. But don't feel bad. My parents just don't trust people. They find me a new teacher every few months. They have a lot of secrets."

"Like what?"

"I think my ba takes bribes. He's a big guy in the government." He paused. "You won't tell anyone, right? You seem trustworthy, that's why I'm telling you. I still need his money to go to the United States. That's the only way I can escape from them. My ba said he'll send me to the U.S. after I graduate from high school. That's why he cares so much about my English."

"If they have so much money, why don't they spend some decorating the house?" I thought of the shabby leather sofa in the living room and the underpowered air conditioner.

"Adults are much trickier than us, don't you think so?" He looked puzzled.

I was glad he didn't categorize me as an adult.

"May I call you Sister Chen?"

"Of course," I replied, feeling suddenly sympathetic.

⌒

Miao Yan didn't show up on campus until the last week of the summer break. For a while I thought I would miss her so much that I wouldn't be able to do anything except mope. But I survived, thanks to books, her dissertation, my violin, and teaching Ar Yu. Toward the end of the break I thought I would hate her so much that I wouldn't want to speak to her anymore. But when I saw her I greeted her with boundless joy, forgetting all my misery, loneliness, and cursing.

She was only on campus for less than a week before telling me that she was going to Shenzhen for a one-month internship.

"Wow, that's great," I said.

"It's a private-owned company. I hope they can get my dossier from the university. Without the dossier I won't be able to stay in Shenzhen." She didn't look as happy as I thought she should have. "It's my last chance."

"Of course, they can do that."

"I wish you were our university's chancellor." She sighed. "Or, better yet, Minister of Education. It's much more complicated than you might think. But I'll try my best."

"No pain, no gain. Isn't that the old saying?"

She nodded but I could tell that her mind had drifted off. She left the next day, taking a big suitcase filled with her expensive suits.

I was now in my second year. With fewer mandatory classes I had more time for my own reading. I began to subscribe to *Foreign Literature Review* and became fascinated by modernism. I read whatever I could find—Eliot, Camus, Kafka, Beckett, Pound, Kerouac, and other authors my foreign literature professor wouldn't discuss in class and my classmates didn't know. The more philosophical and abstract the books were, the more interesting I found them. I was at the age when life seems meaningless unless constantly examined, evaluated, and adjusted.

On a warm day in early September I headed for West Five from the library. The sun hid behind clouds and tinted their edges. The breeze brushed my hair back behind my ears. From the speakers installed on lampposts came Beethoven's *Ode to Joy,* then a girl's gentle voice reading a poem from Tagore's *The Crescent Moon.* The broadcast went off three times a day: fifteen minutes before the first class at eight in the morning, at lunchtime, and between five thirty and six thirty in the afternoon. Now it was lunchtime.

Wearing a short-sleeved white shirt, beige pants, and white plastic sandals, I held a thick, hard-backed copy of *Dream of the Red Chamber* over my chest. Last week the professor teaching the novels from the Ming and Qing Dynasties assigned us a few classic novels, including *Dream of the Red Chamber*. I had often tried to read it before I came to university but could never finish it. The conflicts between the feudalistic families seemed too intricate and out-of-reach to me. But I liked the poems in the book and even wrote a few in a similar style.

"Ming!" I heard someone yell from behind me.

It was Pingping. She was wearing an orange T-shirt with the university's logo on it and a pair of green workout shorts. Seen from a distance, she looked like a big carrot. Before she reached me she jumped down from her old bike, which she had bought from one of her hometown acquaintances for ten yuan not long ago. The bike had rusty handlebars, severely scratched chrome trim, and no bell. When she was riding it, it shook all over, making weird sounds like those a desperate mouse might emit when caught in a trap. The girls in my class nicknamed it "ambulance" because when other bikers saw her coming they would stay as far from her as possible. A few months earlier she had bought a brand-new bike for two hundred yuan but it was stolen a week later. She reported it to the Security Department only to be told not to bother—there were too many cases like hers. "It's a big university. There are all kinds of people here," they said. After that she had sworn she'd never spend more than twenty yuan on a bike.

"Aha, you got the book!" Pingping stood in front of me. "I was just in the library, wondering who was so quick."

"I read fast. You can have it in three days." I smiled.

"Cool. It'll take me at least two weeks to read such a difficult book."

"Are you going to the gym?"

"Yes. I went there yesterday, too." She showed me her leg.

"Do you think it looks a little thicker?" Knowing the answer herself, she lowered her skinny leg and sighed.

"What a change! You never used to go to the gym."

"It's different now. The men's basketball team trains there every day for their big games. They all look so handsome. When they're sweaty, they sometimes take off their tops. My, you should see that!"

"No wonder you're there."

"That's why I'm wearing bright clothes—so they can see me. You never know when you'll hit the lottery." She wiped the sweat from her forehead and grinned.

Though Pingping and I weren't good friends, I had begun to like her more and more because she was optimistic and so full of energy.

"Where is Donghua?" I asked.

"That workaholic! She has to finish knitting a long list of stuff for her unborn nephew. Finally her sister-in-law is pregnant with a boy."

"Don't her brother and his wife have two girls already?"

"No one really follows the one-child-per-family policy in their village. They'd rather be homeless than not have a boy in the family. The more boys, the merrier. Even Donghua thinks so. I'd be curious to know how all these men are going to find a wife someday. According to my prediction—" She stopped and tilted her head. "Listen! Something interesting on the speaker."

I listened. It was a male voice: ". . . leaders from the Education Ministry. We welcome and look forward to their inspection. To make our university a first-rate university nationally and internationally, it's critical to build a healthy and positive environment for our students. For a university student, it's as important to achieve excellence in your major as it is to have

103

the correct attitude toward life and the world. Studying science and arts should be combined with cultivating socialistic ideology . . ." His voice was stern, like the news announcers from China Central Television in Beijing.

"What's interesting about that? Don't they say that every day?" I said.

"I heard it's a little different this time. There's a nationwide competition among universities for the Top Ten Campus Award. It seems our university is really serious about it. I read in the university newspaper that many new rules will be enforced."

"Like what?"

"Like smoking is prohibited, lovers can't hug or kiss or even hold hands in public, and girls can't wear revealing clothes or makeup. Oh, yes, and we have to keep our rooms tidy every day. The Student Association will inspect all the dorms frequently. Poor Donghua, she really has to do something about her mess. Anyway, we'll have to wait and see." She got on her bike, one hand holding the handlebar. "I have to go now. The basketball team will finish training soon."

"Good luck!" I said.

I listened to more of the announcement on my way back to the dorm. The broadcaster's serious voice was alarming, contrasting with the relaxing scenery of such a beautiful early autumn day. I took out my radio and tuned in to a classical music channel. Mozart's *Magic Flute* instantly filled the air.

A lot of students were gathered around the poster board as I passed. Some looked indignant. They must have been reading the new rules. I noticed that the once-crowded lawn was completely empty. A middle-aged man wearing an orange vest and a cap stood on the edge of the lawn, a small flag in his

hand and a whistle in his mouth. He must have been employed by the university to prohibit people from walking on the lawn, so it would be at its best when the inspectors arrived.

Though I thought it ridiculous to try to enforce these rules, I didn't think they would affect me much. I didn't smoke or wear makeup or have a boyfriend. To me, life would be just as it had been. Also, I didn't believe that the university would act on the rules—we were old enough and should have the freedom to do what we liked.

The inspectors from the Education Ministry arrived a week later. By now not only was the lawn closed but a guard post had been set up at the main entrance—visitors had to register when they came in and sign out when they left. Street sweeping had increased from once to twice a day. The day before the inspectors arrived, the cleaners even came to West Five to wash the hallways and stairs with detergent.

The Student Association checked the dorms frequently, so we had to keep our rooms tidy at all times. During the day we took down our mosquito nets and folded our blankets into a square, as soldiers do. We also bought a few bottles of air freshener to make the room smell better. These days Donghua often complained about not remembering where she had hidden her belongings. "I'm missing a sock. Anyone seen it?" she would ask, a bare foot high in the air.

A group of uniformed workers from the Security Department patrolled the campus and would stop students who were smoking, or wore makeup, or broke any of the other new rules. They would threaten to report these students to their departments—as one of the punishments, they had to write a letter of apology to the university and read it aloud in front of their class. More seriously, a permanent record was included

in their dossiers so that they would have trouble getting a good job when graduating. In the evenings, these security workers would raid the woods where lovers liked to go. Once, as I was walking back to West Five, I saw them in a half-circle, quietly approaching the woods along the roadside, their torches off. When they were close, they suddenly turned on the torches and shouted, "Freeze!" More than a dozen students, boys and girls, fled. Some unlucky ones were caught. If I hadn't seen it with my own eyes, I wouldn't have believed that it was happening at a university. My heart sank, seeing the university treating students like criminals.

Feeling powerless and frustrated, I turned to books. At the time I was obsessed with *Ulysses*. Out of its intricate and obscure sentences, from those fabricated figures and plots, I sought the significance of my existence and the meaning of the universe. I was in a dark and desperate mood when I was immersed in that book.

While the campaign was going on, I spent a lot of time in the Central Library so I wouldn't be disturbed by it. It was the biggest library on the campus, a five-story rectangular building roofed with red slate. Its ten spacious study rooms could hold more than three thousand students.

I soon found my favorite seat in Room One on the first floor. It had six big windows all looking out over a row of eucalyptus trees, and only one door, opening to a poorly lit hallway. On the other side of the hallway was the reference room where rare publications and documents were kept. I often used the reference room when I was working on Miao Yan's dissertation. In Room One there were sixteen rows of desks and my favorite seat was in the first row, next to the first window. There were only two chairs near the seat, one across the desk, the other on the right. Both chairs had broken legs and

so were always empty. The library staff hadn't bothered to replace them.

Miao Yan was in good spirits when she returned from Shenzhen in mid October. The company in Shenzhen had promised her that they would talk with the university about her dossier. By then, the inspectors from the Education Ministry had left. Soon after they left, the security guard at the main entrance and the uniformed workers disappeared, the lawn reopened, and the long waiting line outside West Five reformed. Everything went back to normal.

I didn't tell Miao Yan about my frustration with the campaign but she seemed to have detected it from my unusually taciturn manner—she must have heard about the campaign when she was in Shenzhen. She came to see me almost daily. Only she could pull me out of my imaginary literary world and make me laugh. I accepted her, admired her, worshiped her—even her vanity and materialism—wholeheartedly. When she had time for me, we would go by bus to coffee bars downtown, chatting there for hours over one drink or loitering on the street aimlessly to kill time. One week in late October she visited me at least twice a day, as if I was the only person she knew on the whole campus and in the whole city of Guangzhou. And I, like a dying plant in the desert, longed to see Miao Yan as such a plant would long for water.

My first publication in a literary magazine came at the end of October. It was the poem that Miao Yan had read in the university newspaper when we first met. Though I had been published in the university newspaper before, I couldn't contain my excitement when I opened the letter, and went to see Miao Yan immediately. She happened to be in her room that day, filling out some forms the company in Shenzhen had sent her as part of the background review package. Since she had returned from her internship she had been attending her classes regularly and had even begun to take notes. When I saw her, she was frowning at the paperwork on her desk.

I almost stammered when I told her the good news.

"That's great! Let's go to Shamian Island to celebrate! I need fresh air, too." She pushed aside her paperwork.

She always liked to go to Shamian Island and said it was the most beautiful place in Guangzhou. She knew where each foreign embassy was situated and how many statues stood along the beach.

We took Bus 208 to Shamian. The dim sum restaurant we had planned to go to had a two-hour queue. "We'll eat something fast for now, then come back for evening tea," Miao Yan suggested. Having lived in Guangzhou for more than a year by that stage, I knew that "evening tea" was actually a dim sum meal. Old Cantonese people eat five meals a day: morning tea, lunch, afternoon tea, dinner, and evening tea, though for dim sum they typically order only two items.

After much debate, we ended up eating yang rou pao mo, a dish of hand-broken bread in mutton broth, most popular in northern China.

"A friend of mine in Shenzhen likes this dish a lot," Miao Yan said after the meal, applying new lipstick with her compact in her hand.

"Who is this friend?"

"It's not important. I don't see him much myself."

I wondered if this person was the same as the one who had read *Fortress Besieged*. I wanted to ask but she stopped me by saying, "Don't ask more."

We walked past the European-style mansions and rows of luxuriant banyan trees, their aerial roots hanging from outspread limbs like an old man's beard. Every few steps there were bronze statues. One was of a Chinese girl and a Western girl greeting each other in their own traditional ways. Miao Yan stood next to the Western girl, mimicking her while I played the Chinese girl, folding my hands together at the waist and bending my knees.

Standing on Pearl River beach, Miao Yan executed a few graceful pirouettes. "I'll buy a house here someday." She laughed.

We found a patch of newly planted lawn and lay down side by side. A pallid full moon hung in the sky like a curious eye watching us. Near the bronze statue of "Beauty of the Century," which showed three women of different generations, an artist was playing gu zheng. The music was *Fisherman's Evening Song,* slow and expressive. I was glad the music was not intrusive; it was even romantic.

"Your dissertation—" I thought she would like to know about its progress. I had written more than fifty pages already. I had spent so much time in the library's archive room that the librarian had reserved a seat for me.

"Boring," Miao Yan yawned. "Can we talk about something else?"

I looked at her sleepy eyes and realized that I had always wanted to know why she was interested in being friends with me in the first place. So I asked.

She was amused. "You play the violin and you read books."

"A lot of girls play the violin and read books."

"You write poems. You know how to write."

"Were you thinking about asking me to write your dissertation from the very beginning?"

She laughed. "What a clever guess!" She patted the back of my head. "I feel safe being with you. I know you won't hurt me."

"No one will hurt you."

"You don't know. This world's more complicated than you think," she said. "But I can always trust you, right?"

"Of course you can. You're my best friend. Actually you're the only friend I have in Guangzhou," I said eagerly.

"Really? That's too much responsibility for me. You should meet other people."

"Responsibility? What are you talking about? I can take care of myself perfectly well."

"Wonderful. You know what people would say? They'd say our being together is like a white daisy in a black dye vat." She played with the grass that grew around the rock next to her. "You're a top student, a published poet, a violinist, a person with a lot of talent and ambition. Who am I? I hate studying, I do things no teachers or parents would like to see their kids do. Aren't you afraid that you'll become a bad girl under my influence? You know, sometimes I think it'd be better for you if you didn't know me."

"That's nonsense! You're not a dye vat. I'm no white daisy, either." I squeezed her arm gently and leaned over to whisper in her ear, "I like being with you. We're like sisters."

"Well, that's nice," she said absentmindedly, not looking at me, her face as blank as a mask.

I sighed. Apparently she was not in a good mood tonight. I

figured she must have been having problems with the company in Shenzhen. "Let's talk about colors," I said, trying to cheer her up. "What's your favorite color?"

"Black? Red? Dark purple? I don't know. I used to like white, but not anymore. Dramatic colors suit me better." After a pause, she said, "I think we were connected in a previous life. It's our destiny to be each other's best friend."

"Don't be so superstitious."

"I'm a non-practicing Buddhist. I believe in fate." She picked up a small stone and hurled it into the darkness. "Ming, do you know how much I admire you?"

"Admire me? Why?"

She buried her head in her arms, her hair spreading over her back like a small blanket. At that moment the moon moved behind a thin veil of cloud and was obscured, cut into patches of different sizes. I felt a cool breeze brush my face. Against the soft light of the moon, Miao Yan's silhouette was curvaceous and graceful, like a scene from a dream world.

"I just do. Not growing up is a good thing sometimes."

"Well, you're the one who's always telling me that every girl will grow into a woman sooner or later."

"Do you love your parents?" she said, changing the subject.

"Of course. They're my parents."

"You love your ba?"

"I guess so, though sometimes he's annoying. He treats me like a ten-year-old. Do this, don't do that. Stuff like that."

"Tell me more about him." She propped her chin on her folded hands, looking at me intently.

"After being a teacher for so many years, he talks like a teacher even at home. All we talk about is school and books. We seldom talk about other things. When he talks with me, he leans back in his chair, holding a cup of oolong tea with both hands while I sit across from him. He stays in his study a lot, not always reading or writing. Sometimes he just sits there, eyes closed. Whenever I see him like that I wonder what's on his mind. He's probably thinking of the tough years on the farm, or books that he never got published. I don't know. But overall he isn't bad. He buys me all the books I want and he cares about me." Then I realized where her question might have come from. I quickly added, "Just like your ba, my ba would spank or scold me if I did something wrong. He isn't perfect. No father is perfect."

"Did he ever spank you?"

"You bet. When I was little he spanked me a few times with bamboo rods because I couldn't recite the ancient poems he'd asked me to learn. He was strict. Those bamboo rods were thin but hurt like crazy. They'd leave red marks on my skin for a week. Whenever he spanked me he'd feel guilty afterward and buy me sweets and books to make up for it. He never said sorry to me, though. I guess it never occurred to him that a father needs to say sorry to his own children."

She smiled slightly. "Isn't that true?" she said. "When was the last time he spanked you?"

"Hmm, I don't remember. Maybe when I was eight or ten? After we returned to the city he never spanked me again. Well, perhaps the isolated life on the farm made him get depressed and angry more easily."

"So you don't hate him anymore?"

"I don't think I ever hated him. I guess no one is perfect and one must learn how to forgive." I looked at her and hoped she would agree with me.

But she didn't respond immediately. She stared at the road for a while before saying, "You're lucky. Do you know that?"

I thought she was talking about my father, so I nodded.

"After all, you're not from Yunnan and you're not a minority."

"What's wrong with Yunnan? What's wrong with being a Miao? You have the world-famous Stone Forest and the Dali Butterfly Spring. The Miao costumes are so beautiful. Oh, also, Shen Congwen, the contemporary writer who wrote *Border Town* and *Long River*, isn't he a Miao? I've always wanted to visit Yunnan. You can be my guide—" I was about to tell her that I had saved enough money for a trip to Yunnan.

"Forget about it! They have nothing to do with me. I hate Yunnan, I hate everything about it." She turned her back to me. "We live in different worlds."

I knew that the best way to comfort her when she was moody was to leave her alone for a while. Lying on my back, I stretched my legs and arms a few times and clasped my hands behind my head. The pale, round moon was still covered by wispy clouds. I stared at it and its dark craters and thought about all the fairy tales I had read about the moon when I was little. I felt safe, relaxed, happy. My eyes started to get blurry, then I sensed a light drizzle. I opened my eyes. A dark cloud was moving slowly over the sky. It approached the moon, cut its edge, floated over it, and moved away. I tilted my head and saw Miao Yan lying beside me with her knees up against her chest. She looked slender and curvy; her waist and upper body formed a smooth half-circle. Her hips were narrower than her shoulders and were tightly wrapped by a pair of well-fitting low-cut black jeans—I could see her skin at her waist. It surprised me that she looked so small and vulnerable—I had always thought of her as much bigger and more muscular since she was half a head taller than me.

Ten minutes later I got up and squatted in front of Miao Yan, thinking about asking her what was wrong. Then I realized she had fallen asleep. I sat down beside her, my legs crossed, listening to her even breathing. She wore a black embroidered cardigan over a white shirt, the top two buttons undone. Half of her face was exposed in the moonlight and her skin was as delicate as fresh wax. Her lips were slightly parted as though she had fallen asleep when she was speaking. The lipstick on her lower lip was smeared and went slightly beyond the lip line—she must have been biting her lip with her teeth, as I remembered her doing before. I stared at her lips and suddenly wanted to kiss them. I brushed a few strands of loose hair from her forehead and moved my hand near her nostrils to feel the warmth in her breath. Then I lowered my head toward her lips. I jumped up with a start when I saw her tightly closed eyelids twitch slightly. But she didn't wake up; she just murmured and moved her hands from her side to her chest, as if she was cold.

It was the first time that I had ever felt the urge to kiss a girl. But at that moment it seemed so natural, so pure, like I wanted to kiss a beautiful flower or a white snowflake falling on my hand from the sky. Afterward, when I went back to my room and lay down on the bed, I began to wonder why I'd had the desire to kiss her. I didn't panic or anything like that; I just thought it was odd that I had wanted to kiss her.

Pingping had a boyfriend! One Friday night around seven o'clock, I heard Dama's voice from the speaker: "301, Wang Pingping. Shu Zhong is waiting for you in the duty room."

Pingping was putting on makeup near the window. She jumped up from her chair, one hand holding a lipstick, the other her mascara. "It's him! It's him! He's here!" she screamed at Donghua and me.

"When did you start seeing him? How come I didn't know? Who is this guy?" Donghua dropped her knitting and sat up on the bed.

"We met on the train to my hometown during the summer break. He was on his way to Harbin to visit relatives and happened to sit across from me. He's in law school. You'd have seen him. He's everything I want in a man. He said he'd come to see me after school started and here he is! What should I do?" Her voice was so eager and nervous that I was afraid her vocal cords would jump out of her throat.

"You'd better change your clothes now," Donghua said.

"I am!" Pingping jumped onto her bed and began to take off her T-shirt.

"Wow!" Donghua looked away. "What about putting down your net first?"

Pingping slipped into a blue dress with puffy sleeves and little white flowers printed all over it. She twisted her body a few times to zip it up at the back. "How do you like this dress?"

It wasn't a nice dress but she looked slender and delicate. Her bony face shone with pink patches on her cheeks; her whole frame trembled with excitement. For the first time, her scrawny body looked pretty to me.

Both Donghua and I nodded our approval. Pingping smiled shyly. After quickly combing her short hair and checking her makeup in the mirror, she said, "Wish me luck!" and disappeared out the door.

Pingping returned a few minutes after curfew. I was lying on my bed listening to Mozart through headphones. Donghua was knitting by the light of her torch. She was half done with

115

a green wool sweater for her mother. For over two weeks she had eaten only instant noodles to save money for the yarn. "It'll be a New Year's gift for her," she had told me. "She's never had a wool sweater in her life."

Though it was dark I could see the happiness in Pingping's face. She tossed her handbag on her desk, then threw herself on the bed. "You know what? We held hands today!" I heard her whisper to Donghua.

The next evening the speaker crackled again, asking for Pingping. She returned around midnight. Under Donghua's relentless interrogation, Pingping finally admitted that she and the law student had kissed.

"You two were fast! It doesn't sound right to me to kiss the second time you meet," Donghua said, spreading out the wool sweater on the bed.

"What's wrong with kissing on the second date? Passion's what matters. I've known him since the summer break. He even called me while he was in Harbin. We're not little kids. Some of the girls I know who didn't go to college have already done *it* with their boyfriends. They're about our age."

I knew what "it" meant.

Maybe because it was dark or because the music I was listening to was soothing, I felt like asking Pingping and Donghua about men. Oddly, though Miao Yan often bragged about her love life she never talked about her physical involvement with men, apart from the single time that she mentioned the teacher kissing her when she was thirteen. Once we went to see a movie together and she laughed at a scene in which the male and female protagonists kissed passionately. She said the acting was fake but wouldn't tell me how they should have kissed. "You'll know when the time comes," she said.

116

Another time, when she told me that she'd lost her virginity at fifteen, I asked her what she meant by losing her virginity and how it had happened, but she became angry and made me promise that I would never ask her such questions again. She acted as if she didn't want me to know what goes on between men and women, as if she was trying to protect me from some kind of danger that perhaps she herself wasn't even sure about.

I thought of what she had said to me on Shamian Island about her being a black dye vat and me being a white daisy. Did she view herself as a danger to me, as a black dye vat might be to a white daisy? Did she secretly admire my innocence and ignorance of men, knowing she could never return to that period of her own life?

"Pingping, what was it like when he kissed you?" I finally mustered the courage to ask.

"Was he a good kisser?" Donghua added.

We all laughed.

"More than just good. I almost suffocated." Pingping chuckled.

Her answer drew boos and hoots from Donghua and me. Donghua recited a line she had just penned dramatically, "You! You! Like fire, melted my lonely heart." She sat up on her knees, both hands on her chest, and let her body fall heavily on the bed. I'd never seen her be so funny.

"How did you feel when his tongue . . . his tongue touched yours?" I asked.

"My goodness, what an embarrassing question! I can't tell you that."

"Come on, Pingping, we're roommates and you should just tell us what it's like to kiss a man," Donghua said.

"Okay, I guess there's nothing I can do but sacrifice my privacy and tell you something about romance." Pingping moved her chair to the middle of the room, halfway between my bed and Donghua's.

"Shoot!" Donghua and I both chanted.

"What I'll tell you isn't suitable for kids. You either stop me right now or you have to let me finish. Neither of you is allowed to cover your ears, understand?"

Donghua and I nodded eagerly.

"Before his lips touched mine my heart was beating so madly that I thought it was going to jump out of my chest. I was surrounded by heated airwaves and I had nowhere to escape. The moment his lips touched mine I felt like a match had been lit on my lips. You wouldn't mistake this moment for any other moment in your life. In fact, not just my lips, my whole face, my whole body felt like it was on fire.

"Then he forced his tongue into my mouth. I resisted at first but the feeling was so good that I soon accepted his tongue and kissed back fiercely and wholeheartedly. Our tongues were intertwined, darting desperately in and out of each other's mouths. Our bodies were pressed against each other's and I could hear his heart beating. I thought I was going to faint from suffocation. All my thoughts and feelings were evaporating and fading away. Time and space didn't exist anymore. I was like a candle burning from both ends and I was melting quickly, melting into a patch of liquid wax . . ."

Her voice was getting quieter and quieter as the narration continued. By the time she was finished she was whispering. I couldn't see her eyes but I imagined that they must have been clear and shining like diamonds. After she finished talking, none of us spoke or moved for a minute.

"Wow, the irresistible power of love," Donghua said.

"I wish I could live in that moment for the rest of my life. It was so sweet, like a poem," Pingping said.

At that moment Donghua blurted out, "Pingping, you won't get pregnant, will you?"

"What are you talking about?"

"I'm worried for you since you two kissed so much," Donghua said indignantly.

"Haha, you're worried that kissing could make a person pregnant? You stupid girl! My stomach's hurting. Haha . . ." She covered her head with a pillow.

I laughed as well. What a ridiculous question Donghua had asked! Of course kissing wouldn't make a person pregnant. A man and a woman would have to sleep together to get pregnant. I kept laughing until two questions I had never thought about before came to me. Why would sleeping together result in pregnancy? What do a man and a woman do when they sleep together? I didn't have the answers. In middle school, I took physiology classes but girls and boys took the class separately. In the girls' class, the teacher only taught the chapters about a female's physiological structure, such as how her breasts would grow and how her hips would widen during puberty. The remaining chapters were for after-class reading. Since the class was optional and we didn't have exams, I never bothered to read the rest of the chapters. I thought it was time to solve my puzzle. "Pingping, how does a woman get pregnant?"

"You're kidding, right? Don't tease me like this."

Pingping stopped laughing—she realized that Donghua and I weren't joking. She cleared her throat and announced, "Pregnancy is the process of a male's sperm and a female's egg merging."

"How do they merge?" Donghua asked.

119

"I don't know what to say." Pingping breathed a long sigh. "Making love means that the guy takes his thing, you know, and puts it into the girl, between her legs. Then the guy's sperm travels to the egg and fertilizes it and the sperm and the egg merge. After that you won't be a virgin anymore. Losing your virginity means you've made love with a man. Don't ask me any more questions. I'm still a virgin, I swear. I've learned all of this from magazines. I also overheard my older girlfriends talk about how to make love to men. They said it's a lot of fun."

"Stop it, you dirty girl!" Donghua said. She drummed her feet against her bed so hard that it sounded as though the bed might collapse.

"Don't blame me. You asked me to tell you about it! I told you it wasn't for kids," Pingping protested.

I said nothing. I was trying to imagine what "making love" was like. I pictured a few scenes in my mind, but they seemed weird to me. I laughed.

"I can't believe you're laughing. Making love is nothing to be ashamed of. Sex has existed since the world began. Human beings, cats, dogs, birds, and every other animal in the world need to make love to have babies," Pingping said.

"I don't want to get pregnant. I don't want to have sex," Donghua said.

"Don't want to have sex? I don't believe you for a second. You aren't a nun. Of course you'll have sex someday," Pingping said. Then she lowered her voice and said secretively, "You know what? You don't need a man to get pleasure. You can make love with yourself. That's called masturbation. And you can even reach orgasm through it. Have you tried?"

I remembered the night I'd seen Donghua touching herself on her bed. I had never tried but didn't want to admit it. I suddenly felt ashamed that I knew so little.

"I've tried. But I think it's a dirty thing to do. Some girls in my village said you'd die early if you did it more than once a month," Donghua said reluctantly. "Sometimes I enjoy it but I'm not sure if I've ever had an orgasm."

"I can always have an orgasm after reading porn magazines. I have something for you guys," Pingping said. She walked to her bed and dragged a black suitcase from underneath the bed. The suitcase was locked. She shook out a key from a pen-holder on her desk and unlocked the suitcase. From under a pile of clothes she pulled out a few magazines, throwing one to me and one to Donghua. "It cost me a fortune to get them from the black market on Zhong Shan Fifth Road. I can take you there if you want to buy some. You two must keep your mouths shut. If our department finds out we'll all be expelled. I'm not joking."

I switched on my torch and picked up the magazine. It didn't have a front cover and its pages were thin and yellowish. The back cover was still there, half secured by a staple. There was a naked woman on it. She was bending over, her behind high in the air, her huge breasts dangling like two sandbags. Her hands were crossed over her pubic area. Seen from the space between her fingers, the area was shaved. She looked frightened; her eyes were wide open and her tongue was sticking out from between her red lips. There were numerous creases on the cover, some cutting through the woman's body and face, creating a strange scarring effect. It was the first time I had ever seen a picture of a naked woman. The first word that popped into my mind was "prostitute."

I had often seen naked women as a child. The house where my parents lived, from the time I was in primary school to middle school, was in a neighborhood without a hot-water supply. In winter everyone would go to the local public bathhouse to take a shower. When it was too cold to take a cold-water shower at home, my mother would take me to the bath-house every Wednesday and Saturday afternoon. Most people there were middle-aged women, many overweight. A few were so fat that their poorly shaped breasts would dangle over their potbellies, and the fat on their thighs would move up and down when they walked. The blue veins in their legs spread underneath their skin like earthworms. In the bath-house, I would squint and try not to glance at them.

It had never occurred to me that a woman's naked body could be arousing. When I thought about naked women, I thought about those overweight middle-aged women in the bathhouse. But this time, holding the porn magazine, I felt different. At the first sight of the naked woman, I felt my body getting warm and my heart rate rising. There was an inexplicable tumult within my body.

I looked at Donghua out of the corner of my eye. She sat on her bed motionless, holding the magazine with both hands. I couldn't see her expression but I assumed that she must have been feeling as helpless as I was.

Pingping sat at her desk, facing me, whistling. She shook her head periodically as if she was ridiculing something in the magazine in front of her. She must be laughing at Donghua and me, I thought.

I opened the magazine to a new page and saw a photo spread of white men and women. Though the torchlight was weak and the print quality poor, I could still make out all the naked bodies in different positions. In one picture, a man was lying beside a woman, one of his hands holding his penis while the other rested on the woman's pubic area. The woman seemed intoxicated; her eyes were closed and her hands touching her balloon-like breasts. If Miao Yan had seen this picture, she would have yelled admiringly, "At least 40D!" I frowned at this page. How disgusting!

I flipped quickly to the next page. It was a full-page picture: two naked Asian women were kissing, one touching the other's breast.

I wanted to turn the page, but I couldn't—my hands weren't following my mind. My breathing was getting heavier and I was becoming agitated. My bra and underwear seemed tight, which made me want to go to the bathroom. I took a deep breath, trying to force myself to calm down, but my hands were trembling helplessly and the magazine slipped from my hands onto the bed, then landed on the floor with a thud.

Both Donghua and Pingping raised their heads, looking at me. For a few seconds I heard only my own breathing.

"You're frightened by a few pictures!" Pingping laughed aloud. "You're a little kid!"

Donghua laughed as well, but her laughs were short and dry.

"That's not true." I was struggling to find an explanation. "The pictures don't frighten me at all. I wasn't holding the magazine properly, so it slipped from my hand. I—"

"It's just sex. I think it can be fun. Actually . . ." She hesitated. "What the hell, I'll just tell you guys. When he kissed me, I felt his erection through his pants. You know what I mean? It was big and hard. I was so aroused that I wanted to touch it. I wanted him to be inside me."

"Oh my goodness!" Donghua exclaimed.

Pingping picked up the magazine from the floor—unfortunately it was open at the page of the two women kissing.

"I see," she said, holding the magazine closer. "They're homosexuals."

"Homosexuals? I've heard about them. They have a mental illness," Donghua said. "They must be Americans. I heard there are a lot of them in the U.S."

"These two women are Asians," Pingping said disapprovingly.

"Women? Disgusting! They must be Japanese then. Only capitalist countries have homosexuals and AIDS. China doesn't."

"How do you know?"

"I read it in the newspaper."

"That's propaganda. I don't believe that's the case. China's so big. There must be homosexuals around. You never know."

"But why does a girl want to make love with another girl? It doesn't make sense. Can't she just touch herself?" Donghua said.

"Don't ask me. How do I know? I'm not a homosexual." Pingping giggled. "I have a boyfriend."

"Don't show off." Donghua threw her magazine back to Pingping. "I think sex is dirty and men are dirty. I don't want to have sex with a man."

"If your ma thought the same way, you wouldn't have come into this world. I don't want to become an old maid. I like having a boyfriend, maybe even more than one. I want to get married and have babies. If China allowed a couple to have more than one child, I'd have at least three." Pingping tucked the magazines back into the bottom of her suitcase, locked it, and pushed it underneath the bed.

"Three kids? My! You really have to make love with your husband every day to have three kids," Donghua said.

"You're jealous, aren't you? It's none of your business how

many times I'll make love to my husband." Pingping threw a pillow at Donghua. Donghua caught it on her bed and threw it at me. The pillow hit me right on the head and fell on the floor.

"Ming, are you okay?" Pingping stopped laughing and walked over to pick up the pillow.

"I'm all right. I'm okay. I'm just a little sleepy." I managed a big yawn.

"Are you sure?" Donghua asked.

"Don't take those magazines seriously," Pingping said. "The models are prostitutes. They do it for money. If I'd known you'd be upset I wouldn't have showed them to you."

"I'm sleepy. I'm going to sleep now," I said. I put down the mosquito net and covered myself from head to toe with a blanket.

The picture filled my mind. It was unacceptable and obscene for two women to touch each other like that, I thought. Though I had read about homosexuals I had never thought such people really existed. Like Donghua, I had also read that they didn't exist in China. I retraced in my mind all the books I had read and tried to recall if any had ever mentioned a sexual relationship between two women. Nothing came to mind. Then I assured myself that Miao Yan and I were close and intimate because we cared about each other and wanted to help each other out. I hadn't the slightest desire to see her naked or touch her naked body. But then I asked myself why, if that was true, I sometimes wanted to touch her or even kiss her. Since I'd met Miao Yan I hadn't been interested in having a boyfriend. Though it hadn't seemed to me a problem before, I now thought it a little puzzling. I wrapped myself tightly in the blanket and forced myself not to think for a while by counting sheep. That somehow helped. At the end I was so exhausted that I fell asleep.

When I woke next morning, the first thing I said to myself was that I would have a boyfriend by the end of the semester. This resolution relaxed me magically.

⌒

"That company in Shenzhen won't hire me." Miao Yan came to my room the following afternoon with the news. "True or not, they said they couldn't get my dossier from the university." She shrugged. "I knew all this from the beginning."

"Don't give up. There are a lot more opportunities," I said, consoling her.

"Yeah, we'll see."

After that day she began to skip classes again and was off campus most evenings. She told me that she had found two part-time jobs. One was teaching a fifth-grade girl composition and English, which paid twelve yuan an hour; the other was doing odd jobs at a jewelry store owned by someone from her hometown. I didn't know how much she got paid for the latter, but I doubted she would get much, for it was such an easy job—all she had to do was put price tags on newly arrived merchandise.

I disliked the jewelry store owner at first sight. He was at least forty years old, coarse-voiced, bald, heavy-set, short—I was taller than he was—with a Japanese-style beard beneath his big, flat nose. The gold necklace he wore was as thick as a dog collar. He had three gold rings on each hand—the rings were so big that they made his fingers spread out. When he walked, his feet pointed outward in opposite directions, forming nearly a ninety-degree angle. Whatever the angle, he matched exactly the despicable image of a nouveau riche in my mind. I tried to persuade Miao Yan to quit the job but she kept saying he was much better than most of the men she knew.

The man often invited Miao Yan to dinner at upmarket restaurants and would drive his red BMW to pick her up at the university's main entrance. Miao Yan never turned down his invitations. In fact she would spend hours putting on makeup and choosing a dress. Sometimes she would ask me to walk her to the entrance. By the time we got there the man would be waiting in his car. On seeing us, he would smile a toothy grin, get out, and open the door for her. Then Miao Yan would step into the car like a celebrity, full of pride, pretentiousness, and privilege. How I hated it!

Whenever the man invited Miao Yan he would also invite me, but I turned down his invitations without bothering to offer an excuse. Miao Yan knew that I disliked her hanging out with him but she laughed it off and never wanted to discuss it. "Don't act like a jealous lover," she would tease me. "I just like sitting in a BMW. What's wrong with that? Tell me, do you know any other girls who go riding in a BMW?"

One Thursday night in early fall, not long after school started, Miao Yan asked me to go shopping with her at the Guangzhou Department Store on Beijing Road, one of the most expensive malls. Normally she wouldn't have wanted my company because, she said, I had no patience, style, or taste. "It's no fun shopping with you. You don't know good stuff and never buy anything. You're so frugal," she once remarked.

These days, whenever she showed me an expensive purchase, she would say that the jewelry-store owner had just given her a good bonus for her work, or the family of the girl she was teaching had just handed her a red envelope because the girl had passed a major exam. I didn't believe her but kept my mouth shut, trying not to be bothered by my own speculations, though my doubts and concerns were growing. At one point Miao Yan even made me promise that I wouldn't ask her where her money came from. Though I obeyed her, naturally, I knew we would have to talk about it sooner or later.

"Yan, where did you get so much money?" I asked finally, inside the store.

She was trying on a dark blue suit. She turned back and forth before a full-length mirror on the wall, her eyebrows knotted into a frown. The suit was priced at six hundred and forty yuan—more than twice my monthly allowance. I knew she had expensive clothes but I never thought they were as expensive as this.

"Silly girl, what do you think? I work hard to pay for everything. Money doesn't fall from the sky," she said, not looking away from the mirror. She stretched the suit at her waist with both hands, looking for creases. Her red fingernails flashed with each movement.

"Don't try to fool me. No part-time job can pay you that much. I don't know of any other students who spend as much as you do. I think there's something you haven't told me."

"Lower your voice!" she said. She walked to a corner near the emergency exit. There was no one else around.

"Can we talk about it after shopping? If I'd thought you'd make a scene I wouldn't have asked you to come with me." She crossed her hands behind her head and leaned back.

"I know it's fashionable for girls to find themselves a 'sugar daddy.' "

"What do you mean, 'a sugar daddy'?" She laughed, poking my head with the index finger of her right hand. "When did our innocent Ming start to know about this kind of thing?"

I didn't laugh with her. "I don't care if you only flirt with guys. But I don't want to see you do anything improper with them."

"Like what?"

"Like . . . like . . ." I bit my lower lip until it hurt. "Like going to bed with them."

"Is this all you've been worried about?" Her voice turned cold and hard.

"Don't act like you don't care."

"Why should I care? I told you I became a woman at thirteen. I know how to take care of myself."

"Why do you think you know how to take care of yourself? I don't think you do." There was a lot I wanted to say, like telling her to quit smoking and drinking alcohol, telling her to spend time in the library and stop seeing the jewelry-store owner. But instead I said something else: "The teacher kissing you on the forehead doesn't make you a woman and it wasn't your fault to begin with."

"What wasn't my fault? What do you know?"

"You didn't know what you were doing. You were too young. Your baba shouldn't—"

"Shut up! I don't want to hear!"

But I couldn't stop. "It wasn't your fault to begin with. You didn't know—"

"I said shut up!"

Silence fell between us.

"You've never gone to bed with the short fat man, right? Tell me you've never gone to bed with him," I whispered, almost begging.

"For God's sake, I'm twenty-four years old! I don't need another ma. You don't have the right to interrogate me. You know so little about me."

"I only want you to say that you don't sleep with him. I know you're a good girl."

"If you think I'm a good girl like you, you're wrong. I can never be like you and never want to be like you. Just as you can never be like me, even if you wanted."

"Just answer my question."

"Why do you care?"

"Of course I care. If you sleep with him for money, you are . . . a whore!" I realized too late what I had just said.

"How dare you!" She took a step toward me, staring, then grabbed my throat with one hand and my arm with the other, shoving me against the wall.

I had wanted to apologize for using the word "whore," for reminding her of the horrible incident eleven years ago, but when she grabbed my throat and pushed me I felt sorry for myself, for how she treated me in return for all my affection for her.

When she finally loosened her grip I backed away. I avoided eye contact, looking at the rows of clothes hanging nearby. I suddenly missed sitting in the library, where it was always so quiet and peaceful.

"Have you ever loved somebody? Have you ever tasted the bitterness of love? Do you know what love means? You know nothing! You're a snail hiding in your shell of fantasies. What do you know about the world other than what you have read in your books? You haven't even been in a relationship. You don't have the right to tell me what to do or not do." Her voice was low but trembling with anger. While speaking, she turned her head and touched her back pocket with one hand—she was looking for a cigarette. When she realized that she was not wearing her own clothes she licked her lips with her tongue.

"I can say whatever I want to say to you. I care about you. That's why." I tried my best to soften my tone. I even managed a light smile. But my heart was burning with anger and resentment. The light smile on my face was nothing more than a stiff grin.

"Is that so? Who are you to me? Are you my parent? No. Are you my sibling? No. Are you my boyfriend or lover? No. I know how to take care of myself. Please do me a huge favor and stay out of my business."

"Don't you worry, I'll stay out. I just want you to answer one question. Do you go to bed with him just for money?"

She narrowed her eyes to slits, like a cat before it pounces on a mouse. "Little sister, what are you going to do if I'm the kind of person you *good* girls despise?"

It was not the answer I was expecting, though I was not really expecting any answers. Everything about this conversation was so dramatic, so fake, it was as though we were rehearsing our lines for a stage play. I felt my heart sinking. I wanted to end the conversation. I was feeling sick and wanted to throw up. The glaring light penetrating every corner of the store was upsetting my stomach, making me want to rush out for fresh air.

"If you're that kind of person, then . . . then we're not friends anymore," I said eventually, but the words were weak and didn't match the seriousness of the message I had wanted to deliver. They sounded like a joke. I stared at her. I didn't move my eyes from hers until she began to speak.

"Really? Sounds good to me." She leaned back against the wall, her arms crossed over her chest, her knees relaxed. She ran her fingers through her hair exaggeratedly all the way to the back of her neck, then shook her head to make her hair fall like a black wave. She looked stunning with her silky hair and luminous skin.

I was standing only a few feet away, so close that I could see a few tiny, reddish pimples on her forehead above her left eyebrow. I looked at her, my spine stiff as steel. She towered over me, either because she was wearing a pair of absurdly high-heeled shoes or because the blue suit flattered her figure so perfectly that I had to bend back to look up at her. Then it seemed she was moving away from me inch by inch. Her blue figure became blurry as I looked at her and I felt I would never be able to touch her again.

I swallowed hard, turned, and walked determinedly toward the elevator. The moment I turned, tears filled my eyes. Before they streamed down, I erased them with the back of my hand. I heard a voice from my heart. "Be brave! Don't be afraid of breaking up with her!" Then other thoughts ran through my mind. What a fool I was! Why was I even attracted to her? She didn't like books, she knew nothing about literature, she was flirtatious and materialistic, and she wasn't even honest with me. How much did I know about her? She had told me almost nothing about her family. I didn't even know if she had any siblings. While I, the biggest fool in the world, put aside my homework and reading plans to stay with her, to write her dissertation. So many nights I'd worked on it until the small hours. Where was she on those evenings? She must have been out fooling around with those rich men, like the ugly and vulgar man with the red BMW, flirting with them, even going to bed with them. What a fool I had been!

I thought of the magazine pictures of naked people. She'd have her pictures printed in that kind of magazine if she got paid. I trembled with disgust. Thinking back, I felt that I had been deceived since the first day I met her and that every single day thereafter had been nothing but lies and dishonesty between us.

Standing in front of the elevator, I managed to compose myself. I even felt like laughing. I began to feel the whole thing was my own fault. I met her on the rooftop and without knowing much about her I decided to devote my friendship, trust, and loyalty to her. She was everything to me, while to her I was nothing. All she cared about was her vanity and desire for money. I was the one to blame and to be laughed at. Now I understood why her expression had been relaxed. She must have felt freed. I had discovered her secret, the dark truth. Now, in front of me, she never needed to put on a mask.

The mall was closing in another ten minutes. A dozen people were waiting at the elevator. When the door opened I walked into the crowded elevator without looking back. The remaining space was filled in no time. Before the door closed, two people with shopping bags squeezed in forcefully, triggering a roar of complaints. Standing in a corner, face against one wall, weight on my toes, I had trouble breathing. I turned around, finally, to face the elevator doors.

The elevator moved slowly. Looking at the different shapes of people's heads from behind, listening to their heavy breathing in different rhythms, I thought of the day when I first left

my hometown to go to university in Guangzhou a little over
a year ago.

Back then, no trains went directly from Nanchang to
Guangzhou. Between the two cities, the only trains that
stopped at Nanchang came from Hangzhou and stopped
there only three times a week. Since many people wanted to
go to Guangdong to make money, these trains were always
packed—not only were all the seats taken but the aisles were
crowded with people standing. There were even people on
the baggage racks and under the seats. In Nanchang, almost
no tickets with assigned seats were sold through the ticket office. Even if there were such tickets, they were sold at the
black market at a much higher price or bought through "back
door" deals. In peak season, when the train pulled in, the
porters wouldn't even open the doors for fear of not being
able to control the crowd. People wanting to get on the train
had to climb through the windows.

I didn't fight my way onto the platform until twenty minutes before the train's departure. My parents and uncle were
carrying my luggage for me. I had never seen so many people
in my life. The whole station was full, all the way to the street.
People were everywhere, pushing each other forward and
backward. A few times I had to grab somebody's clothes to
keep myself from falling. I saw the train at last, with no doors
open. Even the windows were closed tightly because the people inside feared the train might break down if more people
got on.

"Not good. Too many people," my uncle said to my parents. "But Ming can't afford to delay her trip to the university.
I'll try my best to get her on the train. You wait here. I'll push
her in through a window."

My father sighed and nodded. Arthritis had been troubling

him these days and he couldn't walk fast. It was a disease he'd developed on the farm.

As my mother handed me a bag of fruit and combed my straggling hair with her fingers, she said, "You're leaving home for the first time to start your life in a strange city. I hope you'll become more mature and take good care of yourself."

She put her hands on my shoulders and looked at me for a few seconds. I could tell she was trying hard to hide her tears. Then she said calmly, "When you're out alone, you need to learn how to make decisions for yourself. Don't always expect other people to understand and approve of your choices in life."

Before I could react, the train whistle sounded, meaning that it would pull out in ten minutes. I had only a brief moment to turn my head and say goodbye to my parents before my uncle, a tall and heavy man, held me by the arm and pushed forward into the crowd. He was half a head taller than most of the people around, which helped. Soon we were next to the train.

One hand dragging my two big suitcases, the other knocking on the windows, my uncle shouted at the top of his lungs: "Please open the window. My niece is going to college in Guangzhou. The classes start in two days. She can't afford to miss the opening of school."

The windows remained shut. Through the dirty glass I could see people shaking their heads: no. Finally, one window opened a small crack. From inside came a man's voice: "Climb up here."

My uncle released a long breath. "Thank you. Thank you. Thank you." He lifted me up as if I was a lifeless object and squeezed me in through the narrow crack. Two or three people sitting near the window grabbed my hands and pulled me inside. My head went through the crack first, then my chest, behind, and legs followed.

The people in the luggage racks and under the seats craned their heads to see who the newcomer was. I was embarrassed and offended by the attention, but I could only close my eyes tightly—I was still up in the air, pushed by my uncle from outside and pulled by a few strangers inside. Finally my feet touched something solid. I opened my eyes and found myself standing among a bag of oranges, food wrappers, empty bottles, and a few crumpled hand towels on a table. Two middle-aged men lifted me down to the floor. On the way down, I unwittingly kicked the back of somebody sleeping on the floor, his head on his tightly drawn-up knees. He raised his head and looked at me with half-opened eyes, then dropped his head and went back to sleep.

From the platform, my uncle was handing up my luggage through the window. I heard him say, "Sorry for the trouble. My niece has never left home before. This year is her first at college. Most of her luggage is books. Please take care of her on the train. She's only sixteen and has never left her parents before. Thank you, thank you."

After that came a roar of shouts, scoldings, and complaints. I looked back over my shoulder—several people on the platform were trying to climb in through the half-opened window. All the passengers sitting next to the window stood up. Two forcefully loosened the hands clutching the sill and others pulled the window down. People were calling out inside the compartment. One person on the luggage rack said, "Don't let them in. There's no more space. Not even room for a fly." Another said, "Definitely not this compartment. Tell them to try other windows." Still another said, "The train's about to pull out. They might get injured. Don't be so cruel."

Then came a hysterical shout from the platform: "Son of a bitch. You're all sons of bitches. How could you be so vicious as to push people down—" The rest of his words were cut off by the window, which was now completely shut, and the train began to lurch forward.

I hadn't said goodbye to my uncle but it was too late. Through the dirty window glass everything looked blurry. As the train gathered speed, I saw the sea of people still on the platform, a few poles passing by, dilapidated houses along the railroad, then fields—infinitely expanding fields of green or yellow. The whole trip lasted twenty-four hours and I stood in the same spot throughout. I might have napped briefly, standing, or leaned against the table in the compartment to rest my feet, but I didn't eat, drink, or go to the toilet during the whole trip. I also remember what the table looked like. It was rectangular, with a green plastic top. Its original yellowish wood showed beneath the peeling paint around the edges.

What I didn't remember were the faces of the other people in the compartment or any conversations among them. All I could think about was what my mother had said to me before my uncle took me away. She was never a person to talk about general principles. My brain was like a phonograph and it kept repeating: "Don't always expect other people to understand and approve of your choices in life."

For a few days after our argument in the department store, I thought I wouldn't want to see Miao Yan again and I would be perfectly fine without her companionship. I told myself that she was not a worthwhile person and that nothing could

137

save our friendship. It was perhaps a good thing that I no longer needed to see her. I could catch up with my reading. I could go back to my peaceful student life. I no longer had to worry about being her friend or being intimate with her. I could meet other people and make new friends.

When I hadn't heard from her in over ten days, though, I began to regret my actions. I blamed myself for driving her away by calling her a whore. Why was I so foolish as to have used this taboo word? There were a million other words I could have used to make her feel bad about herself without hurting her so much. I knew perfectly well that nothing was more painful to her than thinking about her past. If I had just given her time to explain how she got the money and if I had just calmed down enough to have a rational discussion with her, maybe we wouldn't have ended our friendship.

Then I recalled how her cold hand had gripped my throat and how she had stared at me with fire in her eyes. My heart broke. It seemed she didn't care about me at all. I was a no-body to her, like a piece of clothing she could dispose of at will.

I spent hours and hours on my bed, in the library, in classes, thinking back and forth about Miao Yan. Sometimes I thought I knew how to get her back and would do whatever it took. Often I was lost in endless self-questioning and self-blame. Other times I thought I would be better off without her. After all, the world I had enjoyed before—the rooftop, the violin, and my books—was so much easier and simpler.

Another week slipped by. I could no longer maintain my pride. I went to Miao Yan's room but she was not there. Her roommates told me she had gone to Shenzhen. I asked when she would be back and was told that only God knew the answer.

I still went up to the rooftop to play violin some evenings and stayed there late. Every time I passed the corner Miao Yan used to sit in, I would stare at it for a few minutes and pray in my heart, wishing she would magically appear there, smiling at me.

It was late November. The winter break was only one month away. I didn't hear anything from Miao Yan—no phone calls, no letters, nothing.

Without Miao Yan as a distraction, I went to classes punctually every day, though I spent most of the time daydreaming.

One Wednesday afternoon, windy and freezing cold, I went to a class called "Shakespeare and His Sonnets," one of the two courses on foreign literature that semester. I sat in a window seat in the back row. From there I could see the overcast sky, a cluster of red-brick buildings far away, and the heavily dressed passersby.

I didn't like the teacher. He would start the class with a roll call and boast about his overseas experience whenever he could. His name was Gao Jie. Seven or eight years our senior, he was already an assistant professor, the youngest in the department. He had been sent to the U.S. as a visiting scholar for a year and a half. Afterward, his title changed from lecturer to assistant professor. But we never addressed him as Professor Gao. We called him Gao CK, since after he returned he told everyone that his favorite fashion brand was Calvin Klein.

After calling the roll and noting absent students, Gao CK began to read aloud a sonnet in English and asked us to repeat it after him. When he spoke English, he emphasized all the syllables and drawled every vowel. I didn't read after him; instead, I scribbled on my notepad to kill time—I had forgotten to bring a novel with me. A few of my classmates in the same row were reading their own books, using the textbook as a cover. I quickly lost interest in scribbling and decided to draw something, though I was terrible at drawing. I'd always had difficulty passing my drawing exams in primary school.

I drew a big circle and five smaller circles around it—all together, a flower. Then a long stem, a few leaves, and some intersecting lines on the leaves as veins. After studying my drawing for a few seconds, I added more layers of petals to the flower; I didn't stop until the five-petal flower became a huge sunflower filling the whole page.

At that moment I thought of Miao Yan. I thought of her hat decorated with a sunflower—the one she had worn the day she danced in my room. I thought of the morning light pouring into my room as she whirled before me, the morning light so soft and transparent, like her gentle eyes.

I decided to draw a picture of her. I flipped to a new page and drew a half-circle. Miao Yan had an oval-shaped face. She always said she had too much fat on her cheeks and needed to lose weight. Sometimes, examining herself in the mirror, she would inhale deeply to suck in her cheeks, then tilt her head back and ask me to look at her—implying that if her cheeks were less fleshy she would be an absolute beauty.

Then her hair. Her hair was dense and curly on the sides and she often piled it high on top of her head to make a chignon, using a big hairpin to secure it. When she wanted to be cute, she would braid her long hair and tie it with hairbands—the color of the band depended on the color of the clothes she was wearing. But the hairdo she wore most often was the free-fall style, with a part in the middle. That was the hairstyle I was drawing. I spent at least five minutes drawing the hair. Gao CK was now talking about those seminars he claimed to have attended at Stanford University with first-class scholars from all around the world.

Her eyes. The first time I saw them they seemed twice as big as normal people's. When she put on makeup, she would use eyeliner and mascara, which made her eyes look even bigger, like those of the characters in Japanese anime films. The two things that most satisfied Miao Yan about her appearance were her five-foot-nine height and her enormous eyes; she was least satisfied with her 34A cup size. She collected ads for breast enlargement and said she would have the surgery someday if she could get the money.

I felt uncomfortable and guilty when I thought of Miao Yan's bra size. I pushed open the window behind me to let in fresh air. Miao Yan never hesitated to change her clothes in my presence. Even when removing her underwear she would hardly turn her body away. When she saw me cover my eyes with both hands she would sometimes ask me to scratch her naked back or massage her bare shoulders. Once, with her bra unfastened, she asked me to look at the few rice-size moles between her breasts and near her navel. The more embarrassed I was the more excited she would become. "Why not look at me? I'm just a girl like you. You have everything I have on my body." She would mock me. I was often too embarrassed to know how to act and what to say.

I drew eyebrows, ears, nose, and mouth. Now the drawing didn't look like Miao Yan anymore. I was disappointed but continued to work at it. I added two parallel vertical lines under the head—the neck—then drew the torso, hips, arms, legs, and a pair of high-heeled shoes. She always said she wanted her hips to be fleshier, so I widened the hips and made the thighs thicker. Despite all the work, everything below the neck looked deformed—the arms were too thin and too long, the torso too short and too thick. The whole drawing seemed to have been done by a toddler.

I held the drawing up and examined it. Something was missing. Apart from the long hair, no other features indicated that the figure was female—she had no breasts. I twiddled my pen over the paper, then remembered the porn magazine Pingping had shown me. I had never talked about that night with Miao Yan, fearing that she would make fun of me. I rapidly drew two big circles on the person's chest and penned in dots in the middle of each circle as nipples. When I was done, I could feel my heart beating faster.

I was concentrating so intently on the drawing that I didn't even hear Gao CK call my name.

"Ming . . ." Pingping, sitting right in front of me, rocked my desk with her back.

My first reaction was to tear the paper into pieces. But Gao CK had started to walk toward me.

"Chen Ming, please stand up." He crossed his hands over his stomach when he stood beside me. His small eyes narrowed.

I stood up, hurriedly shoving the paper inside my bag. All my classmates turned to look at Gao CK and me. Those who had been reading kung fu novels earlier had put away their books. I bent my head, staring at my textbook. I lifted my right knee to push the bag a little farther into the desk drawer.

"Did you hear my question?" Gao CK placed his right hand on my desk.

I shook my head.

"What were you doing when I called your name?"

Somehow I felt he wouldn't make things too difficult for

me. After all, I was one of the best students in the class and he knew it.

"I wasn't doing anything."

"If you were listening to me, how come you didn't hear the question?"

I was silent.

He turned to face the class. "Could any of you tell Chen Ming what the question was?"

I knew he was trying to save my dignity.

Nobody answered his question. The classroom was so quiet it was as though every possible sound had been sucked into a black hole.

He waited a few seconds, then turned and faced me, his tone stiffened considerably. "What were you doing when I called your name?"

"I was writing a letter."

"To whom?"

"To a friend."

"Give me the letter."

"Sorry. It's a private letter. I won't turn it in." I was hesitant, but finally raised my eyes to his and defied him. I saw intense seriousness in his eyes. I put my hand into the drawer and gripped the strap of my bag, wishing the paper inside it would turn to ashes.

Gao CK extended his hand toward me. "Give me the letter in your bag. Don't write love letters in class."

A wave of whispering and giggling rustled over the classroom.

"I wasn't writing a love letter. I was writing to a friend," I said, a little resentful of my classmates' lack of sympathy.

He stretched his hand farther toward me. I took out my bag and hid it behind my back, grasping it with both hands.

"If you don't turn in the letter, you will have to leave the classroom. Now!"

I felt as though I had to say something to defend myself, but my mind was blank. I looked at Pingping and Donghua, both of whom were making gestures suggesting I turn in the letter.

Left without options, I walked toward the back door, holding my bag over my chest with both hands, my legs shaking. Before I reached the door I heard Gao CK's knuckles hit the desk: "How can a student like you be a top student? I will have to talk to the Dean. You will have to deal with the consequences!"

Surprisingly, his words cooled me down. My legs stopped trembling. I walked out of the classroom, then out of the building. I didn't stop until I saw Violin Lake, then I removed the drawing from my bag. Without looking at it, I tore it to pieces and threw all the pieces into the nearest trash can.

That night, the picture in the magazine of two naked women touching each other came to me repeatedly. It was obscene that I had drawn a naked picture of Miao Yan. I blamed myself. I was lucky that my classmates hadn't seen it or they would think I was a homosexual and would humiliate me. Not just that, they might think I had a mental disorder. The university might even send me to see a doctor. I didn't dare think further.

Then I reasoned that drawing Miao Yan naked might just be an intimate joke between friends instead of something sinful and disgusting. I never had the slightest desire to touch her the way the two women were touching in the magazine picture. I just wanted to be close to her. I was afraid of losing her as a friend. That was all. Perhaps I just missed her too much . . .

After class the next day I went to the library to look for books on homosexuals but didn't find any. On my way back, I glanced at every passing girl—they were all unattractive and irritating.

Ar Yu came to visit me a few days later. We hadn't seen each other since my summer teaching job ended. As he had predicted, his mother insisted on finding him another teacher though he got quite a few As in English under my tuition. "She thinks you know too much about our family," Ar Yu said sadly in our last class. Since then he had called me every week but we never got together.

When I saw him he was standing on the curb outside West Five, hands in his pockets, looking at the passing girls. It had been only two months since I'd last seen him but he seemed taller, his leather jacket a little tight on him and his khaki pants too short.

As we were walking toward the stadium—I had offered to show him around the campus—he was quiet. He nodded when I pointed out different buildings along the road but talked little. When we were near the woods across from the stadium, he said, "I've come here to say goodbye. I'm going to the U.S. next month."

"Next month? I thought you wouldn't leave until after high school."

"I thought so, too. But I guess my parents are worried that the government will find out about my ba's bribery. Some months ago a few people in my ba's unit were arrested for corruption. My aunt in the U.S. had prepared all the supporting documents. I got my visa last week and will study in Michigan."

I wanted to say "Congratulations," but it didn't sound right, so I said only, "I see."

"My ma has been crying every day since my aunt sent over the documents." His eyes were wet. "I'll miss my parents. I'll miss you and all my friends here."

"Maybe you shouldn't go." I felt sad. Though I had known him for only a few months, he felt like my little brother. America seemed really far away to me and I felt as though he would disappear like a bubble in a pot of boiling water as soon as he stepped on the airplane.

Ar Yu was silent. From his expression I knew he had made up his mind. "I have to go. I want to meet girls and I want to have the freedom to decorate my own room."

His reasons sounded childish but I couldn't think of anything to say.

"I do have one worry, though." He kicked away a little gravel on the road. "I'm only five foot six."

"What's that to worry about?"

"American boys are much taller than I am. I'll be bullied."

"You poor thing! What a worry!" I laughed.

"I'm serious. I've been taking kung fu classes. I'm also worried that I won't be able to find a girlfriend there. American girls are big, too." He looked gloomy.

"You're only fifteen. You'll grow for another three or four years. American milk and beef will make you grow faster. You'll be at least five foot ten by the time you go to college."

"You think so?" He stared at me, half convinced. "Would you find me a girlfriend if I can't find one in the U.S.?"

"Sure. I'll post an ad for you on campus."

"If nobody replied, would you be my girlfriend?" He winked at me, smiling.

My heart skipped. "You silly boy! Of course not. I'd never want to have a boyfriend who's younger than I am. You're still a kid."

"I'm not a kid!"

"Okay. You're not a kid. You're a man. You're going abroad by yourself. That's quite something, isn't it?"

He was pleased. "I'll become a man soon. Sooner than you can imagine. I started to shave regularly a month ago. Can you see?" He pointed to his chin. "By the way, how come you're so old-fashioned? I wouldn't care if my girlfriend was older than me."

"Good for you. In that case I'll post an ad for you at a senior center."

"A grandma girlfriend! She'll cook for me every day. My ma would be happy."

It was getting dark. We hadn't paid attention to where we were going as we talked and I realized we were off the main road and far into the woods, on a quiet little gravel road inlaid with irregularly shaped blue bricks. On both sides of the road were densely planted silk cotton trees, eucalyptus, and the branches of evergreen bushes struggling out from between them. Despite my little knowledge about where students went on dates, I knew this road was nicknamed Lovers' Lane and was frequented by both students and people from outside the university looking for a private place to be together. I had walked this road only once and it was with Miao Yan.

I took Ar Yu's hand and was going to walk back but he was not moving. I followed the direction of his gaze and saw two people kissing fiercely behind a tree about twenty meters from the road. They were so passionate and so involved that they didn't detect us approaching. I let go of Ar Yu's hand immediately and turned, but he grabbed my wrist, his fingers like pincers. He frowned and gestured for me to follow him behind a bush. Afraid of alarming the lovers, I had no choice but to do as he asked.

I thought the couple would finish kissing and leave but they started to touch each other aggressively. They must have thought the dim light in the woods at sunset would protect them from being seen. I watched the man's hand fondling the woman's chest as she unzipped his pants and put one hand inside his crotch. The man's hand slowly moved downward to reach under the woman's long skirt, and stayed there. The woman tilted her head back. The man used his other hand to unbutton her blouse, then her bra. The black bra must have been strapless, because it slipped to the ground.

The scene made me dizzy. I had to lower my head and close my eyes to take a break. When I opened them again, I turned to look at Ar Yu. Staring at the couple without blinking, he seemed to have been possessed by a ghost. His grip on my hand loosened.

At this moment, from the opposite direction, came a ten- or eleven-year-old girl with a ponytail, a red backpack on her back. She must have picked this road as a shortcut home. She was humming and hopping toward Ar Yu and me. I elbowed Ar Yu and tilted my head toward the girl. When Ar Yu came back to himself and saw the girl he ground his teeth and said in a strangled voice, "Damn it! Damn it!" The girl and the couple saw each other almost at the same time, then immediately spotted Ar Yu and me. The girl screamed.

"Hurry! Run!" Ar Yu sprang up from behind the bush, grasped my hand, and darted toward the main road, his hand strong, his strides long. I could barely keep up with him. After hitting the main road we didn't stop but kept running until we took shelter inside a kiosk near the library. When we had caught our breath, Ar Yu burst out laughing, and so did I.

Finally he stopped laughing and stared at me. There was something strange in his gaze, something I couldn't understand—hope, desire, doubt, bewilderment, or a little bit of everything. I backed away from him. "Let me show you the library and my department," I said.

He mumbled something.

"What did you say?"

"I want to kiss you." His voice was firm this time. Before I could react, he stepped forward and pulled me close, his arms surprisingly strong for a fifteen-year-old. Not that I had any idea how much strength a fifteen-year-old boy should have— no man had ever grabbed me like that. Then he quickly moved his hands from my arms to my waist. For a moment I thought he was going to lift me but he only lowered his head to find my lips, his breathing short and heavy.

I struggled out of his arms and kicked him hard in the stomach—so hard that he backed up a few steps and sat on the ground. "Those people aren't students. We shouldn't have walked in the woods. You shouldn't even have come to visit me. You'd better leave now."

"What's wrong? I like you!" He looked hurt. I could see my dirty footprint on his white polo shirt under the jacket.

"It isn't funny!"

"I love you!"

I couldn't help laughing—what did a fifteen-year-old know about love? I walked to Ar Yu and extended my hands. He pushed them away and stood up.

"You don't know what love is," I said, remembering how Miao Yan had said the same thing to me when we were quarreling in the department store.

"You don't need to have a girlfriend to know about love!" He turned away.

"You don't love me. You only like me as your sister."

"I don't need a sister. I need a girlfriend."

149

"You'll have one someday."

"I love you and I've missed you."

"You're a little boy. You're like my little brother," I said, trying to hold his hand and turn him around.

He shook me off. "I'm not a boy!" His voice was a little husky.

"You are." I smiled, thinking it was like a game instead of an argument.

"I'm not! You are!" He turned, his eyes a little red. "You don't want to have a boyfriend. You don't want to grow up. You're a kid! You'll become an old maid without a boyfriend."

Much as I felt bad for him, I felt worse for myself. I walked out of the kiosk, leaving him there alone.

"You hurt me! You don't know about love. You're a kid!" Ar Yu shouted at my back as I walked away.

⌒

The same week as Ar Yu's visit, at six thirty on Saturday afternoon when I was writing a review of *Dream of the Red Chamber* in the library, I heard a knock on the window. I looked up. Miao Yan was standing outside!

"Where did you go? I couldn't find you anywhere. How've you been?" I jumped up from my chair, managing to keep my voice down. I couldn't help smiling at her.

She poked her head through the window. "Still want to see me?"

"Of course! I missed you every day."

"You did?" She chuckled.

Before I could say more she extended her hands through the window and impatiently gathered my books and pens into a pile on the desk. The happy expression on her face told me that something special must be happening tonight.

Walking out of the library I saw a guy, about Miao Yan's height, with tanned skin and a crew cut, standing next to her on the stairs. He had a thin, angular face. His eyes weren't big but the gleam in them was penetrating and magnetic—a pair of eyes I hadn't seen in any other man. At that moment I couldn't think of words other than "bright" to describe them. Later, words like "sensual," "mature," and "profound" seemed more accurate. He wore a silver, double-breasted wind-breaker, unbuttoned, over a black turtleneck.

He strode toward me, offering a handshake. "You must be Chen Ming. Miao Yan has mentioned you at least one hundred times. It's a pleasure to meet you finally, the mystery girl, in person. My name is Du Sheng. You can call me Big Brother Du." He looked into my eyes with the confidence of a salesman describing his products. His voice was a baritone, powerful yet musical. When he spoke, he rolled his tongue slightly to make pronounced "er" sounds, like Ping-ping.

Miao Yan stood beside him, head against his shoulder, both hands gripping his arm, and smiled at me. She wore the blue suit she had tried on in the department store. Her high-heeled shoes were the same blue, a silver heart-shaped buckle on each side. This Big Brother Du must be her secret wealthy boyfriend, I thought.

"Here's my business card." Du Sheng took out his wallet and gave me a card with gold foil print on it.

I glanced at the card: his title was Director of General Merchandise.

"Ming's a student, not a potential client," Miao Yan said sweetly.

"That's right. I didn't think about that. It's a habit."

I put the card in my pocket. "It's the first business card I've received. I'll keep it as a souvenir. I can also use it as a bookmark."

Du Sheng put one hand on Miao Yan's shoulder, the other on my back. "Let's go. My treat. I'm so hungry I could eat a horse."

When we hit the road leading to the university's main entrance, the streetlights went on, shedding a yellowish light.

Miao Yan suggested that we eat on Food Street—a side street near the main entrance. The street was no more than a mile long but hosted over a hundred restaurants and food stands. Along the street, white bulbs on strings crisscrossed over the trees like stars. Food stands were extremely popular with students because they were cheap and the service was fast. They were offshoots of small restaurants whose owners would set up tables on the pavement to attract customers in the evenings. On weekend nights, the footpath would be jammed with tables and chairs, along with hundreds of customers—mostly students.

Winter is the best time to eat hotpot. We fought our way among tables, chairs, and people. At last we sat down under a big oak tree. We ordered lamb hotpot with two different soups—one spicy, for Du Sheng, the other plain, for Miao Yan and me.

When Miao Yan sat down she turned and embraced Du Sheng, both arms around his neck. "Ming is still mad at me. You need to apologize to her for me."

"What are you talking about? I'm not mad at you at all," I said, embarrassed by their intimacy in public, though it seemed natural to see Miao Yan with a handsome and mature guy like Du Sheng. I didn't feel jealous, as I had thought I would. Perhaps I was just happy to see Miao Yan.

"For my sake, you two little girls should just forget about your argument. Come on, give your brother a big smile. Let's use tea as alcohol and toast to everlasting friendship." He gently detached Miao Yan's hands from his neck and lifted the teapot to pour jasmine tea into our three cups.

Miao Yan pursed her lips and shrugged, but didn't complain.

We raised the teacups high. "Friendship forever!" we said together, and sipped the tea.

"Big Brother Du, where are you from? How come you like spicy food?" I asked.

"Liaoning Province. The northeast is cold in the winter. Everybody eats spicy food there. After coming to Guangdong, though the weather is warm, I still can't change my eating habits. No spice, no appetite." He uncapped a bottle of spicy barbecue sauce and poured half the bottle into his bowl, then mixed the sauce with two big scoops of reddish chili oil. To me, that would have tasted like fire.

"You can tell he's from the northeast at first sight. Loud voice, big temper, stubborn—all characteristics of northeasterners. If he decided to do something, nothing could make him change his mind," Miao Yan said.

"Miss Miao, didn't we agree earlier that we wouldn't argue in front of Ming? Someday I'll come up with ways to describe you people from Yunnan." Du Sheng caressed Miao Yan's hair with one hand, smiling at me.

Miao Yan turned away from him.

Finally, a shiny aluminum bowl was placed on the table, on a small charcoal burner alive with blue flames. A stainless steel wall divided the bowl in half. One side held whitish soup, plain, for Miao Yan and me; only Du Sheng dared to dip food in the other side. A moment later the waiter put a dozen dishes of hotpot ingredients on our table: sliced lamb, shrimp, pork blood, sliced beef stomach, fresh bean curd, dry clear noodles, mushrooms, bean sprouts, baby taros, fresh eggs . . . the variety excited us. "Bravo!" exclaimed Du Sheng. We began to place the food into the bubbling bowl of soup. In less than a minute we used our spoons to scoop out the hot food. We ate busily for a while, fully content. Between mouthfuls, Miao Yan drawled, "Yummy! Yummy! Dirty or clean, done or rare, it's all good for my stomach."

After eating a little more lamb and bean curd, Du Sheng put down his chopsticks and said to me, "Yan told me you like reading."

"Ming is much more knowledgeable than you are," Miao Yan interjected. "You're a company man, thinking about how to climb the corporate ladder every day. You don't have time for anything."

I smiled at their bantering and said to Du Sheng, "I do. When I was growing up, books were all my parents had. Also, I'm a student. I have time."

"Don't be so modest. He always thinks highly of himself and is so arrogant. You need to help me punish him." Miao Yan kicked my leg playfully under the table.

Du Sheng didn't look at Miao Yan. He said, "My undergraduate study was in philosophy. I used to read Dostoevsky, Kafka, and Sartre. Later, forced by the job market, I changed to business and management."

I was peeling a shrimp that I had just scooped out from the boiling soup. The shrimp was like burning charcoal in my fingers, and then in my mouth. After swallowing it and gulping water, I said, "I like those writers, too."

"Don't listen to him. He's pretending he has good taste in books. I've been with him for ages and he has never mentioned their names to me."

Du Sheng ignored Miao Yan. "Let's talk about books some other time. My job has been keeping me busy. It's hard to find time to read. Shenzhen is a materialistic city and the people there only care about money. It's good to be a student. When you study, you have time to read. When you don't study, you wander around spending money." He poured almost half the bottle of chili sauce into his bowl, spread green onion on top, and stirred the mix with his chopsticks.

"No wonder my ears are burning—somebody is bad-mouthing me. Mister Du, what's going on? You have a problem with me spending money? I've yet to depend on you for a living," Miao Yan said, caressing Du Sheng's cheek.

Du Sheng didn't smile.

Miao Yan gazed at him for a moment and lowered her hand. She stood up, circled around the table, and stood beside me. She bent and put her hands on my shoulders. "Ming, you're the only person in the world who treats me nicely. Nobody else cares about me." She took a pack of Camels from her handbag, moved the bowl from the burner onto the table, and leaned toward the charcoal to light the cigarette between her lips. The charcoal darkened where it touched the cigarette, forming a black circle, then glowed again, brighter than before. Miao Yan put the bowl back and exhaled a plume of smoke. The smoke and the steam from the bowl mixed and rose, like a hand waving.

Du Sheng blew away the white cloud. He said to me, "Perhaps you should take Miao Yan to the library occasionally, so she won't waste time hanging out with bad people. If she doesn't change, she'll be in trouble sooner or later."

I didn't know what to say—it seemed wrong for someone to say such things about his girlfriend.

Miao Yan seemed to be completely ignoring Du Sheng and me. She raised her right hand, cutting the smoke from her mouth slowly. She looked serious, as though she was creating art.

The charcoal was still burning but a thin layer of white ash dimmed the brightness of the flame. The soup in the bowl was boiling, lifting the food with each bubble, but all three of us had had enough.

Du Sheng went back to Shenzhen early the next morning. That night Miao Yan called from the duty room, asking me to meet her on the rooftop after curfew.

When I got to the rooftop Miao Yan was already there, sitting in the corner she usually sat in, a half-smoked cigarette between her fingers. I sat down next to her. It had been a while since we had last met there. I noticed that her eyes were red and swollen. She and Du Sheng must have had a fight after the hotpot.

"You once told me that your ma said something to you when she sent you off at the train station. You said her words made you think for a long time. What did she say exactly?" she asked.

"Why does it interest you?"

"Just curious. My ma never talks much with me. I'd like to know what other mothers say to their daughters." Miao Yan dropped the half-smoked cigarette on the cement, put her left foot on it, and twisted it a few times to crush it.

I told her what my mother had said.

She was silent for a while, then said, "I wish my ma would say something like that. She isn't a mute but she doesn't talk much. She never has a chance to talk anyway. My ba is boss at home. We're all afraid of him. Whenever he beat me or my brothers, my ma would hide in the kitchen. She'd cry. That's all she did. I don't blame her. She has no education and doesn't know any better. Your ma is an intellectual. That's nice. I guess she wanted you to become a strong-minded person. Really, you can't please everybody. Some people are doomed not to be understood and liked, like all the geniuses."

I nodded.

"Do you think it's easier for normal people like you and me to be understood by others?"

"I guess so."

"I think it's the opposite. We normal people don't believe strongly in what we do in life. We're fragile. We get scared and lost when others don't agree with us."

"Are you scared and lost?"

"All the time." She laughed. "But it doesn't matter. I'm nobody."

"You're somebody to me."

"You're so sweet to me," she said, her eyes fixed on the cement. "But what's the point of getting yourself understood? What does that get you? Do you dare to open up and make yourself vulnerable to others?"

I had no answers to her questions but she didn't seem to expect any. She continued, "Perhaps whether you can be understood by others or not isn't important at all."

I stared at her, silent.

"You know what? Even if you wanted to be understood, who would want to listen to you and try to understand you anyway? Nowadays, who cares what you think and what you do. You're on your own. If you must struggle, suffer, cry, or even die, that's your fate, your destiny."

I didn't know how to interpret her words. I wanted to say something positive, something like "people are always trying to help each other" or "that's why friendship matters," but none of those replies sounded convincing. I muttered only, "I'm always here for you."

"Will you go to Yunnan with me?" She raised one eyebrow, her voice suddenly cheerful.

"Of course. I can go there with you in the winter break. I've saved enough money for the trip." I was glad that we had finally dropped the earlier subject and switched to something fun.

"Will you live there with me?"

"You're not going back forever. You'll find a job here. You'll stay here with me," I said jovially.

She rested her head against the wall and her mind seemed to be somewhere else. "Ming, do you want to be understood?"

I sighed—she had reverted to the earlier topic. I said, "I don't know. I don't think about it. Maybe I'm too young to think about it. I'm not worried. I'm happy with who I am, especially now I have you as my best friend. I don't need anybody else in my life."

She shook her head. "I think you need a boyfriend."

"I don't have time to date."

"You're either with me or studying at the library. How can you find time to meet boys?"

"I don't want to meet boys. I can't think of one I'd fall in love with. At least not right now. What's good about them anyway? They're only interested in shallow girls. I must look like a geek to them. I like being with you. We always have so much fun together." I suddenly thought of the naked picture I had drawn of her in class. I blushed and bent to retie my shoelace.

"Don't like me too much. It's dangerous. You've spent too much time with me. Your parents wouldn't be happy if they knew that. You should meet other people, to talk about books and literature. And you should meet boys. Not all are immature and shallow. Believe me, you're attractive and there must be lots of boys dying to get your attention. You won't grow up until you begin to learn how to love. You can't live in your books forever. Being with me doesn't help you grow up. Lovers and friends are different. You need a lover. I'll find you a boyfriend. It's good for you. I want somebody to take good care of you when I'm away."

"You're talking nonsense now. You'll certainly find a job here."

"What do you think of Du Sheng?" she asked suddenly.

"Du Sheng? He seems nice."

"I can tell he likes you. Remember, a long time ago you told me about your ideal boyfriend and I laughed at you. Actually, he's pretty close to what you described."

"Don't say that! He's your boyfriend." I covered my ears.

"He *was*."

"Don't joke about it. I'm sure he'll come to visit you soon. I can find myself a boyfriend if I want."

"I bet you can." She smiled. She put her right hand on my waist and moved it up my spine to my neck. Her hand was soft and warm. She rested it on the back of my neck, caressing my neck in small circles, then withdrew it quickly.

"Ming, I'm starting to like you too much." She laughed.

I bent forward, head on my knees. I had been holding my breath when her hand was on my neck. The few seconds her hand was there seemed eternal.

"By the way," she said, "your hair is too long at the back. You need a haircut. Let me call my stylist and make an appointment for you. I'll go with you sometime next week."

She was silent for a while, then clapped her hands. "Now," she said, her eyes beaming, "tell me something about me. Tell me what kind of person I am."

"You're pretty, sexy, funny—"

"No, no, no." She shook her head sharply. "Not that superficial stuff. Say something deep about me. Something that would explain why you like being with me and why you think I'm different from the rest of the people in your life." She straightened up and gazed at me with intensity.

"Easy!" I said, but as soon as I'd said the word I hesitated. I was searching frantically to catch fleeting words and phrases to describe her. I realized that I didn't know much about her. We had had lunches and dinners together, we had skipped classes and wandered about together, we had joked and laughed together, but I had never spent time thinking about what kind of person she was.

She was waiting for my answer and disappointment was beginning to show on her face.

"You don't really know me. You just think it's fun to be with me. You need my friendship just as much as I need yours. No one knows me." She looked away from me. "You don't need me. You'll have a better life without me. You only need your books, your violin, your rooftop. Your world is full of smiles and sunshine. During my twenty-four years, no one ever asked me why I'd become today's Miao Yan, why I thought the way today's Miao Yan thinks. But even if you knew me well, what difference would that make? You're still you and I'm still myself."

My first impulse was to deny all her statements but nothing came out of my mouth.

"He doesn't need me, either." Her voice was low. I knew "he" meant Du Sheng.

She stood up and walked toward the other side of the rooftop. Before she reached the wall, I rose and followed her. I was afraid she would do something silly.

She leaned on the wall and turned to look at me. I stopped. She put a cigarette between her lips, inhaled, and blew the smoke at me. I didn't wave it away as I would have normally. The smoke was thick at first, then thinned as it dissipated in the darkness.

The air was still, like before a storm. With a few long stripes of black cloud on its uneven blueness, the sky looked like a scarred face.

"I'm pregnant," she said.

Finals were around the corner. These days, the library was packed. It now opened at six, instead of the normal six thirty, and didn't close until midnight. In the mornings the waiting crowd would form by five thirty. Once the door was opened, I would have to fight my way through to sit in my window seat in Room One.

Somehow this year's winter was especially cold. For a few days the temperature dropped to one or two degrees Celsius, and exhalation was no longer transparent but a cloud of whitish mist. For the Cantonese, this kind of cold weather was very unusual—the familiar winter was typically about seeing more fallen leaves on the ground than in the autumn.

Everywhere on the streets vendors sold eiderdown coats. One night I couldn't stand the cold weather any longer and bought a jacket from one of them. Students pedaled their bikes rapidly, forming a stream rushing toward the libraries and classrooms. The sounds of their loud bells rose and fell. Only the rows of palm trees remained unchanged. They wore the same summer yellow outfit, sparse leaves on the head, against the cold air.

Then it began to rain a lot, mostly just drizzle. No raindrops were visible but they were there: on tree leaves, sticking to walls, seeping into the earth. The whole world was a big wet sponge. Occasionally the ocean currents of the South China Sea brought showers and storms. Raindrops as big as beans would pour down. Sometimes, when it rained hard, wind would accompany the rain, to create a bigger mess. I liked the heavy rain. I would spend hours looking at the window glass being beaten by raindrops, blurry with each new splatter.

I didn't see Miao Yan for over a week after the night she told me she was pregnant. That night when she broke the news, I didn't feel surprised or anxious; it was as though getting pregnant was as normal as getting a period. I asked her only what she wanted to do next.

"Disco!" she said.

"Disco?"

"Let's dance. Let's dance a hell of a lot. Why should I care if nobody else cares?" Her face was red and her eyes burning.

We headed to the bus station, which was swarming with students going to the city for the nightlife. Miao Yan ran into the traffic and stopped a red Volkswagen taxi. We got in. "You idiot! Stop honking," she shouted at the car behind us before closing the door. Then she said to the driver, "Beijing Road. Dynasty Ballroom."

On the way she clenched her hands over her chest, leaning forward, gazing out the window on her side. She frowned at every red light and cursed every traffic slowdown. A few times she burst out with a remark like, "Let's have a good time. Tonight, let's have a good time."

The door of the Dynasty Ballroom was blood red. Two big red lanterns hung on each side, with the name of the ballroom written in extravagant calligraphy like a figure of a ghost. At the entrance I heard rip-roaring heavy-metal music coming from inside. Once we entered Miao Yan left me. Before I could stop her she ran through the lobby and the hallway as though called by a voice only she could hear. She was quickly with the dancing crowd. At first I could still see her among all the other people—she was waving her hands, inviting me to join her—but then she was pushed away to the far side of the hall. The moment I blinked, she disappeared.

Seeing hundreds of people squeezed together in a tiny space, twisting their bodies like snakes, I lost my desire for dancing. Miao Yan once asserted that my blood type must be B and said that explained my passive personality—preoccupied, pensive, difficult to get excited and all that. As for herself, she said her blood type must be O, and that people with this blood type were passionate and adventurous. When she told me that I laughed it off; now I felt that what she had said might be true.

I found an empty table and sat. Visibility inside was obscured, partly because people were smoking, partly because the dance hall had a dry ice machine to create a mysterious ambience. On the table was a red candle, its soft yellowish flame quivering with the music: Michael Jackson's *Dirty Diana*.

"Excuse me, would you like to smoke?" Somebody was yelling in my ear. I turned my head and saw a girl with dyed blonde hair in a sky-blue miniskirt. She carried a square blue bag with "Marlboro" printed on the front. She wore heavy makeup: thick black eyeliner circled her eyes, silver powder covered her eyelids. Her severely plucked eyebrows tilted upward in the middle and flattened toward the ends. I knew from Miao Yan that this kind of Western eyebrow shape was in fashion. She smiled at me—a hurried but polite smile, her teeth slightly exposed between dark purple lips.

She was sizing me up. Following her eyes, I looked at my brown sweater and black flat-heeled leather shoes, the toes of which were worn and scuffed. A little embarrassed with my unfashionable appearance, I pulled my feet out of view under the chair.

"Where is Miao Yan?" she asked. Her smile had been replaced by an indifferent and casual expression. She glanced at the bar where two bartenders were busy serving drinks, sat down with her Marlboro bag on her lap, and crossed her legs slowly and elegantly.

"How do you know Miao Yan?" I asked.

"She used to be a sales representative here, promoting foreign cigarettes. Part-time, of course. Fifty yuan an hour. Quite a good deal, isn't it? Some rich clients even give generous tips. It's much easier to make money this way than going to someone's house to teach their stupid kids English or selling instant noodles to first-years. But Miao Yan was fired after a few months. I don't know what the real deal was, but I think she'd got into an argument with a client." She paused, staring at me for a few seconds. "Why did she bring you to such a place?" she said.

"Why can't I come here?"

"It's not a place for you good girls." After a big yawn, she began to smoke.

"Give me a cigarette," I demanded.

"Are you sure?"

I nodded hard.

Though it was the first time I had smoked, I inhaled and exhaled like a chain smoker—maybe because I had seen Miao Yan smoke so many times. I even managed to exhale toward the girl's face. As I registered her amazed expression and thought about my "bad girl" pose, to my surprise I felt proud of myself.

"How do you know that Miao Yan and I came here to-gether? Did you see us walk in?" I asked.

"Who doesn't know the two of you? You're the only girl that Miao Yan hangs out with." She giggled in a voice that made my skin crawl. "She *likes* you."

"Don't talk like that. She and I are good friends. Her boyfriend is in Shenzhen and his name is Du Sheng." After a short pause, I added, "I have a boyfriend as well. He's in my hometown."

"You don't need to explain. I don't care how many boy-friends you have. Miao Yan has a lot of lovers. She wouldn't blink if she needed to go to bed with a guy she barely knew. All these months she's been looking for a local to marry her so she can stay here. She's from Yunnan, you know. Too bad that you're not a local, or a guy, otherwise she could have married you." She laughed, the powder on her face white and patchy.

I wanted to explain further about Miao Yan and me being just friends, but a more important question arose. "Why does she have to marry someone to stay here? If she finds a job, she can stay, right?" I remembered Miao Yan once told me that she admired me because I was not from Yunnan.

She shrugged. "It doesn't matter if she can find a job here or not. She has to go back anyway unless she finds somebody to marry her. She's tried to look for a job but I don't think she'll get anything. This year's assignment policy is that all students from Yunnan must go back. After they go back, the local Personnel Bureau will arrange their jobs locally. Students from other remote and backward provinces must also go back to where they came from. Actually, for Miao Yan, since she's also a minority and got into university because of her ethnic background, she would have to return to Yunnan even if this year's policy was different. She knew that the day she was admitted. Everybody wants to stay here. For sure a smart girl like her wouldn't just go back."

"Why did Miao Yan never tell me this?"

"Who are you? What can you do to help her? Her only bet is to marry a guy with permanent residence in Guangdong. The guy you just mentioned, Du something, should be okay. I met him once. He's handsome and has money. I wish he was my boyfriend." The girl giggled, the silver eye shadow on her eyelids flashing like fish scales. What an ugly face!

"If Du Sheng marries her, she can stay?" I asked.

"I think so."

"Any other options?"

"Well, connections help. But her hometown is one of the poorest places in Yunnan and she's a minority. I don't think her family can help her much. She has made some money and may have tried to bribe the guy who's in charge of job arrangement in her department. But she needs a lot of money, you know. Her father is permanently paralyzed because of a stroke and her mother doesn't have a good job. She also needs to support her brothers in school."

"How do you know so much?"

"I just know." She stood up, crushing her cigarette butt in the ashtray. "I have to go now."

"Are you also from Yunnan? Are you graduating next year? You must have found somebody to marry you," I said suddenly.

"None of your business! I only wanted to say that Miao Yan is manipulative. She'll dump you if she doesn't need you. I know she was looking for somebody to write her dissertation. I guess she found you, you poor thing. Look, I can't chat any longer. If my boss saw me chatting, I'd be fired. Say hi to Miao Yan. See you later." She took out a pack of cigarettes and threw it on my table. "On me." She turned and walked away.

"Wait a second. What's your name? Which department are you in?" I yelled at her retreating back. Either because the music was too loud or because she pretended not to hear, she didn't turn around. She quickly reached the other side of the dance hall, her hips swinging, her ponytail swaying from side to side. In no time she was gone.

The music was rap now. Fragmented humming-like talking and deafening drumming made me feel squeamish. The dry ice machines, installed on the ceiling and at the four corners of the hall, began to emit clouds of white mist that looked like ever-changing masks in the light. The music was getting louder, the crowd getting crazier.

Then I saw Miao Yan. She was dancing inside a circle formed by seven or eight men. She was wearing tight, low-cut black jeans and a half-transparent black tank top—so short and tight that her waist and her navel were exposed at each dramatic movement. Inside, in the disco light, her white bra became glittering purple. The men surrounding her clapped, laughing and shouting hysterically. One had Miao Yan's jacket on his head. When he danced, the jacket's two drooping arms waved like two broken wings.

It suddenly became clear to me that she was indeed pregnant and would be expelled from the university. The fear resulting from this realization was so strong that I became breathless and sweaty. I stood up, staring at Miao Yan. How I wished she would stop dancing. How I wished we were somewhere else—sipping coffee in a quiet bar, chatting, and laughing. How I wished she would tell me everything about her family and her life, say that she always counted on me for support. But the next moment I doubted I had ever met her on the rooftop or spent much time with her. With only shouting distance between us in this overcrowded and smoky disco bar, she seemed unreal. I was trying to conjure pictures in my mind of her hometown, her paralyzed father, her timid mother, and her brothers in school. I was trying to connect my past and present with hers. But my brain was foggy. I couldn't think clearly. I was filled with anger, disappointment, frustration, compassion, and other unspeakable emotions. I subconsciously walked forward a few steps, exposing myself to the light.

She must have seen me—she misstepped, facing me. But she didn't raise her head or stop dancing. With a swift toss of her hair, she swirled away, toward the farthest corner of the hall, followed by all the men surrounding her. The rest of the crowd quickly filled the space they left behind. She was out of my sight in a few seconds.

By the time I had run out of the ballroom and jumped into a taxi, I had decided to go to Shenzhen to visit Du Sheng the following day. I had got an entry permit from the Student Management Bureau one week earlier because I thought it would come in handy if I needed to go to Shenzhen to look for Miao Yan. I had a few classes on Monday but I didn't care. The sooner I saw Du Sheng the earlier I could save Miao Yan from those vicious men. I wouldn't let her abandon herself like a prostitute. Du Sheng seemed a nice guy. Maybe Miao Yan was pregnant by him. Maybe he was compassionate and responsible and would marry her, though he no longer loved her. Maybe Miao Yan wouldn't be forced to leave the university. Maybe she wouldn't need to go back to Yunnan.

All my earlier frustration and bewilderment about my intimacy toward Miao Yan was now replaced by an urgent need to save her. In the face of this urgency, everything else became trivial.

The whole night I tossed and turned and had fragmented dreams. When I got up around seven o'clock I couldn't remember any of my dreams. I had expected that Miao Yan would knock on my door to apologize for leaving me alone at the disco or at least leave a note of apology. But neither of these things happened.

It hadn't rained for a few days and the temperature was rising steadily. Before stepping onto Bus 25 for the train station, I took out the business card Du Sheng had given me the night we had hotpot—his office address was 701 East Lake Road.

The timing was perfect. When I arrived at the station, the eight o'clock train to Shenzhen was about to leave. An attendant in a blue uniform greeted me at the door of my compartment and waved me in after checking my ticket, entry permit, and student identity card.

There were many empty seats. A young mother and her son sat across from me. The boy had a girlish face with pink cheeks and long eyelashes. He wore a matching blue flannel jacket and pants, and a cap with a duck embroidered in gold thread. He couldn't sit still. One second he was on top of a seat pretending he was riding a horse, the next second he jumped down and ran the length of the compartment or took up his toy gun, shooting at imagined enemies. His mother got up often to apologize to other passengers for her son's naughtiness. I watched the little boy with admiration. Not growing up is indeed a good thing, I thought.

I turned to look out the window, trying to cheer up. The train stopped at a few stations to let passengers on and off. The empty seats filled up quickly. Two hours later the train pulled into Shenzhen station.

I waited in line to go through the border control. Some people were complaining about the difficulty of getting an entry permit. "It's like getting a visa to the United States. Why must Shenzhen be so special? Aren't people here Chinese like us?" I heard someone say. Ahead of me in line, some people were denied entry for lack of proper documentation. When they were trying to argue with the uniformed officers, security guards pulled them away. A young woman with a big suitcase sat on a bench against the wall, crying. "My husband is in Shenzhen. Why won't you let me in? He's rich now and wants to get rid of me. When he was in graduate school I saved every penny for him. I have to see him." She didn't leave until a female security guard talked with her for a while.

I passed through without any trouble. I ran out of the sta-

tion, up to the viaduct in front of the Shangri-La Hotel, eager
to look at this first special economic zone, transformed from a
fishing village a mere ten years ago. Miao Yan had told me that
it was an immigrant city, where most people spoke Mandarin.
She had also told me that the first McDonald's in China had
opened here two years earlier.

Everything looked glistening white. Within sight, the
Shangri-La Hotel was the only building that could be called
"unique"; the other high-rises all looked like square boxes,
devoid of character. A big crowd sat on the stairs outside the
station, baggy luggage beside them—obviously new immi-
grants looking for opportunities to make money in the
wealthiest city in the country.

I was depressed, partly because of the dreary view, partly
because of the sad wife at the border control. I began to feel
that my decision to visit Du Sheng was too hasty—I had
only met him once and didn't even know if he was in Shenzhen right now. But it was too late to change my plan.

After asking for directions, I got on a bus. The view im-
proved when the bus drove away from the train station—as in
most other cities, the train station was located in the worst
part of town. The wide streets were clean and beautifully
landscaped and, unlike Guangzhou, there were no traffic jams
and endless honking from cars. Near and far, clusters of skyscrapers and half-built residential high-rises gleamed in different colors against the sky. On the way the bus passed by a huge
billboard overlooking a luxuriant park; on the billboard
Chairman Deng, surrounded by flowers, was waving with a
broad smile on his face.

Half an hour later I stood before the sliding glass door of
Du Sheng's company. "Director Du? He is in a meeting right
now. May I ask who wants to see him?" The receptionist was

friendly. After I told her who I was she ushered me into a waiting room near the lobby. I sat down on a long brown leather sofa, one of a set of seven along the walls. In the middle of the room was a mahogany table with a big china vase in the center holding dozens of plastic flowers pointing in all directions. From one of the flowers drooped a golden ribbon with "prosperous business" written on it in black ink. In each corner of the room was a vase the same size but with a different pattern. A floral oriental rug extended from under the table to the sofas.

After drinking the water the receptionist poured for me, I got up to look at the company photographs on the walls. I spotted Du Sheng here and there. He was wearing a suit in every picture, smiling the same smile as everybody else in the pictures. For some reason I began to question the favorable impression I had of him. I knew almost nothing about him.

I walked back to the sofa and sat down, hoping I wouldn't need to wait too long.

"Ming? What brings you here?" Du Sheng hurried in at that moment. In a well-tailored black suit with a blue striped tie, he looked handsome and dignified.

"One of my relatives lives nearby, so I thought I'd stop by to say hello." I had conjured up this reason when I was on the train.

"Did you come with Miao Yan?" He scanned the room.

"She didn't have time. I came by myself."

"Isn't today Monday? Don't you have classes?"

"The professor of ancient literature is sick and no substitute is available."

He loosened his tie and sat on one arm of the sofa. "Is she okay?"

I didn't answer.

172

"Well, there must be something wrong but I guess you don't want to tell me right now. We can talk about that later. It's lunchtime. Want to try Japanese food?"

I hadn't eaten breakfast and my stomach was growling, so I agreed.

We went to a restaurant a block away. There was a long queue but we were immediately seated at the sushi counter, thanks to Du Sheng's acquaintance with the owner.

Du Sheng selected a few dishes from the passing parade and put them in front of me. He also tore open the paper wrap of my chopsticks and poured tea for me.

"I can do it myself." I frowned.

"You're my guest today." He smiled and helped himself to a salmon roll. "If you have time, I can take you to Splendid China or Folk Culture Villages this afternoon. Whenever I have guests I always take them there. I'm an excellent tour guide and you don't even need to tip me."

"I'll go there with my relative."

"Which relative?"

"My uncle, my father's youngest brother." I did have a distant uncle in Shenzhen but I had never seen him nor did I know his name or address.

"Which part of the city does he live in? I could drive you there after lunch."

"Don't bother. I can take a taxi." I knew I sounded rude but I couldn't help myself.

"When did you become such a big spender, like Miao Yan? When I was in college I never took a taxi. Taxis aren't cheap in Shenzhen. You must be from a wealthy family."

I didn't reply. I used my chopsticks to push around the sushi and wasabi on my plate, wondering how to ask him to marry Miao Yan.

"Did Miao Yan send you here?" He mixed wasabi with soy sauce on his plate, not looking at me. "Is she in Shenzhen? You don't seem to be yourself today. You wouldn't visit me if it wasn't for her."

"I told you, I came alone. She'd never ask me to see you for help," I said, my eyes watering a bit.

Du Sheng handed me his napkin, looking concerned. "Something is wrong. You'd better tell me."

"It's because of the wasabi," I said, covering my eyes with my own napkin, but soon my anger overwhelmed me. I put the napkin down and looked into his face. "Frankly, I know everything that's happened between you and Miao Yan. I hope you take responsibility for it."

"What responsibility?" He raised his eyebrows.

"Why do you pretend to know nothing? I thought you were a responsible man." My face was warm with anger.

"What happened?"

"She's pregnant by *you!*"

"Wait a second, she is . . . what?"

"Don't tell me you're innocent!"

"Damn it!" he said, his fists clenched, head buried in his folded arms on the table. "Why did she do that? What a fool!" His voice was low but pounding in my ears.

"You didn't—"

He raised his head and tore his chopstick wrapper to pieces. "Waiter, bill please."

"Everything will be okay if you marry her," I said, confused by his reaction. "You know she loves you."

Du Sheng stared at me, looking stunned and disgusted, as if I was asking him to kill someone. At last he said, "Let's go."

He paid the bill and strode out. I followed, one step behind him.

174

We walked a few blocks and arrived at a community park. He stopped at a wooden bench near a fountain. I stopped, too. He took out a cell phone from his pants pocket. "Tell Director Wang I have some personal things to deal with this afternoon and won't go back to work afterward. You can reschedule this afternoon's meetings to tomorrow."

After speaking on the phone, he turned to face me, hands behind his back. "I know Miao Yan is your best friend and you won't believe me no matter what I tell you, but I must tell you that the baby isn't mine. Also, I can't marry her so that she can stay here. We did have sex but the last time was eight months ago. We tried to get back together but it didn't work out. Each time she came to see me in Shenzhen, we always ended up arguing. We agreed that we should just be friends, not a couple. For some reason she asked me to pretend we were still a couple when we three met for the hotpot. I think she didn't want you to worry about her. She often told me how much you care about her and how much she's afraid of hurting you."

He was lying, I told myself. If he and Miao Yan had sex, the baby could be his. Didn't Pingping say that having sex would make a woman pregnant? He was trying to fool me!

"I don't care when and why you two broke up. If you had sex with her the baby could be yours." I felt thankful to Pingping for what she had taught me that night. Otherwise, I wouldn't have been able to confront him.

To my surprise, he smiled. A helpless smile. "I forgot—I'm talking to a teenager," he said.

I was furious. "What do you mean? Are you afraid now? If you think every girl is so naive and credulous, you're wrong. I feel bad for Miao Yan to have mistaken you for a responsible man."

He stopped smiling. He looked away from me and began

175

to pace back and forth. I didn't move; I was waiting for him to apologize.

After a few turns he stood in front of me, scratching his head. "What can I say? I am telling you the truth. First, having sex doesn't necessarily make a woman pregnant. There are many ways to control birth—men wearing a condom or women taking pills. I guess none of the novels you've read has told you anything like that. Second, the last time she and I had sex was eight months ago. If she was pregnant by me, she'd be at least eight months pregnant now and you'd be able to see it easily. Third, I can't marry her just because I had sex with her. I loved her but our relationship didn't go as well as I had hoped. Though I care about her and want her to stay in Guangdong, I can't marry her just for that."

I knew that he was telling the truth. I felt terrible about my ignorance of sex—I had just made a fool of myself. But I couldn't stop being angry at him. After all, if he hadn't broken up with her and if he had taken good care of her, she wouldn't have done something stupid like going to bed with someone she didn't love.

We caught a bus to the train station. Du Sheng wanted to call a taxi, saying he would pay for it, but I insisted on taking a bus. On the bus, we sat in separate rows. He tried to talk to me but I didn't feel like talking.

"You won't hate me, will you?" he said when we were waiting for the train on the platform.

"It's between you and Miao Yan. It's none of my business."

"I can tell you're still angry at me. I'm ten years older than you. There is something you don't understand right now."

"Though I haven't experienced as much as you have, it doesn't mean that I know less." I raised my head, looking away from him in the direction of the approaching train.

He put a hand on my shoulder. "Sorry. I take back what I said. I always wanted to have a little sister like you, who lives in a world of books and is never bothered by the outside world. I wish I could be like that."

His hand weighed heavily on me. The heat from his palm quickened my blood.

He sensed my uneasiness and withdrew his hand awkwardly. "Oh, you know," he said, smiling, "for a moment, I really thought you were my little sister. I remember when I was a kid I begged my ma for the longest time to give me a sister. No girls in my family. All boys. Three of us. I'm the eldest. My younger brothers are both married and don't need me around anymore."

His good-natured smile touched my heart. "You're luckier than I am. I'm by myself. When I was little I also wanted to have a brother or sister. But the one-child-per-family policy was very strict then," I said, less angry at him.

"I can tell you're an only child. You're stubborn, aren't you?" He stuck out his tongue and made a face at me. I couldn't help laughing. If I had had an elder brother, he would have been just like him.

The whistle of the coming train reminded me of the purpose of my trip. "How can we help Miao Yan?"

"She must get an abortion or she'll be expelled. There is no other option. An unmarried woman with a child is simply unacceptable in China. I don't even know if she knows who the man is. She must have been drunk when it happened, otherwise she wouldn't have done anything so stupid. I'll talk to her and take her to the hospital."

"An abortion? Is it dangerous?"

"Don't worry, I'll take care of her. I'll make sure everything goes well. I promise."

I looked at Du Sheng and nodded. How I wished he would agree to marry her so she could keep the baby and, even without the diploma, at least stay in Guangdong. But I didn't tell him what I was thinking—his serious expression stopped me. I still believed he should marry Miao Yan if he had made love to her but I knew he wouldn't do that and it wasn't even a good idea if he no longer loved her. How disappointed I felt with myself, at my failure to find a way to help Miao Yan!

The train pulled into the station. Passengers on the platform started to board. Before walking to my compartment I asked Du Sheng, "Why don't you love her? Why did you break up with her? She was hurt when she was thirteen years old and she can't afford to be hurt anymore."

He didn't answer. He shook his head, as if he didn't know what I was talking about.

The train pulled out of the station and a few moments later entered a long, dark tunnel. I stared at my reflection in the window and wondered why I was on this train.

With only ten days to the finals, students were busy, shuttling on bikes between the libraries, classrooms, and dorms.

It rained heavily the afternoon I came back from Shenzhen. I went to see Miao Yan as soon as I got into the dorm but nobody was in her room though the door was wide open. I went up to try my luck again after dinner but this time the door was locked. On the fourth morning after my return I saw a note on my door: "I'll be in Shenzhen these days. Don't contact me. Don't try to find me. Good luck with your finals. Good luck with everything. Miao Yan."

It was the first time I had seen her handwriting. It was surprisingly coarse and childish, each character as big as a five-fen coin, each stroke stiff as if carved. While some characters went up, others went down. There was no pattern in her handwriting.

It had been a while since I had visited the rooftop. I hadn't felt like going up there. Whenever I walked into my room I would glance at my violin case, once so beloved and dear to me, now as dark and cold as the weather. One day I took it from under the desk and put it beneath my bunk instead, so I wouldn't see it right away when I walked in.

The evening Miao Yan left for Shenzhen, I went to the library without eating dinner. Around nine o'clock I felt nauseous and distracted, so I returned to the dorm. Nobody else was in the room. On Pingping's desk was a bunch of red roses, eleven of them, in a black heart-shaped ceramic vase—eleven was a lucky number among college lovers because it represented loyalty. The roses must have been there for at least a few days since the petals were drooping and ready to fall. It surprised me that I hadn't noticed them until now.

Donghua's bed, as always, was messy, covered with yarn and half-finished knitting. I was often afraid that one day she would be stabbed by her own sharp knitting needles. She had also gotten herself a boyfriend recently. They had met the day I went to Shenzhen. Later, she told me that she was bored that day so she bicycled for an hour to visit a friend at another university. They went to see a movie, along with a group of her friend's classmates. Among them was a fair-skinned, bespectacled thin guy. He kept trying to speak to Donghua. He was majoring in computer science and was also in his second year. Donghua liked the way he spoke—soft-voiced and slow-paced—and was attracted to his broad knowledge of world affairs. After returning, she compared their horoscopes and birth dates and was convinced that they would be a good match. Later that day the guy showed up in the duty room and asked her if she'd like to be his girlfriend. She agreed. Since then he had come to see her three times. After telling me how they met, Donghua quickly added, "I told him that I wouldn't have sex with him until we get married."

I took the violin case from under the bunk—it felt heavier than I remembered. Then I realized that it was raining. I put the violin away and grabbed my raincoat.

The rain was heavier than I thought. Though I was wearing a raincoat with a cap, I hesitated for a few minutes before stepping onto the rooftop.

The sky was unusually white, shining like pebbles in a creek. The wind was soundless. Threads of rain, tilting and dense, fleeted past my eyes. I had always thought a rainy sky would be dismal and dark. It was the first time that I had seen such a brightly white rainy sky. This brightness cheered me up. Like a kid I started to run and jump, despite the rain that hit my face and trickled down my neck.

When the rain stopped I leaned against a wall. I put my hands on the top of the wall and bent over to look down. Seen from the rooftop, the duty room looked like a toy house and the grand iron door like a rusty knife. The few bicycle parking lots inside West Five were covered with puddles. Many of the bikes had fallen on top of each other.

Miao Yan always liked to look down from the rooftop. Sometimes, to scare me, she would sit on the wall with her legs dangling on each side and even swing her body left and right, making horrible falling sounds. Whenever she did this I would beg her to come down. She wouldn't stop until I screamed at her, then she would tease me for being such a coward before jumping back onto the cement rooftop. She often said there was crazy blood in her body.

Apart from *Fortress Besieged,* she once took another book from my bookshelf—a short story collection authored by college students. One piece, "A Life's Lightness," contained a scene of a student jumping from a high building.

After reading the story she said to me, "If you could choose how to die, what would you do?"

"I don't want to die," I replied. "Nobody wants to die."

She laughed hysterically.

"Okay, now you tell me what you'd choose," I said.

"I'd jump from a high place—a skyscraper, a bridge, a mountain, somewhere in the sky. The higher the better. I'm a wild goose. That's my name. That's my fate. I have no fear because I know how to fly." She had shrugged and waved her arms up and down as if she indeed knew how to fly.

Remembering her words, I gripped the wall even more tightly, as though a whirlwind might come from nowhere and carry me down from the rooftop.

Suddenly, I heard a female's piercing scream from downstairs, then the sound of a motor starting. The sound faded away rapidly.

I looked down and heard one girl shout, "Dama, what happened?"

The stocky Dama ran out of the duty room. In seconds, her hoarse voice broke the sky: "A murder! Somebody just committed a murder! Help! Call the Security Department! Call an ambulance!"

With her voice still resonating, a stream of students, including me, ran down the stairs, making a clatter like guns firing, and hurried outside.

A girl lay against the brick wall, groaning. Her long green

181

sweater was stained with mud, her face hidden by a veil of hair. A red umbrella covered half of her body. Dama lifted the umbrella and from the girl's stomach blood oozed between her fingers.

"Blood! Blood! Get her to hospital!" a girl screamed and began to throw up at the sight of the blood.

"She lives on our floor. She was okay a few minutes ago. I even said hello to her in the hallway," another girl cried.

The injured girl was no longer groaning but she closed her eyes slowly. When Dama asked her what had happened, she didn't answer. She only twisted a corner of her mouth a little and managed an almost imperceptible smile.

Ten minutes later an ambulance and two police cars arrived. Sirens screaming, they took away the girl.

At eleven thirty, Pingping and Donghua walked into the room, bringing the latest news, which they had heard in the duty room. The victim was Wang Mei, a senior who had recently found a job in Shenzhen. The man, also in his senior year, who had run away on the motorcycle was her boyfriend and they had been together for more than three years. He was from Xinjiang, the most northwestern province in China, and as required by the government he had to go back to his hometown after graduation.

The day before the incident, Wang Mei told him that their relationship had to end because she would never want to go to Xinjiang with him. The next afternoon the guy rode a borrowed motorcycle to visit her. He said he understood why she didn't want to continue the relationship and only wished they could spend one more night together. She agreed. First he drove her along the Pearl River, then took her to one of the most expensive bars in the city, where they danced intimately. Afterward, he drove her back to the university.

Outside the duty room, he asked if she would reconsider her decision. She answered that they had to break up because she could never live in a backward province like Xinjiang. The guy nodded and let her return to her room. An hour later he walked into the duty room, pushed Dama away from the phone, and dialed Wang Mei's room number. He said on the phone how much he loved her and that he only wished to see her one more time, after which he would leave her alone. She went down to see him and he stabbed her.

One of Wang Mei's roommates told the story. When Wang Mei had parted with the guy earlier in the evening and returned to her dorm, she told one of her roommates what had happened. The roommate also heard the guy's voice on the speaker and had warned Wang Mei not to go down to meet him, but she wouldn't listen. The roommate said, "My instinct told me that he might do something bad to her but I never thought he'd stab her. His voice was so sad. I might have gone down to see him as well if I had been Wang Mei."

After sharing the story, Pingping said if she ever had a loyal boyfriend like this guy she would go to Xinjiang with him.

"That's a big lie," Donghua said from her bed, putting down her knitting. "You're practical. I don't think you'd be so silly as to give up the opportunity of staying in a big city for a man. Didn't you come to this university because you wanted to stay in Guangdong?"

Pingping hesitated, but soon said, "If you're with the person you love, the rest isn't important."

"Okay. Say I'm a man and you love me. You go to my village in Sichuan with me. There are no shopping malls there, no refrigerators, no color televisions, no washing machines, you make little money, you have to work in the field, you have to feed pigs, you have to have at least one son or you'll be looked down on. Will you still love me?"

"That's not realistic. We're university students. We won't be assigned to the countryside."

"You see, love isn't enough. The difference between Xinjiang and Guangzhou is just as big. Since I was little, my parents have told me that their greatest wish is that I become a city person. My ma even said I could marry a cripple, a blind man, as long as I work in the city she'd be happy for me. You're lucky to be born in a big city. You don't know what life is like in the country." Donghua's face turned red. She climbed down from her bed and poured some water from her thermos.

"How come you're so worked up?" Pingping mumbled. "We aren't talking about you."

"Anyway," Donghua said. "The guy shouldn't have stabbed her. Now his future is ruined completely."

I was lying on my bed listening to their conversation. I chimed in, "Do you think the girl ever considered going to Xinjiang with him?"

Donghua shook her head. "I don't think so. There are so many men in the world. If you can't stay with this guy, there must be another guy somewhere waiting for you."

"My goodness, are you practical yourself, or what? No wonder you spend so much time knitting. You want to have enough sweaters for all of your potential boyfriends!" Pingping dragged a half-done sweater from Donghua's bed and waved it like a battle flag. It turned into a chase around the room, with a lot of bumping into desks and knocking down chairs. Pingping then said she had never tried cheek-to-cheek dancing and suggested a demonstration, so Donghua put on a pair of high-heeled shoes and danced with her. They whirled with their cheeks touching, their arms around each other's waists.

Next morning I overslept. It was eleven thirty when I got up. After brushing my teeth and washing my face, I picked up my bag, ran down the stairs, and grabbed my bike from a messy heap of them. I was perched on the saddle, about to rush to the library, when I saw an announcement posted near the window of the duty room. It was written in red ink and the headline blazed WARRANT FOR ARREST:

Li Zhe, male, twenty-two years old, a senior, from Sihezi City in Xinjiang Province. This student is suspected of stabbing a female student (name undisclosed) in front of the dormitory of West Five at about ten in the evening on December 24, 1992. The victim is still in a critical condition. According to witnesses the suspect escaped on a red Honda motorcycle after stabbing the victim. The City Police Department has ordered the arrest of Li Zhe. If you know where he is hiding or can provide any information regarding his whereabouts, please contact the City Police Department or the Security Department on campus immediately.

To the left of the announcement was a small photograph of Li Zhe. He had a square face and big eyes that looked slightly to the left. His lips, thick and full, were closed tightly, as though he was determined not to open them. The masculinity of his face was, however, balanced by feminine features: his eyebrows were thin and curved, his nose was small and straight. A face full of conflict.

On my way to the library, I saw an identical notice on every dorm and office building I passed.

Finals ended on a bright, sunny afternoon. Though I thought of Miao Yan even when I was taking the tests, I did well in all my subjects. By now, Miao Yan had been gone for more than a week. I often went to a pay phone and dialed Du Sheng's cell phone, but hung up on the first ring. Though I worried about Miao Yan, I didn't want to speak with him. I was afraid of him. The way he had looked at me, the way he'd put his hand on my shoulder, seemed to suggest he knew me—perhaps better than I knew myself.

Once I dialed his phone and waited till I heard his voice on the other end before hanging up without saying a word. I even heard him shouting, "Ming, is that you? I know it's you. Why not speak to me? Don't hang up . . ."

Whenever Dama saw me she would say, "There's another call for you today. Same guy from Shenzhen. He's been calling for a few days now, but when I ask him if he wants me to take a message he always says it's nothing important and he'll call back." Then she would smile and say, "Is he your boyfriend? Did you have a fight?"

According to undergraduate tradition, when the evening finals ended we would play a poker game called "Tractor" all night long till dawn. Since finals had begun, we'd had no curfew, so we didn't even need to buy candles. All the rooms were full of loud laughter and happy screams. Pingping, standing barefoot on her desk, was decorating the window with some tiny twinkling light bulbs. Donghua was moving chairs around and putting away all the textbooks and examination materials. A few other classmates were sitting on Yishu's bed, debating who would team up with whom in the poker game—to make the game more competitive, they had invited students from other departments. Both Pingping and Donghua were good players, so they decided to play in separate rooms to guarantee higher winning odds for our own department. Pingping had asked me to join the game but I didn't feel like celebrating.

I fumbled around my bookshelf and took out a paperback copy of Camus's *The Stranger*—I had decided to go to the library. The book was thin. I rolled it into a tube and tucked it in my pocket. It was much colder out than I had thought—perhaps close to zero. I wore only a sweater and a thin jacket but I didn't want to return to the dorm to put more clothes on.

The sky was starless. I turned up the collar of my jacket, put my hands into the pockets, and walked along the graveled footpath circling Violin Lake. Nobody else seemed to be around.

I sat on a stone bench at the edge of the lake. The chill from the stone immediately penetrated my jeans, ran up through my chest, and reached my nose. I sneezed aloud. The echo reverberated over the lake and into the woods, making a continuous *wung, wung, wung* sound, as though all the trees were sneezing as well. The lake was calm, its surface like a steel board reflecting the sky. I stared at the lake, bent low, neck drawn back, and hugged my jacket around my body. I sat like this for ten minutes or so till two lovers, leaning on each other, walked by. They kept looking at me over their shoulders so I stood up. My legs were numb. I touched my face—cold as ice. It took me a while to massage away the numbness and then I trudged to the library.

Room One was only half full but my seat was taken. When I walked in the person sitting there raised his head, looking

surprised, then smiled. It was the guy who usually sat on the
end seat in the front row, near the door. Sometimes, walking
by, I had glimpsed the books on his desk—mostly physics
books, often piled up high. Once or twice I ran into him in
the hallway but we never greeted each other.

Occasionally Pingping and I had been in the library together when he was there. Later, Pingping said she was sure
that he liked me. One reason she gave was that he had walked
to the window next to me three times within two hours to
look out. "It's dark outside. What could he possibly see?"
Pingping said secretively. "He was peeking at you and your
books."

His own seat near the door was empty. Why was he sitting
in my seat? Was his seat not available when he went in? I told
myself to sit somewhere far from him but for some reason I sat
across from him, as if wanting him to feel guilty about taking
my seat.

"Hello," he said.

"Hey," I said nervously. I took the Camus book from my
pocket and thumbed through it—I had read it four or five
times already and could remember the story by heart.

A few minutes passed and I was still staring at the same
page. The unnaturally bright fluorescent lights seemed to have
sapped my energy and made me feel listless, isolated, and exposed. I shouldn't have come to the library tonight. I wished
I had gone to Shenzhen with Miao Yan but I knew she
wouldn't have allowed me to. There were so many questions
in my mind. Had she decided to get an abortion? Would she
bleed a lot? Could I trust Du Sheng to take good care of her?

The guy was observing me from the corner of his eye. He
had well-chiseled features and tanned skin. On any other day
I might have felt uncomfortable with such attention from a

stranger, but tonight I felt like speaking to someone. Anyone. I needed a companion.

As I was pondering this he pushed a piece of paper toward me, folded neatly into a square.

I unfolded it: "Ming, I'm sorry for having taken your seat. When I walked in your seat was empty, so I thought you wouldn't be coming to the library tonight." The note was signed "Sang Wei."

His handwriting was delicate and accurately formed, each character the same size and the spacing between characters perfectly measured.

He knew my name and my seat! I glanced at him again and met his eyes—he looked friendly and intelligent. I quickly lowered my head.

I wrote on the back of the paper: "You needn't apologize. That seat isn't assigned to me and anybody can have it. You came first, of course it's yours."

He smiled when he saw my note. He took out another piece of paper and wrote: "I've noticed you and your seat. I wanted to introduce myself but didn't get a chance. I'm not the kind of guy who knows how to approach girls. I'm glad we finally talked."

I replied: "Want to go out for a walk?"

He took my note. "Good idea," he whispered. He pushed aside his books and stood up.

We walked to the library's outdoor garden. He was almost a head taller than me. In a dark blue sweatshirt and black jeans, he looked thin but athletically built.

The garden wasn't very big but had a variety of plants. Succulents bordered the reddish tiled ground. Evergreen plants such as holly and camellia prospered, forming a dense wall behind the succulents. In one corner, a broad-leafed ivy made its way to the top of a silk cotton tree. In the middle of the garden was a tiny pond with water lilies. There were no benches, but flat-surfaced rocks here and there served well as seats. When I was studying in the library I often came here for a short break.

"Why did you sit in my chair?" I asked when we were standing next to the pond.

"When you sit there you always seem absorbed in your books. I thought I'd be much more productive if I sat there. And it was true. I completed a tough paper within a few hours."

I knew he was mocking me. "How do you know my name?"

"Your books told me. I also know that you like reading literary reviews. I thought all girls in Chinese literature read love stories every day. You don't know how much we science students admire you arts and humanities students."

"Are you studying physics?" Thinking of the books on his desk, I had blurted out my question.

"How do you know? Did you notice me as well?" He looked happy.

"You just look like a person who might study physics." I blushed.

"Do you mean I'm boring?"

"Oh, no." I could feel the warmth on my face.

More people came to the garden. It was nine, a good time for a break.

"Let me walk you home," he suggested.

We walked toward West Five. The streetlights stretched our shadows into two long, thin poles. He held the handlebar of his bike rigidly with both hands while I walked on the other side of the bike.

"You—" I said.

"You—" he said at the same time.

"Ladies first." He smiled. His smile was natural and amiable—the kind of smile that makes you feel safe.

"Tell me something about yourself," I said.

"I'm in the last year of graduate school. Twenty-three years old. I did my undergraduate study in Qinghua University. Physics as well. I grew up in Suzhou and live ten minutes from the Lingering Garden. I have one older sister." He spoke rhythmically.

"You don't have to tell me that much. I'm not a police-woman." I was amused.

We were now walking along Violin Lake. He parked his bike against a tree, then extended his arms forward, stretching them a few times. "Do you come here a lot?"

"Hardly ever. Too many couples come here," I said. Not far away, a couple was kissing behind a tree.

"You're too nice. I sometimes come here just to disturb them."

"Are you jealous?"

"A little, maybe." He stopped and stared at me. "You don't have a boyfriend in your hometown or somewhere else, do you?"

"No," I said after hesitating briefly.

"I don't have a girlfriend, either. Frankly, I'm a little afraid of girls. I had a bad experience with a girl once."

We circled the lake, discussing books and movies. He had read many of the books I liked, including *Wuthering Heights* and Nietzsche's *Thus Spake Zarathustra*. At some point we talked about our childhoods. Like my parents, his parents were also exiled during the Cultural Revolution, but to a farm in the most northeastern Heilongjiang Province. On a map of the country, the province was like the head of a rooster.

191

"You were lucky," he said. "Your farm had much nicer weather. In Heilongjiang we had blizzards for months."

"I've never seen a blizzard."

"Believe me, you don't want to."

"Our farm was near a river," I said. "Sometimes I went there to fish or catch shrimp with other kids. In the summers my ba took me swimming there. I never learned how to swim, though. He was too protective."

"We had no rivers, but a lot of mountains. My sister and I liked to pick mushrooms and listen to our echoes from the mountains when we called out. We also went to the woods to steal honey from wild beehives. We were always hungry. Once bees stung me so badly that for a week I had to cover my face, all except for my eyes, when I went to school."

It was the first time that I had felt comfortable being with a guy. When we wanted to sit, there were no available benches—they had all been taken. We were surrounded by lovers who were cuddling and kissing.

We walked back to the main road. When we passed a cypress tree near a basketball court, Sang Wei stopped and took my hand unexpectedly. My mind raced. Was he going to kiss me? On my lips, or cheek, or forehead? What should I do if he kissed me? What should I say to him if I didn't want to be kissed?

I thought of the kissing scene Pingping had described. No, I wouldn't let him kiss me on the first date—if tonight could be called a date. I had just met him, barely knew him. Even Pingping and her boyfriend didn't kiss until their second date.

He must have sensed my uneasiness. He let go of my hand, looking embarrassed. "I don't want to scare you away. Let's be friends first."

I nodded, appreciating his concern, and walked ahead.

We were approaching West Five. From the road, Miao Yan's room could be seen—it was dark, so none of her roommates were home. They must have been playing poker somewhere, or partying at a club. They didn't know what she had gone through. They didn't know anything about her. They were just jealous of her beauty and her pretty clothes. They wanted her to go back to Yunnan.

I was suddenly anxious about her abortion. Why did she tell me not to contact her? Would she do something stupid? Something stupid like . . . my stomach ached. She wouldn't kill herself, would she? I shook my head hard and quickened my pace. No, she would never do anything like that. She was so young and pretty. I had to call Du Sheng to see how she was doing, once I returned to the dorm.

"Sorry, I didn't mean to make you uncomfortable." Sang Wei had caught up with me.

"Oh, sorry, I was just thinking about my best friend. She's going through tough times," I said apologetically.

"Who is she? You always go to the library alone."

"You wouldn't know her. The campus is so big."

"You can't be sure. I've been here for a while."

"Her name is Miao Yan. I bet you don't know her."

"Miao Yan? A final-year student?"

"You know her?"

"I used to," he said curtly.

My heart fell—they must have been more than just casual acquaintances. "How did you meet her?" I asked.

"At a party for graduate students. She was an undergraduate and I didn't know why she was there."

"That was it?"

"I don't understand how the two of you can be good friends. You're so different from each other."

"In what way?"

He stood closer. "Ming, you shouldn't be with her."

"What happened?"

He stared at me for a moment. "I'd better tell you. That night, unlike the other girls who were waiting to be invited, she offered to teach some of the guys to dance. I'd never seen a girl who was so gracious and kind. Of course, every guy fell in love with her after the party. For a while she frequented our dorm, each time being seen with a different guy."

He paused and held my hand again. "Ming, I have to be honest with you. I went out with her briefly as well. I don't know why. Perhaps I just couldn't resist her beauty. She was never serious with me or with any of the other guys. Later she dumped us all. There were no explanations, no excuses. It was like she was taking revenge on us. Or I guess none of the students were rich enough for her. It was also said that she was looking for someone to marry so she could stay in Guangdong. There was a lot of gossip about her. You don't want to know what we called her at that time. Ming, you shouldn't be with her. She's a terrible person."

"That is not true!" I shook off his hand. Two scenes invaded my mind's eye: a group of strange men at the disco bar surrounding Miao Yan, laughing frantically, and Miao Yan lying bloodstained on the operating table, moaning in pain.

"She isn't that kind of person! She wouldn't stay with a guy just because he's rich or because she wanted to remain in Guangdong! You don't understand her. You don't know anything about her. She doesn't want to go back to her hometown because she hates her father!"

Sang Wei stared at me, a little taken aback by my sudden fury. For a few minutes neither of us spoke.

"Did you have sex with her?" I asked.

"Ming, let's drop the subject." He averted his eyes. "She isn't worthy of your friendship. She's materialistic and immoral. She only uses people to get what she wants."

"That's not true! That's not her! There must be other reasons why she left you. You don't know her at all. You're just like the other men who only want to go to bed with her. I bet you didn't know that her father was paralyzed. I bet you didn't know that she has to make money to support her family. I bet you didn't know that she was badly hurt emotionally when she was thirteen. She's the sweetest person I've ever known. Now she's suffering and I'm here doing nothing about it."

Sang Wei opened his mouth twice, but nothing came out. Tears streamed down my cheeks before I could wipe them away.

"I have to go back to the dorm. It's late," I said.

I left him. At West Five's big iron gate I stopped and detoured toward a row of trimmed bushes near the student canteen. I smelled the leaves, then sat against a bush. The earth under me was as damp and soft as a swamp; it felt like it could swallow me.

Through the space between the bushes I peeked at the road near the lake, where the lampposts looked thin and fragile. The pale yellowish light in the air was strangely dim.

The road was empty, as if a heavy rain had just cleaned everything I had left behind.

The door to my room was open but nobody was inside—Donghua and Pingping were playing poker next door. I heard their yelling and laughter and the sounds of cards being slammed down on the desk. I took off my jacket and jeans, climbed into bed, and fell asleep right away.

• • •

Miao Yan returned a few days later. The abortion was done—Du Sheng had called the night before with a message: it went well.

At lunchtime, Miao Yan showed up in my room. She looked tired and only stayed briefly. She didn't mention the abortion. She talked about her trip to Shenzhen in a way that made it sound just like any other trip she'd made there.

I went to her room the next day. She wasn't in. A note on her desk addressed to me said that she wanted to be alone and asked me not to visit her until she came to see me.

When Du Sheng called again I picked up the phone. "Keep an eye on her. She went crazy in Shenzhen," he said, then told me that more than once Miao Yan had threatened to jump out of the window of the hotel he had put her in. "I took a week off from work to be with her day and night. I was afraid that she'd do something like that."

The temperature plummeted. My parents had heard the forecast and sent me a thick coat, a cashmere sweater, and a woolen shawl.

After finals, Yishu disappeared without saying goodbye to Pingping, Donghua, and me. She had folded her mosquito net and bedding and put them away in the highest storage cell behind the door. She had rolled her bamboo mat into a tight tube and placed it inside a plastic cover. One day when I climbed up to my bed, I noticed that a picture of her and her mother had replaced the picture of her and her best friend. Her glass vase was still on the desk but for the first time there was no flower in it. A week earlier I had heard a rumor about her from a classmate, saying that she was emigrating to Australia with her parents.

Pingping had a fight with her boyfriend before finals. Since the poker night she had rarely gone out of the dorm and often slept through the day. When she was up, sometimes she didn't even bother to change her clothes but walked about in the hallway or the washroom in her pajamas. One night I woke up around three o'clock and saw her standing in the hallway, her hands on the banister. She looked awfully thin, like a dried-out plant stem shaking in the wind. I thought about bringing her a jacket but was not sure if she wanted to be disturbed. The wind was getting gustier and my mosquito net was ballooning as if it would explode and be carried away by the wind. Finally she walked back into the room, shut the door, and pushed in the bolt. She stood with her back against the door for a while before tiptoeing to her bed.

I wanted to ask her if there was anything I could do to help, but I knew there wasn't. I hadn't even been in a relationship. How could I possibly know how to advise her?

I listened to the whistling of the wind, imagining that it was sending leaves down to the water-filled gutters. I wondered where Miao Yan was at this moment. Was she sleepless, like me? What was she thinking right now?

⌒2⌒

My train home was at six o'clock in the evening, the day of my eighteenth birthday. My parents had called earlier and said they would pick me up at the station. They had also asked me not to buy gifts for them so I could travel light. In the past week I had received birthday cards from my parents and a few classmates from middle school and high school. One of them said she would organize a birthday party for me to celebrate my reaching adulthood.

Yesterday I received a letter from Ar Yu. He complained about the blizzards in Michigan. He said he missed me and missed Guangzhou, though he had begun to make friends there. He also said his aunt was stricter with him than his parents. "I have to go home right after my language school and every night I have to watch English news for two hours. The English tutor she has hired for me is older than my grandma and meaner than the headmaster in my primary school. There's no chance for me to meet girls. One piece of good news is that I can finally decorate my own room. I bought two big posters of Michael Jackson last week."

The results of the finals came out. I got a C– in Gao CK's "Shakespeare and His Sonnets"—the only C– in the class, the lowest score despite my past record as his top student. I wouldn't qualify for a "Top Student" scholarship for the coming year because it required that scores in all subjects be B+ or above. At first Pingping and Donghua were indignant for me, saying Gao CK was too narrow-minded and revengeful, then they said I was lucky that he hadn't reported what I had done in his class to the Dean. I was actually relieved and happy—for the first time being a top student didn't mean so much to me.

The cold wind that had been gusting for a few days finally stopped the day before my departure. Around noon the sun came out from behind thick black clouds. After lunch I took down my mosquito net and immersed it with all of my dirty sheets and clothes in a big basin full of detergent. I left the basin in the washroom to let the detergent soak in. When I was in my room packing, the speaker crackled with Dama's voice: "301, Chen Ming. Somebody is waiting—" Then Sang Wei's panting: "It's me. I must speak with you."

198

Both Pingping and Donghua looked at me.

"Boyfriend?" Donghua grinned.

"Oh no, just a friend," I said. "A guy from my hometown and he . . . he wants me to take something home to his family."

It was not a successful lie. Pingping laughed. "Why is your face so red?" Donghua giggled, too. I excused myself hastily and said I needed to go down to get the stuff this guy had wanted me to take to his family.

I walked to the other side of the hallway and looked at the duty room from behind a pole. There he was, pacing back and forth. It was the first time he had come to the dorm to visit me. Since the night we had parted he had written me three letters, each neatly folded and placed inside a sky-blue envelope, but I hadn't opened them; I had put them away with the textbooks I no longer needed. I didn't want to hear his explanation. What could he say about his past with Miao Yan anyway? On the other hand, I couldn't deny my feelings for him.

I stayed hidden behind the pole until Sang Wei left. Afraid that Pingping and Donghua would grill me about him, I went directly to the washroom. As I was doing my laundry I became anxious. Why didn't I dare to see him? Had I fallen in love with him? How terrible was it to fall in love with your best friend's ex-lover!

I washed my clothes so vigorously that I could feel the material squeak in my hands. I hung up the clothes and mosquito net on the wire outside my room. They were dripping and quickly wet the hallway. I looked up at the sun and hoped it would stay for another few hours to dry my things.

When I went back to my room Pingping and Donghua were gone. A hard-covered book was on my desk: Emily Dickinson's *Complete Collection*—Dama must have asked Pingping or Donghua to pick it up for me. I opened the book and saw a little card between the cover and the first page: "My train is leaving in a few hours and I'm off to the station now. It'll be one month before I come back to the university. I don't write romantic love poems. I only hope you can accept me. After all, the past is the past, isn't it? Nobody can afford to live in the past."

I decided to visit Miao Yan. The door to her room was wide open. She was alone, folding clothes. I knocked on the door. She put down a pair of jeans and smiled brightly. "I knew you'd be here. Come right in," she said.

She wore an ankle-length gray sweater-dress, its buttons unfastened and the waist strap untied, slippers on her feet. Under the dress she was wearing a wrinkled T-shirt, fat and long like a rice bag. She seemed to have lost a lot of weight, her fleshy cheeks now sunken. Her bed had only a bamboo mat left on it and the once colorful wall decorated by her suits was now white; all the nails were gone. I looked at her desk— it was bare where her piles of books had been.

"I donated all my suits and books to a foundation for minority students," she said happily.

"What's going on?" My heart jumped insanely.

"Let's talk on the rooftop. I haven't been up there in ages."

I followed her through the dark hallway and up the dimly lit stairs. The moment I stepped onto the rooftop I had to shade my eyes—the sun was strong, intensified, and reflected by the bare cement.

It was the first time I had visited the rooftop in the daytime. For some reason I didn't understand it had never occurred to me to visit it other than in the evenings or at night. After my eyes had adjusted to the brightness I lowered my hands. In the broad sunlight the once mysterious rooftop—

the rooftop that reminded me of the attic in my parents' house—seemed to have lost its dramatic ambience and become normal, even ugly, like a clown without stage makeup and costume. The rusty pipes along the walls, the bare cement, even the sky all looked unreal.

"Want to sit where we met for the first time?" She walked toward the corner and sat down, taking off her slippers. When I stood in front of her she grinned and moved away from the corner a little.

I wedged myself between her and the wall, my left arm holding her right arm. She leaned her head on my shoulder. I wanted to cry.

"You didn't put perfume on today," I said.

"You didn't play the violin, either." She smiled. "I miss your playing."

"You were packing. Where are you going?"

"My train leaves tonight. I'm sorry I can't celebrate your birthday with you."

"Where are you going?" I stared at her.

"Yunnan, my hometown. After I get off the train I'll take a long bus ride to Zhaotong, then another bus to the tiny town where I went to school. It's in the northeast part of Yunnan, at the foot of the Wumeng mountain range. Other minority groups are there, like Yi, Hui, Bai, and Buyi. They have their own languages and customs. When my grandparents were alive we lived in a thatched hut under the mountain and ate a lot of maize and buckwheat. The hut was made of mud-plastered bamboo strips. I cut my fingers so many times when I helped them split the bamboo. We spoke the Miao dialect at that time. My grandma taught me how to do embroidery, wax dyeing, and paper-cutting. She often told me that we Miao women are the prettiest and hardest-working in the world. She made all my and my brothers' clothes. During the holidays the men in my village would play the *lusheng*. Have you ever seen a *lusheng*?"

I shook my head.

"It plays the most beautiful music I've ever heard. It's made mostly of reeds and has six pipes. It varies a lot in length, from ten inches or so to over ten feet. You play it with your mouth, as you do a trumpet. We Miao play it for holidays, funerals, or other special occasions. Sometimes a group of players play their *lusheng* together and the sound is bright, pleasing, and pure. Hearing that kind of music, you forget all your worries and troubles. On those days we also sing and dance all night long. Women wear their most beautiful costumes, jewelry from head to toe, and sing love songs to the men they admire. Miao women are never shy about expressing their love. Men sing, too, wooing the girls they have fallen in love with. My grandma and grandpa actually met after such a courtship. When my grandma was old she had terrible teeth but she still sang like a lark."

I was completely engrossed. "Did she teach you how to sing?"

"She did but I don't remember any of the songs now. After my grandparents died, my parents moved away from the mountain and became city dwellers. We no longer sang."

"What a pity!"

"I decided to go home two days ago and a guy from my hometown got a train ticket for me through a 'back-door' deal. Don't frown. He really is from my hometown. If I'd had to buy the ticket myself I might have had to wait in line a whole day. I've been here almost four years now and have never been back. I miss my family, my parents and brothers."

"How many brothers do you have?"

202

"Two. One's two years older than you. His twentieth birth-day was yesterday. He's smart but didn't get a chance to go to college. He works in the factory my ba used to work in as a bench worker. He's the handsomest guy there and is always surrounded by girls. My other brother is only fourteen and in middle school. He's mature for his age and always writes, ask-ing me to take care of myself. His biggest dream is to go to Qinghua University in Beijing to study engineering." She smiled, looking up at the sky as if her brothers were up there waving at her.

"I heard your ba is paralyzed from a stroke and has to stay in bed."

"He's doing just fine." She looked at me with narrowed eyes. "Who told you that? I don't remember having said a word about it."

"I just know. Does your ma have a job?"

"Yes. She's a cashier at a local department store."

"Does she make enough money to support the family?" There were so many questions I wanted to ask.

"I send money back every month. My ba's factory also gives him money from time to time. Don't worry so much. I'm twenty-four years old and I'm the oldest. With me around my family will always be okay."

"Just tell me if you need more money. My parents send me an allowance every month and I can also get part-time jobs. I also get scholarships every year." I didn't want to tell her about that C–.

"I'll certainly borrow money from you if I need any."

"When are you coming back?" I asked.

"I don't know. Maybe I'll get married in Yunnan and never come back. I like Yunnan guys. They're nice and honest, much better than the guys around here."

"Who will you marry?"

"Haha, you'd better believe in me. Surely I can find a husband, can't I? I'm pretty and I'll have a college diploma. If the governor's son doesn't want to marry me, I'll marry a mayor's son. If I can't marry a mayor's son, there are dozens of bureau officers' sons waiting in line for me." She laughed aloud.

"You're joking, right? Don't marry those playboys. They won't take good care of you. Marry a man you love who's also nice to you."

"You sound like my grandma. She used to tell me that." She rubbed my nose playfully. "I'll ask you to phone-screen the candidates. How does that sound?"

"What did you say earlier? Did you just say you might never come back?"

"Don't worry. I'll come back to visit you as soon as I settle down. If you had a good job in Guangdong and made lots of money you could send me plane tickets every year." She laughed again.

"If you don't come back next semester, how can you get your diploma?" I didn't laugh with her.

"I forgot to tell you that my adviser loved the dissertation you wrote for me. He said he'd send my diploma."

"Even if you don't come back for the next semester?"

She nodded.

"Why did—?" before I could finish, Miao Yan put her hand over my mouth, a mischievous look on her face.

"I should call you 'Miss Why.' Don't think about things that don't make sense to you, will you, my poet?"

"But . . . but you said that you'd tell me everything as soon as I was eighteen years old. I'm turning eighteen tomorrow. You can't leave me like this."

"What do you want to know?"

"I want to know . . . about everything." I gestured with my hands to help me think. "I want to know . . . about men and women, love and sex. I want to know how to date a guy. I want to know about you. You can't leave me without telling me anything."

"Ming," she said, then fell silent. She put her chin on her knees, looking puzzled. "I really don't know any more than you do. I thought I knew, but I don't. I—"

"That's not what you said before. I've been waiting for you to tell me about the secret of becoming a woman. I've been trying to figure it out all these months. I thought that if I was a woman, like you, you'd like me more and tell me everything about your life. I was even trying to get a boyfriend. I thought that if I had a boyfriend you'd talk to me about things like men, women, and love and would treat me equally. I don't want to be a girl anymore. How am I supposed to grow up without you around?" I stood up, afraid that tears would pour from my suddenly flooded heart.

She stood up as well, but only to press me back down.

"Listen to me. You'll be all right. You might even have a better life without me around. I'm a bad influence and a self-ish person. After I leave you'll have time to go to the library, date, get to know other people. What do I know? I don't know about men and women. I don't know what I want. I don't even know much about myself. What can be worse than not knowing about yourself? Don't blame me, Ming. I'm not a good person to teach you anything about men and women. For a long while I was confused, I just wanted to punish men for what I had suffered. When I finally fell in love with Du Sheng I couldn't even make him love me. I'm such a failure."

"If I was a guy I'd marry you, so you wouldn't go back to

Yunnan and wouldn't marry someone you might not like. So we would stay together and be best friends until forever. I don't know if my life would be the same if you weren't around. I don't know if I ever want to make love to a man or ever want to get married." These words came out of my mouth so strongly that I knew I had always wanted to say them. I grabbed her hands, much more tightly than either of us expected.

She stared at me, her lips quivering. I let go of her hands, wondering what she would say. She put her hands on my cheeks, her palms warm and moist—she had never touched my face before, not with both hands, not with such seriousness. I studied her—her eyes, her nose, her mouth, her freckles, every inch of her face. I didn't blink.

She kissed me on the forehead. The kiss, my first kiss from someone other than my parents, was tender, like a breeze. "Silly girl. You're such a silly girl. You'll marry someone you love, who loves you. You'll make love to the man who's destined to appear in your life. It's as inevitable as the fact that you'll be eighteen years old tomorrow. You'll become a woman before you know it."

"Why do girls have to become women?"

"It's not up to us. Every girl will become a woman sooner or later, in her own way."

I didn't want to believe it but I knew it was silly not to. "Do you have cigarettes with you? May I smoke?" I said.

"Of course," she said, but she didn't move, her hands still on my cheeks. We stared at each other, face to face, and neither of us said anything.

"Oh yes, the cigarette." She lowered her hands. She took a pack of Salem and a lighter from her pocket. "You can never change yourself much. I've tried so many brands in the past few months but still went back to the same brand and even the same lighter."

She inserted a cigarette between my lips and struck the lighter.

I inhaled deeply but instead of exhaling, I swallowed the smoke. I coughed severely and Miao Yan had to pat my back to help me cough the smoke from my chest.

"So you've never smoked before." She laughed.

"I don't like the brand," I said, my face red after I had stopped coughing. "Why don't you smoke with me?"

"I quit. Weren't you always at me to quit? There was only one cigarette in this box and it was for you. Look! It's empty." She threw the empty box up, caught it with both hands, and tore it open. "Look! It's empty." She laughed loudly.

I frowned, stared at her incredulously, and laughed with her. We laughed so hard that tears came to our eyes. I hadn't laughed so heartily for a long time.

She held my hand and we walked to the other side of the roof. In front of us was a vista with red-roofed buildings, green trees, and glittering lakes. "How I love this university!" she said. She took a deep breath and opened her arms slowly, eyes closed. When she opened her eyes again she asked, "How do you want to celebrate your eighteenth birthday?"

"No plan yet. I've always wished that something unforgettable would happen that day. Something I'd remember my whole life. I mean, something big and significant that would tell me that from now on I'm an adult. But it looks as though nothing will happen."

"It's too early to say. The most magical things always take place at the last minute." Suddenly she looked concerned. "Can you promise me one thing?"

I nodded.

207

"Can you promise me that you'd never deny someone because of me?"

"Like whom?"

"Just promise me."

"Okay. I promise."

I thought immediately of Du Sheng. Somehow I felt she
was referring to him. I hadn't heard from him since the last
time he told me on the phone to keep an eye on Miao Yan.

"How's everything between you and Du Sheng?" I asked.

"There's nothing left between us now, not even friendship.
We aren't meant for each other," she said candidly.

"But you love him, right?"

"I don't know. I thought so. I'm not sure anymore. For a
while, I desperately wanted him back. I went to Shenzhen to
see him so often, hoping he'd change his mind. I read books
he liked. I even tried to quit smoking. I never thought I'd love
a man like that. But sometimes I asked myself whether it was
really love or more of a reflection of my fear of being hurt
again. Since I started at university, I'd been gripped by the fear
that I would have to go back to my hometown. I wanted to
escape Yunnan, my family, my own memory. I'd been wanting
so much for somebody to protect me. I finally thought it
through when I was in Shenzhen, when I was lying on the
operating table: you can never forget the past unless you face
up to it.

"I wrote a letter to my ba and mentioned the thing that
took place eleven years ago and told him how I had hated him
all these years. The funny thing is that when I called home Ba
said he'd never beaten me like that and never called me a
'whore.' He cried so much that he couldn't speak. Then he
said he loves me and misses me every day. It's the first time he

ever said that to me. How ironic! The thing that has haunted me for so many years has left no trace in my ba's memory."

"So you'll forgive him?"

"I don't know. I only know that I wouldn't be the Miao Yan I am today if not for what happened when I was thirteen."

"Does Du Sheng know any of this?"

"No. That's why I said I'm not sure if I loved him," she said. "Maybe I just can never trust a man. He's a good guy but not meant for me. Maybe no guys are meant for a wild goose like me."

"If you don't love him, why did you threaten him that you'd commit suicide?"

"I can't hide anything from you." Miao Yan laughed and walked back to the corner. We both sat. She said, "I like watching dramas, especially tragic ones, and I often feel as though I'm one of the main characters. But it's tiring to play somebody other than yourself all the time. Since I got to know Du Sheng I'd been trying to change myself to please him because I wanted his protection and love so badly. But I finally realized that I could never be the kind of girl he wanted me to be.

"Remember once I told you that I'm not afraid of death? I lied. The moment I told him I wanted to jump from the hotel window, I knew that I didn't dare. I couldn't believe I was such a coward so I told him again and again that I wanted to jump, each time becoming more and more certain that I didn't have the courage. Now I want to go back to Yunnan so badly, to where I can be myself, where nobody can control my mind. I've been dreaming of the bamboo hut under the mountain and my family, relatives, and friends who've never been out of Yunnan all their lives."

We were silent for a few minutes. I was trying to visualize the bamboo hut where Miao Yan had lived as a child. I had never been to Yunnan but the pictures of it, of her hometown, came so naturally that in my mind I could see her, in a richly embroidered Miao costume, running and singing aloud on the bank of a creek near the bamboo hut she and her grand-parents lived in. The creek was so clear that I could picture the waving weeds and the pebbles in the riverbed. In my imagina-tion I was sitting on a big rock in the creek, paddling and yelling her name.

"Why are you smiling? What are you thinking?" Miao Yan nudged me.

"Nothing." I was still smiling. I thought she would laugh at me if I told her the truth.

"You're trickier than I thought." She smiled, too. "Let's cheer for you becoming an adult and applaud for my return-ing to my hometown." She clenched her right hand and ex-tended it high in the air, holding an imaginary wineglass. I held up my right fist and bumped it against hers.

After downing the imaginary wine, she winked at me. "You know what I want to do when I have a lot of money?"

"Become a model," I replied.

"You silly girl. When you don't have money you want to become a model. But when you have money," she paused, smiling, "you want to open your own business. I'd like to own a boutique, selling women's designer clothes. Maybe I'll have my own brand someday. Something called 'Miao Chameleon.'"

"If you had a store like that I'd work as your cashier."

"A deal!" Then she thought of something else. "Could you do me a favor?"

"Sure."

"When the eighty-story skyscraper in Guangzhou is built, could you go to the highest floor and tell me what the view is like?"

"We can go together."

"I mean if somehow I can't visit you then."

"Yes, of course. I'll do that for you."

"Also, if you can find a café there, remember to order tiramisu for me."

I nodded sincerely—I knew tiramisu was her favorite dessert.

She put her arm around my shoulders and pulled my head against hers. She began to whistle a folk song. I sat right next to her, listening quietly and attentively. She was not a good whistler; it was more like the sound of a mother whistling to make her baby pee. When she went badly off-key she would switch to another song.

At some point my eyes started to get watery, listening to her, wishing it would never end. In the beginning I could still see the rooftop as a big white square expanse but it seemed to be losing its color and shape. Finally I could see nothing but my own tears. As Miao Yan, also tearful, began to whistle *Two Little Rats* she went completely off-tune. I burst out laughing. I laughed and laughed though my stomach was hurting and tears were streaming down my cheeks into my mouth. I knew it would be a long while before she and I would come to the rooftop again.

Around six I walked her to the university's main entrance. She stopped a red taxi in her typical suicidal way of running out into the traffic. When we parted she gave me a white box and made me promise I wouldn't open it until she was gone. I agreed.

"You'll come back to see me soon, right?" I said, holding

her arm tightly. She was wearing the same gray sweater-dress, now buttoned and with the waist strap tied, her hair braided like ropes on both sides of her face. All of her luggage was a small green suitcase.

"Of course. I promise. Once I settle down I'll come back to see you." She rubbed my head and messed up my hair, as people often do to children.

In no time the taxi was gone. Before it disappeared I saw her waving frantically from the window. I ran after it and was still waving long after the taxi had disappeared into the traffic.

After I returned to my room I opened the box. There, folded neatly, were the floral-patterned silk blouse she had worn the night we first met and the French-brand black dress she had made me put on. Underneath was a brand-new *Fortress Besieged*. On the front page she had written: "I stole your copy from your bookshelf a few days ago. Please let me keep it as a souvenir. I don't know what'll happen between us in the future. But I wanted you to know that you're always in my heart."

Inside the book was a birthday card with a 3D bird on the cover. When I opened the card, out came the cheerful "Happy Birthday to You" music. In the empty space was Miao Yan's childish handwriting: "Happy birthday, my poet, my silly girl, my little kitten, my sunshine. Make a wish and maybe I'll have a surprise for you."

I unfolded the blouse and examined it—time to solve the puzzle of her denying its existence. The blouse was handmade and I could see the uneven stitches along the seams and the occasional stray thread emerging from the fabric. Inside the collar where the brand tag would normally have been, were small, embroidered characters: "From baba and mama, 1989."

212

So it had been a gift from her parents when she left home for university.

Sang Wei was gone. Miao Yan was gone. I lay on my naked bed, lifting the silk blouse in front of me against the twilight coming in from the open door. The blouse fluttered in the breeze. I pulled it back, covered my face with it, and closed my eyes, feeling I had walked into a dream: I was swimming fearlessly in an ocean in the purest darkness. I was chasing floating flames on the water, trying to catch them, though the heat scorched my skin and almost blinded my eyes. But I couldn't catch the flames—the waves from nowhere pushed me away whenever I got near.

When Du Sheng asked for me through the speaker I was in a deep sleep—I had fallen asleep with the silk blouse over my face. I got up hurriedly and fumbled for my shoes. It was dark. In a sudden move I bumped my head on a corner of Yishu's desk. The dizziness was instant and fierce, forcing me to sit on the floor. After my eyes adjusted to the darkness I looked at my clock. It was almost eleven.

Neither Pingping nor Donghua was home. The mosquito nets and bedding on their beds had been removed. Maybe the two of them were in the washroom or maybe they were on their trains back home—I didn't remember if their trains were tonight or tomorrow night. I felt my way to the light switch near the door. After switching it on and off a few times I realized that the bulb must have blown. In the darkness I suddenly felt lonely; I was almost eager to leave my room.

Not wanting Du Sheng to see that I had just got out of bed, I went to the washroom and splashed cold water on my face. The water streamed along my arms and wet my sweater and jeans so I had to go back and change. Before I went downstairs I realized that I had forgotten to comb my hair. I went to the washroom again and ran my wet fingers through my unkempt hair.

Du Sheng was leaning against a wall with his hands crossed over his chest. He looked tired. His face was a little paler. His hair had grown a little too long on the sides.

I thought of Miao Yan instantly. "Why are you here?" I said, in such an unfriendly way that I surprised myself.

"Did I wake you up?"

"I was reading."

"It must be a really good book." He smiled, then looked at his watch. "I hope you don't mind me calling you at this hour. Miao Yan asked me to meet her here tonight but there's no one in her room. I was considering camping outside your dorm tonight. Where is she?"

I ignored his sarcasm. "She took an evening train to Yunnan." Having said that, my eyes became moist. I turned away, pretending that I was looking at the sky.

"Really? She asked me to see her tonight and told me that she wasn't leaving until tomorrow. I should have guessed that she wasn't telling me the truth." He stroked his chin. "If you don't have a plan tonight, perhaps we can go to a café somewhere. I don't have many friends in Guangzhou."

I had nothing to do and nowhere to go. The last thing I wanted was to stay in my dark room alone.

"Did you see her before she took off?" he asked when we were out on the road.

"Yes. We talked on the rooftop for a while."

214

"What rooftop?"

"Oh, nothing. It's just where Miao Yan and I first met and used to go often. It's the top of the building."

"What do you see there? What do you do?"

"It's just an empty space," I said. "A boring place, like any other flat roof." As I said it I looked over my shoulder unwittingly—I couldn't see the rooftop. Six hours ago, there on the rooftop, Miao Yan and I had been sitting close to each other. I could still feel her warmth and her touch. "I go there to play the violin. That's it," I added. The rooftop was such a secret between Miao Yan and me that I didn't even want to hear others mention it.

"Oh, I see. Guess I shouldn't be so nosy." He put his index finger to his lips, indicating he should shut up.

We walked side by side toward the library. The thick layers of fallen leaves crunched under our feet—workers weren't sweeping the road as often since finals ended. Only a week ago Sang Wei and I had walked on the same road, in the same yellowish light, around the same hour. Now I was standing next to Du Sheng, another ex-lover of Miao Yan's. How strange and ridiculous!

I was trying to remember what Sang Wei looked like but his face kept merging with images of other people I knew or had seen in the past. I didn't know him well and would never date someone that Miao Yan had dated, I thought. I glanced at Du Sheng. He looked jovial and relaxed.

The air was chilly. My teeth chattered. Du Sheng took off his black wool coat and put it on me. I tried to refuse but he insisted. After resisting briefly I succumbed to the warmth. With his help I put my arms into the sleeves and buttoned it all the way up to my neck. It was long and heavy, almost reaching the ground.

"Aren't you cold?" I asked. He had only a V-neck sweater on with a white shirt underneath.

"Don't worry about me. I never feel cold when I'm with a girl." As soon as he said that his teeth started to chatter. We both laughed, then I told him that I would be eighteen in a few hours.

"So tomorrow you'll wake up as an adult. We should celebrate tonight. Tell me, what's your number one wish? I promise I'll do whatever you want tonight."

I didn't know what I wanted to do. I wondered what Miao Yan would have done on an evening like this. She would certainly have gone dancing. I remembered she once said that dancing was the best medicine. "I want to dance," I said. "Not the disco type of dancing, but social dancing, the type of dancing for adults."

"Good idea. I haven't been to a dance hall for a long time. But . . ." He frowned, looking at my sweater, jeans, and running shoes.

"I have a dress!" I immediately regretted my words, but I couldn't control my desire to put it on. Tonight was my night and I wanted to look pretty.

We walked back to West Five. I closed the door to my room and removed my clothes. Though it was dark, I quickly found the white box. I took out the black dress and put it on. It took me a few tries to zip it up properly. The window was wide open but I felt warm. There was no full-length mirror in my room. I opened the door, letting in the light from the hallway, closed the window, and pulled Yishu's desk to the middle of the room. I stood on the desk and studied my reflection in the now mirror-like window glass.

Shoes! High-heeled shoes! I jumped down and switched on a torch to search under Pingping's bed—she wore my size.

I found a black pair and slipped them on. They fit perfectly. The heels were thin, and at least five inches high. When I stood I almost lost my balance. At first I had to put my hands on the desks or bed frames to support myself, but after practicing for a few minutes I could walk unaided.

One hand holding the torch, I examined my face in the mirror. I combed my hair the way Miao Yan had done for me when I had first tried on the dress. Then I found some dark purple eye shadow and rose-red lipstick in Pingping's makeup box. After applying them, I sprayed jasmine-scented perfume, which I had found on Donghua's desk, on my neck, hair, chest, and hands. Before heading out, I put on a red, knee-length, double-breasted coat and fastened all the buttons. It was my seventeenth birthday gift from my mother. I had never worn it before.

When I walked out, Du Sheng seemed surprised by how quickly I had changed.

"Only ten minutes and seven seconds. You were fast," he said, smiling. "Are you going to dance in that coat?"

"I'm wearing a dress under it, of course!"

"That's nice. What color?"

"Can we go now?" I said.

"Sure, ma'am," he said, still smiling.

We hailed a taxi and I told the driver to go to the Blue Moon Ballroom next to the White Swan Hotel on Shamian Island. Miao Yan had often mentioned this ballroom to me and told me it was the city's best. She must have been a waitress there. Apart from when I went to the Dynasty Disco with her, it was only the second time I had stepped into a dance hall. I didn't even know how to dance basic steps like the fox-trot and waltz.

The taxi stopped at the front entrance. A slim guy in a

white shirt and black vest ran over to open the door. Inside, two rows of girls in traditional blue Chinese dresses stood on both sides of the lobby. One came over to help me remove my coat. I told her I preferred to do it myself. It seemed to take forever to undo all the buttons. When I finally removed my coat and gave it to the girl she looked at me admiringly.

I walked straight toward the main dance hall. With each step I had to place my foot forcefully, as if hammering a nail into the carpet. To resist leaning forward I lifted my neck and stuck out my chest. It was the heels. Without looking down, I could see the ridge that my breasts formed. Because the bottom of the dress enclosed my thighs, I couldn't walk fast but had to perform a catwalk, as Miao Yan had done whenever she showcased her new outfits. I noticed that the passersby, guys and girls, were looking at me. Even the waiters and waitresses smiled and nodded at me as they hurried in and out of the hall.

Du Sheng didn't catch up until I was almost inside the ballroom. He walked silently, turning occasionally to look at me. An usher led us to a table for two. When I sat I had a strange feeling of loss, of losing my sense of who I was and of being transformed into someone else. This new person had a lot more in common with Miao Yan than with me. It was a strange metamorphosis I couldn't understand clearly.

The music was a tango. In the center of the dance floor a man was teaching his partner the steps. He wore a white shirt tucked into a pair of dressy black pants. Every few seconds he would stop and correct his partner's steps, then they would strike a pose and wait until the next rhythm started. He danced like a professional, his head moving swiftly with each turn of the music, his back erect. His partner, however, looked absentminded. She moved casually and swung her legs around, her eyes wandering about. She wore a wide-bottomed silver dress that reached her ankles and a pair of white high-heeled shoes. Her face looked familiar but I couldn't remember where I had seen her.

When the music climaxed, the girl pushed the guy aside and walked off the dance floor. She passed by my table, throwing me an unfriendly glance, and quickened her pace. When she was almost out of the sitting area, she stopped and suddenly turned. We stared at each other briefly, then she smiled like a blossoming flower. She lifted her right hand elegantly, put her fingers to her lips, and blew me a kiss before disappearing beyond the tables into the crowd. I recognized her—the cigarette salesgirl I had met at the Dynasty Disco.

The tango music switched to the slow and romantic "Swan Lake." People got up and swirled onto the dance floor. Du Sheng had been silent apart from ordering wine for himself and apple juice for me. A few times he studied my hands on the table as if he found them interesting. I felt my hands melting under his gaze but I didn't move them away.

The air-conditioning started to blow cool air. Du Sheng asked me if I wanted to dance. I said I only liked to watch others dance. We said no more. Then he downed his glass of wine and ordered a whole bottle. Just as the waiter was about to head toward the bar to fill the order, I stopped him and asked him to bring me a glass.

When the wine arrived, Du Sheng lifted the bottle gingerly and was about to pour me some. Then he changed his mind. He turned my glass upside down and said that as I was not yet eighteen years old, I should not drink alcohol. I said I had never drunk alcohol and wanted to taste it. I said I thought the wine would taste like strawberry juice. I turned my glass right side up, took the bottle from his hand, and poured. I filled half the glass and kept pouring. He took the bottle away. We looked at each other silently. I lifted my glass and gulped the wine. The red liquid flew down my throat into my stomach, leaving a sweet and spicy taste on my tongue. I put down the glass arrogantly, my eyes fixed on Du Sheng's face. I was about to say that the wine tasted just like strawberry juice when I felt heat in my stomach, as if a bonfire had been lit.

Du Sheng kept drinking. Within two songs, he had drunk all the wine in his glass and the rest in the bottle. I joked about how fast he was drinking, saying there wasn't a drought. He said my face was as red as the national flag and he was afraid I would get drunk.

My brain was getting warm, then numb, then swelling as if it would expand into a big balloon and fly from my body, free from the gravity of Earth. The flying sensation made me happy and excited. I stopped a waitress and ordered a glass of wine for myself. After I took a sip Du Sheng took the glass away from me and drank it in one gulp. Then he stood and said he was going to send me back to my dorm for the night.

On our way out he walked on my right, suggesting that I rest my hand on top of his left arm. He smiled and said if he ever had any bad intentions I could use my more powerful right hand to defend myself. I smiled back at him. Miao Yan must have told him about this habit of mine. Whenever I walked with her, I would walk on her left side. She once asked me why but I could think of no explanation other than it being a habit. The next day she showed me a newspaper clipping that said people who liked to walk on the left tended to be more cautious and skeptical. The reason cited was that the right hand was typically stronger and more agile and could react to sudden attacks more quickly.

Though my face and chest were burning I could still walk. But I put my hand on his arm, afraid that my high heels couldn't support my weight. My toes hurt with every step. How I missed my flat shoes! They were so comfortable, so springy. Why must women torture themselves to look sexy? I thought.

We walked through the dance hall. "Happy birthday!" he whispered in my ear.

In the lobby, an attendant brought my coat and began to help me put it on. Du Sheng took over and waved her away. He also fastened all the buttons and moved a few strands of hair from my cheeks to behind my ears. "I have hands," I protested. He smiled.

I told him that I didn't want to go back to the university. I said it was my eighteenth birthday and I wanted something special. He said he would do whatever I wanted. I lifted my hand and pointed to the luxuriously decorated White Swan Hotel across the street. "I want to sleep there. I've never slept in a hotel room," I said. It was the truth. As far back as I could remember, I had never slept anywhere but at home or in student dormitories.

He was thinking hard but finally nodded. I said that if that hotel was too expensive, I wouldn't mind staying somewhere cheaper. He laughed the way that an older brother, if I'd had one, would have laughed. He said I was really just a little girl who knew nothing.

I was irritated. "I know everything and nobody can treat me like a kid," I asserted. I also said I would refuse to speak to him if he dared to treat me like a kid.

He didn't argue. He stood in front of me, smiling, then combed my hair with his fingers. "I wish you were a few years older," he said.

We entered the hotel. While he spoke with the receptionist I sat on a leather armchair in the middle of the lobby. I kicked off my shoes—they were killing me. But when I saw a uniformed bellboy walking by I quickly put them on again. He smiled at me and I smiled back. I crossed my legs, put my arms on the armrests, tilted my head backward—I wanted to look older. When Du Sheng returned, I glimpsed the clock on the marble wall opposite. It was seven minutes to three.

It was just the two of us in the elevator. When it reached the eighteenth floor, it stopped with an alarming *ding* and the sliding door opened. I wanted to ask Du Sheng if he had deliberately booked the rooms on this floor, but I said nothing—my head was heavy, my throat itchy.

I followed him into a room with two queen-size beds. He settled me on one and turned on the lamp above the headboard. He walked to the liquor counter, removed a jug from the cabinet, and filled it with water. He poured the water into a tea kettle, plugged in the power cord, and opened a tea bag. He said, his back to me, that he had booked two rooms and that his room was next door. For a while the only sound I could hear was the sizzling of the kettle as it warmed up.

He asked me if I was feeling better. I said I was a little dizzy but other than that I was feeling great. "Why are you standing so far away?" I asked. He didn't answer. Instead he asked me if I hated him because he had broken up with Miao Yan and hadn't made her stay in Guangdong.

I shook my head and laughed. "Of course not," I said. "Her leaving has nothing to do with you. She left because she didn't like me anymore. I was too naive, a silly girl. I couldn't help her, not even give her any advice."

I felt warm so I took off my coat and slipped under the coverlet with my head on the pillow. Du Sheng sat on the edge of my bed. "Want some tea?" he asked.

As soon as I lay down the effects of the alcohol increased. I had a severe headache. I had never thought I would react so strongly to alcohol. I closed my eyes, hoping to fall asleep, but a string of stacked rooftops appeared in my mind—red, white, gray, blue, and some unspeakable colors—flying in the sky like magic carpets.

Du Sheng touched my cheeks lightly, as if he somehow thought my face was made of paper. I could hear his breathing as he leaned over me and felt the heat of his breath on my cheeks and lips.

I opened my eyes. He was still sitting on my bed, where he had been earlier. I asked why he had left Miao Yan after he had made love with her and why he didn't marry her. I don't know whether I was only thinking about asking the questions rather than saying them out loud, or he hadn't heard what I said, but he didn't respond. He just stared into my eyes. Then I asked him—or, again, I thought I was asking him—if Miao Yan would come back to see me. He still didn't reply.

I sat up, startling him. He jumped up, looking ashamed, embarrassed, and frustrated. He walked to the window, pulled open the thick velvet curtains, and put both hands on the sill, breathing heavily. "What are you thinking about?" I asked. He looked at the window, reflecting my image, and said he was going to send me back to the university. After a pause he added that he might not be able to control himself if we stayed together in the room for another five minutes. His voice trembling, his head bowed, he looked exhausted.

"Make love to me," I demanded. "I want to make love to a man. I want to grow up."

At the window, Du Sheng buried his face in the curtains.

I continued, "I want to become a woman, a real woman like Miao Yan. Make love to me now and make me a woman."

He said something about going to call a taxi to send me home. He said more, but I couldn't make it out.

"Can you make love with yourself, here, in front of me?" I asked.

He turned around and murmured that I was torturing him.

I repeated my question, louder, as though I was asking a class of schoolchildren what water is made from. I was in the mood for talking. I talked about how I always spent time alone in the dark attic when I was a kid. I talked about the night Miao Yan and I first met on the roof. I talked about the porn magazine I had read in the dorm and the class I was asked to leave. I said I had never watched porn videos or movies, had never masturbated because I felt too ashamed to touch my own body and thought it dirty. I said my roommate Donghua would touch herself when she thought we were asleep. I said I was scared the first time I heard her soft panting and her long, satisfied sigh at the end.

I said that I didn't know what making love was about until a few months ago. My parents and teachers never told me anything about it and even Miao Yan wouldn't talk about it with me since she considered me a child. I said Miao Yan had promised to tell me everything when I turned eighteen but had left without telling me anything. I talked and talked. I talked as if I would become mute after the evening, as if talking was the only remedy for all my problems.

Du Sheng slowly turned to face me. He nodded periodically while I was talking.

I was thirsty when I finished talking. Without being asked, he walked to the liquor cabinet, poured water into a glass, and handed it to me. I drank it greedily, gave him the empty glass, and slipped back underneath the coverlet with my head against the headboard.

Footsteps echoed in the hallway outside, mixed with broken dialogue in a foreign language. Water bubbled in the kettle—it had been boiling for a while. I asked Du Sheng to open the window. I looked out and saw the lights of the distant skyscrapers.

He sat down next to me on the bed. "Do you really want to see me masturbate?" he asked, his voice calm and tender. I said yes. He then asked if I would mind if he turned off the light. I said I wouldn't mind. He said I could still see him by the light from outside. He said he had never done anything like this in front of a girl, not even with Miao Yan, and it sounded ridiculous to him at first. "But it didn't sound so ridiculous after hearing your confession," he said.

Du Sheng turned off all the lights. I sat on the bed, the coverlet over my legs. When he passed, he bent and kissed me lightly on the cheeks. He was about to kiss my lips but stopped halfway. He stood so close that I could see his pupils glint and hear his heartbeat. He gazed at me, unblinking, then walked to the other bed, placing a box of tissues on the nightstand.

With his back to me, Du Sheng started to remove his sweater and pants, then his shirt and underwear. He did everything with both hands, slowly and elegantly. He didn't turn even once to look at me.

By the light from outside I could see his smooth skin and bulging biceps. His lean, masculine hips had a nice curve to them. I studied his naked body without embarrassment or nervousness. It was quiet in the room except for the rustling of his clothes.

He lay down. He seemed tired. He spread his legs apart and put his hands on his thighs. He didn't move for a few minutes. As I was wondering whether I should get up and cover him with a blanket, he started to stroke his penis, caressing it with one hand. At first his movement was slow, as if his hand was carrying a lot of weight. But as his penis became erect he quickened his motion. He began to groan, a groan that sounded to me like a mix of happiness and pain, suggesting something meditative and religious . . .

I closed my eyes, slipped under the coverlet quietly, and covered myself from head to toe. I felt I was sleeping on the bare cement of the rooftop of West Five. It must have been past four o'clock. At this hour the rooftop would be empty and lonely as a graveyard. No one, not even I, would visit it at this early hour. There was no moon tonight. I couldn't imagine what the rooftop would look like without moonlight and people.

It was time to make my birthday wish. I wished that when the clock reached exactly five forty-three, my birth time, there would be bright sunshine and my dorm room would be lit up as if newly painted. But I knew it was just a wish. It would still be dark then, as dark as it was right now, since it was winter and the sun wouldn't rise until after six thirty.

I could hold back my tears no longer. I heard myself whimpering. The groaning from Du Sheng stopped.

226

My whimpering became sobbing, then full-lunged weeping. I cried because I knew I would never want to see Du Sheng again. Because I didn't know why things were happening the way they were. Because I didn't know how to face my parents when I went home. Because there were still so many questions that would remain unanswered when I finally turned eighteen . . .

2

All this happened ten years ago and I have not seen Miao Yan since. When I turned nineteen I received a birthday card from her. Her handwriting was the same—coarse and childish. "Happy birthday, my little poet," she wrote. There was no return address, nor a phone number. The postmark was too smudged to decipher its origin. I wondered if she was still living in her tiny hometown with her family, if she was married, what her life was like. I wanted to know all these things yet I was afraid to bring back the memories. Even if she had enclosed her contact information, I doubt I would have called or written back.

At nineteen, I was tormented by the idea that she had abandoned me, like an irresponsible and selfish parent abandoning her child. I was obsessed with the notion that she might have deliberately arranged for me to be with Du Sheng that evening, so she could leave me without guilt. Didn't she say something like "I want somebody to take care of you when I'm away"? That must have been so, or she wouldn't have invited him to see her when she knew she would already be gone. She wanted me to have sex with Du Sheng. Perhaps she thought that was how I could become a woman—having sex with a man. She might have worried that I would end up having sex with a bad guy, as she had, so she picked Du Sheng—a man she had loved and trusted—to help me realize my womanhood and discover my sexuality. But if that was true I couldn't appreciate her thoughtfulness. I saw something else. I saw myself as having been enslaved by my devotion to her, which was why I had always obeyed her and had done what she told me. I saw her fear of my growing up—that she didn't need another woman in her life. My being her white daisy was what she had wanted and cherished. As soon as I grew up, she left me and no longer wanted to see me. She had manipulated me and my devotion to her. As I had become like her, I had lost her and myself.

Or she might have sensed a danger in my attachment to her so she decided to leave me. Didn't she say, "Don't like me too much, it's dangerous"? To have an excuse to leave, she let Du Sheng fall in love with me and arranged for us to spend the evening together so she could claim later that she had to leave me because I was involved with her ex-lover.

I often came up with different theories and speculations, different reasons. Since I couldn't get any confirmation I tormented myself with endless guessing. Out of frustration, I resented her for leaving me and resented my devotion to her.

The week I graduated I received another card from her. The postmark was Beijing. "Congratulations!" she wrote. At the bottom of the card, in small letters, she wrote: "My father passed away a few months ago." Again, there was no return address or phone number.

By now my resentment had faded and I started to think that she hadn't come to see me because she wanted to forget her past, or thought I would do better in my life without her.

If I could, I would have contacted her. But as she had said, she was a wild goose with no sense of home. She might have sent me more postcards—or even letters—after I graduated. If so, they were probably destroyed by the post office because I moved around a lot and with no return address the post office couldn't return the mail to her.

Sang Wei became my first boyfriend. After the winter break when I turned eighteen, he returned to the university and the first thing he did was come and see me in West Five. After that we saw each other often and sometimes strolled around the campus in the evening, as Miao Yan and I had done. The day I confided in him how I spent my eighteenth birthday, we became boyfriend and girlfriend. By then he was teaching at a local college. We never talked about Miao Yan or Du Sheng—they were taboo—but I could sense the uneasiness and awkwardness this careful avoidance had brought to the relationship. Sometimes, in the middle of a casual conversation, he would stop and stare at me with a puzzled expression. Or when we were kissing I would turn away from him suddenly.

He disliked my smoking, a habit I had picked up, though not heavily, during my second year, but I suspected that what he really disliked was how much it reminded him of Miao Yan. One day, at the beginning of my final year, I told him that I couldn't continue our relationship.

"Did you meet another man?" he asked.

"No."

"So it's about Miao Yan?"

"I guess so. I think about her when I make love to you. I feel like I live in her shadow. I feel like I'm sharing you with her. I feel like I'm actually her."

"Don't be silly. I knew her before I met you. It was so brief that I wouldn't even call it a relationship. You said you'd forgive me."

"It's not about that."

"What's it about?"

"It's about me."

"Tell me, then." He sat beside me and touched my face, his hand warm and trembling.

"I can't. I don't know where to start."

"Why can't you?"

"Because I haven't figured it out myself. What if I can never stop thinking about her for the rest of my life?"

"Why can't you forget the past? She's the past, everything about me and her is the past, everything about you and her is the past. We don't even know where she is. We're together now. Isn't that what matters? Why do you attach yourself to the past and refuse to move on? Did you ever ask me how I felt about the night you saw her boyfriend masturbating? You said he didn't touch you. Why should I believe you? For God's sake, what kind of girl would watch her best friend's boyfriend masturbate? When I met you, I thought you were innocent and pure but now I don't know what to think."

He swiped a glass vase from the table with his arm. It smashed to pieces on the floor. That was the last time I saw him.

I didn't go to graduate school after graduation, though all my professors wanted me to. In my final year I suddenly became tired of studying and wanted to explore the real world. By then the job market was booming and it was easy to obtain permanent residence in Guangdong. I took a government job as an office secretary in Guangzhou. It bored me more quickly than I had expected. I was especially averse to the social activities I had to endure as part of the job—all the single girls in my office had to attend dinners or parties held for officials from Beijing or other higher authorities and to drink and dance with them. During one party a high-ranking official put his arms around my waist and asked me to down a glass of hard liquor. When I refused he threw the glass onto the floor. I quit the next day and began frequent job switching—copy editor, reporter, saleswoman, bar waitress, business analyst, freelance writer—until I became exhausted and settled down at an editorial job with a reference and textbook publisher.

With my busy life I gradually forgot Miao Yan, forgot my resentment toward her, and forgot my struggle with my past. I made new friends and became close to some, though I never mentioned Miao Yan to them. Most of my classmates, including Pingping and Donghua, stayed in Guangzhou and I saw them from time to time for coffee, movies, or shopping. Both Pingping and Donghua were married and had a child. I still read a great deal but no longer played the violin or wrote poems—I just didn't feel like it. I'm not sure when the girlishness in me began to fade and I started to walk, speak, and act like a woman. Maturity: that is what people call it.

Along with my frequent job switching I began to be interested in men again and had various boyfriends. We met, sparkled, got excited and involved, then parted in less than a year as my infatuation faded. This became such an entrenched pattern that in the end I had to stop dating to avoid more emotional damage to myself and others. I was alone for a year before I met my husband during an assignment editing a medical reference book. He was the author and a cardiologist.

If my parents hadn't urged me to get married I would probably have remained single. But they called daily, sometimes twice a day. I hated to upset them—after all, I already lived so far away. They often said Guangzhou was a complicated capitalist world and I should be with a man whom I could trust and depend on.

For them my husband—then my boyfriend—was perfect. He was in his early thirties, had a degree in medicine and a successful career, and—most important—he was honest and trustworthy. So we got married the year I turned twenty-six and soon moved into a two-bedroom condo his hospital had assigned to him downtown. Sex was all right but we never got really passionate about it. He often worked late in the operating theater and was exhausted when he got home, while I always thought there was something wrong when we made love—the position was wrong, the foreplay was too short, the timing of the orgasm was off . . .

We never talked about our sex life. We hardly talked at all—he was a quiet person. When I was cooking he would sit on a stool in a corner of the kitchen, reading newspapers to keep me company. He cared about me and would buy me flowers and expensive gifts for no particular reason. When we could spend a whole evening together we sometimes cuddled on the sofa watching a movie. Neither of us was eager to have a child right away, so life continued smoothly. Day in and day out we went to work and came back home, ate dinner separately most of the time, went to bed at different hours, ran errands or visited friends together on the weekends, and made love when we felt like it, which was not often.

After we had been married for about a year I found myself thinking of Miao Yan occasionally when I was cooking, watching TV, talking with friends, or even at work. The same old questions returned—where was she? Was she married? What did she look like now? These were never more than fleeting thoughts. Life and work kept me busy.

One night I woke in the middle of the night and looked at my husband beside me. Listening to his periodic snoring, I wondered what life really meant to me. I asked myself if I loved him, if I was happy and content as everyone thought, if there was something missing in my life. When I let my mind wander, I thought of Miao Yan and felt an aching longing to see her—to tell her about my life, my lackluster marriage and job, and hear what she would say. I missed her unrestrained laughter, her perfume, the rhythm of her high-heeled shoes on the floor, her nicknames for me. I missed the passion and intimacy that I had never felt with anybody else, including my parents, my other girlfriends, my ex-boyfriends, even my husband. Then it occurred to me that life without her was a bore.

Four months later, my husband and I divorced.

Sometimes I wonder if what I was really yearning for was the kind of devoted passion I no longer possessed as an adult. "Not growing up is a good thing," as Miao Yan had said.

⌒

I call home on Friday the week before I am to fly to the United States—I have been admitted to a university in New York to study comparative literature. My mother picks up the phone. I tell her: it's hot in Guangzhou and every day the temperature is above thirty-five degrees; the price of meat has gone up ten percent compared with last year; motorcycles will

233

be prohibited on major streets; car prices have gone down and many of my coworkers are buying cars; the apartment building I'm living in will be torn down next month.

"Your father's and my salaries won't be enough for us to live there. We've been teaching for more than twenty years yet your salary is three times ours." My mother sighs but soon cheers up. "You've got to come home to see the newly renovated Eight One Square. It's very grand. Your father sometimes takes his students there and tells them the history of Nanchang."

"How's Baba?" I ask.

"A literary journal just accepted one of his papers on Lu Xun. Nanchang University is inviting him to teach a summer class. These days he writes day and night. He says he must make up for lost time. He's in his study right now. Let me put him on the phone."

"Don't interrupt him. I'll talk to him next time."

"We worry about you. You don't know anybody in the U.S. It's hard for a woman your age to get a PhD. If you had gone straight to the PhD program after graduating it would have been better. Also, now you're divorced—"

"I'll be fine."

"Are you sure you don't want us to see you off at the airport?"

"It's high travel season. Guangzhou's jammed with workers from other provinces. You'll have a hard time getting tickets."

"Then promise your father and me that you'll come back home every . . ." Her voice dies into an almost inaudible croaking.

"I promise," I say, holding the telephone tightly. I am silent for a while, then ask: "Ma, do you recall telling me not to expect others to approve of my choices in life?"

"Did I say that?" She stops sobbing, then laughs. "I don't remember. I'm getting old. We have only one daughter and we want you to be happy."

We chat a little more and I tell her I will call every evening before my trip.

After hanging up I go down to a noodle place across the street. A young Cantonese couple owns it and they greet me in their poor Mandarin. I order a bowl of fish porridge and a plate of shrimp-stuffed flat noodles. Nothing tastes better to me than warm flat noodles with soy sauce. Nowadays all my Cantonese friends have learned to speak Mandarin. They criticize me for not learning Cantonese. "Bad attitude," they often say. I argue that they all speak Mandarin so well anyway and there are probably more native Mandarin speakers than native Cantonese speakers in Guangzhou. Truthfully, though, there is no excuse but my own laziness.

By the time I've finished eating it is nine o'clock. I decide to take the ferry downtown. The boat is much bigger and newer than the one Miao Yan and I took years ago. The fare has gone up from fifty fen to three yuan. I don't know where I want to go until I am on Beijing Road, a pedestrian-only street in the evenings. The nightlife has just begun—neon lights blazing, loud music blaring from the stores lining the street. I keep walking, hearing passersby speaking all kinds of different dialects—Cantonese, Mandarin, Shanghainese, Kejia, Fujianese, Hunanese, Sichuanese, and other dialects I can't recognize. I see foreigners, too. They look around like little kids, constantly distracted by the noise and action around them. When I pass by a crowd outside a store I stop. Two girls in white miniskirts and pink knee-high boots are standing at the store entrance, clapping their hands to attract attention. They are promoting a new selection of fruit-scented condoms. "Ma, are those candies?" asks a passing nine- or ten-year-old boy. His mother does not reply but pulls him closer and quickens her pace.

I am going to visit a gay bar I've read about on the internet. According to the article it is also for heterosexuals but people there are liberal toward homosexuals, who still live underground, afraid of revealing their sexual orientation, though homosexuality is no longer classified as a "mental illness." Comrades: that is how homosexuals refer to themselves.

The cover charge is high and the bar, with its muted lighting, artsy decor, and handsome waiters and waitresses, looks much like other upmarket bars in Guangzhou. Most customers are in pairs—man and woman. I sit and order a glass of merlot. To my surprise, I don't see the expected scenes of same-sex hugging and kissing. In a corner two girls sit closely on a bench but they're not doing anything other than chatting. They look awfully young, perhaps in their late teens. The short hair of the girl on the right is dyed bright red and she wears a nose-ring. At the table next to me is a young couple sharing one beer, the woman giggling at something the man has just drawn on a napkin. In front of them a group of mixed gender seem to be celebrating someone's birthday.

I am the only one who is alone, which makes me uncomfortable. I finish the wine and order a bottle of Qingdao beer. After a few sips, I begin to smoke—I plan to leave in a few minutes.

"Hello." A woman walks elegantly toward me.

"Hey," I respond. For a fleeting moment I think I see Miao Yan. The woman is just as tall, about the same age, and has the same length hair. But of course she is not Miao Yan. Her face is thinner and paler, her eyes smaller, and her breasts protrude from her tight black top.

"How about a light?" She sits across from me, a cigarette between her fingers.

I light her cigarette.

"Expecting someone?"

"No." I meet her eyes.

"I've never seen you before."

"It's my first time here."

"I see." She nods meaningfully, then leans forward. "Nice earrings. Where did you get them?"

"Tibet. A coworker bought them for me as a gift."

"They look nice on you. May I touch them?"

I thank her for her compliment and am about to remove my earrings.

"A little innocence always makes a woman more alluring." She laughs. "I want to touch them when they're on you."

I watch as she inhales and exhales slowly, as though trying to refocus her thoughts, her eyes narrowed slightly.

"You remind me of an old friend of mine," I say, smiling. "We used to be very close."

"Where is she now?"

"Another continent. I've not seen her for years."

"Why are you here?" She taps her cigarette on the edge of the ashtray on the table.

"Just curious."

"Did you love her?"

"I loved her as my best friend."

"Nothing going on?"

"Like what?"

"What do you think?"

"Oh, no. It never occurred to me."

"Did you ever want to touch her or kiss her?"

I hesitate. "Sometimes."

"Did you want to have sex with her?"

"No." I lean back. "Never."

"Did she want to have sex with you?"

"I don't think so. She always had boyfriends. I don't think she was interested in girls. We liked each other as sisters, as family."

"You never know. Perhaps she wanted you but was afraid."

I shook my head.

"Did you ever make a move?"

"I had no desire."

"I've seen many women like you. You don't have the guts. You're too timid and too baffled." She takes my beer with her free hand and sips it slowly from where my lipstick is left, her stockinged leg stroking mine under the table.

I withdraw my leg.

She puts down my beer. "My first girlfriend was just like you when we started. She and I knew each other for many years before that. She later went to university here. A smart and pretty girl. But she couldn't face it and went to Australia."

I suddenly know who the woman is. That summer noon. Her dangling red purse and eye-catching yellow top as she walked around the campus with Yishu.

"I'm sorry to hear that, but I have to go," I say.

She raises an eyebrow and nods. "Will I see you again?"

"Probably not," I reply.

After putting a tip on the table, I start for the door, feeling her eyes on my back all the way.

I stroll down Beijing Road as the deepening night chills

the summer air. My high-heeled shoes are hurting so I hail a taxi. I ask the driver to drive around Shamian Island, Up and Down Ninth Street, Zhong Shan Fifth Road, Tianhe Book City, and a few other places I like to go to for shopping or leisure. I have never wanted to see the city as much as I do today—it's nothing close to perfect but it's where I'm most comfortable.

When I arrive at the eighty-story Citic Plaza, I get out of the taxi. The building, massive, blue, glimmering, stands like a door to a mysterious universe. I order espresso and two slices of tiramisu at a café on a high floor. Outside the huge floor-to-ceiling windows, the city spreads before my eyes: a vast collection of skyscrapers and neon lights, jammed traffic, sparsely distributed parks, and pedestrians at every corner.

I visit San Francisco during my first spring break. A few days before the visit I find myself losing sleep and becoming easily irritated. It is snowing heavily when I leave New York, but in San Francisco it is bright and smells of sunshine. As suggested by my guide book, I take the cable car to Fisherman's Wharf, then a bus to the Golden Gate Bridge. Surrounded by tourists like myself, I feel relaxed and comfortable. Nobody knows me. Nobody will judge me.

After dinner I take a bus to Chinatown. I don't know if Miao Yan still owns a boutique here or if she has moved out of San Francisco but I am not worried. Didn't she say that we had been connected in previous lives? If there is a thing called fate, I would put myself in its hands today. I know, when we meet, that I will have a good time—catching up, joking about my anxiety and frustration toward her, hearing her stories of moving around since university and her plans for the future, sharing the loss of innocence and the excitement of living in a new country.

I will talk with her like a woman, her equal, confidently, wisely, maturely, as if I was her twin sister. I have plenty of time and energy to stroll every street, every block, and in my mind's eye, there she is—appearing out of nowhere, just as she did when I saw her on the rooftop for the first time—examining a delicate dress with her long, thin fingers in the gentle light from above.

Acknowledgments

I feel extremely fortunate to have Toby Eady as my agent. I am forever inspired by his enthusiasm, wisdom, and, above all, boundless passion for enriching the communication between the West and the East. Thanks also go to Jennifer Joel, for her trust and hard work in introducing the book to the U.S.

I am grateful to Laetitia Rutherford, Jo Jarrah, Mary Verney, and especially Johanna Castillo, whose editorial acumen and dedication have made this book possible. And I would also like to thank Judith Curr for taking a chance on a new voice, and her staff for being so helpful and efficient.

Thanks to John Joss, a British-born writer and a fearless motorcyclist, for his editorial advice and friendship. From the very beginning, he has believed in my work.

My gratitude also goes to Alan Cheuse, Porter Shreve, and Tom Parker, all writers and teachers, whose encouragement came when it was most needed.

241

I must thank Sandra Cisneros and Xinran. They are women of class and kindness.

I am appreciative of my friends Daniel Barnett, Ryan Foon, Alfonso Lopez, David Dupouy, William Opdyke, Celia Chung, and the Macondo Workshop fellows for reading my writing.

I'm most thankful to Bernice Tsai, with whom I can share joys and sorrows, and An, Pey-Ning, Yu-Ling, Howard, Swati, Peg, Christine, Ed, Bill, and Sue for friendship.

And, finally, I am profoundly indebted to Mattias Cedergren, for his love, patience, and unwavering confidence in me.

february
FLOWERS

Fan Wu

A Readers Club Guide

QUESTIONS AND TOPICS FOR DISCUSSION

1. The narrator of *February Flowers* begins her tale with the words "After my marriage ends ..." (page 1), situating the reader in the midst of her life, akin to beginning "Hansel and Gretel" in the midst of their search for bread crumbs, trying to find their way home. Why do you think Ming chooses to begin her story in the middle and not at the beginning or even at the end? What does it tell us about the kind of story that we are about to be told? What effect does it have on us as readers?

2. Ming is portrayed as a cautious, serious, and even withdrawn teenager. Between her and Yan, it seems that Ming is the "good" girl and Yan is the "bad" girl. To what standards are both Yan and Ming conforming? Against what is each girl rebelling? What from Ming's past might be the cause of her evident caution and even disdain toward both the world in general and specifically toward men?

3. Why do you think Yan decides to embrace her sexuality and womanhood while Ming prefers to deny hers? What impact do you think their upbringing had on their notions of female sexuality? Does *February Flowers* seem to say that our childhoods impact how we view ourselves as we grow up, or that our natures are strictly innate?

4. Throughout the book, Ming makes many references to high heels, associating them particularly with Yan. "The sound of her heels clicking on the rooftop cement lingered in the air even after she had disappeared" (page 20). And at the end of the story, when Ming herself has taken to wearing high heels, she writes, "My high-heeled shoes are hurting ..." (page 239). Discuss how high heels could be viewed as a metaphor for Ming's perception of womanhood and sexuality.

5. Discuss Yan's attitude toward authority, specifically male authority, and contrast it to Ming's approach. Based on their histories, do their respective attitudes make sense to you? Why or why not?

6. What do you think is at the root of Yan's and Ming's relationship? If, as Yan seems to think, everyone uses everyone, of what use is Ming to Yan? What does Yan hope to gain through her friendship with Ming? Do you think Yan was as attached to Ming as Ming was to her?

7. Throughout the book, Ming is touted as the intellectual, while Yan is more sensual. Which approach to life, if either, do you think the author is advocating in *February Flowers*? Based on the book, which approach seems smarter? What exactly would you say constitutes intelligence in *February Flowers*?

8. Why do you think Ming, at the age of seventeen, has never experienced, as she says, "camaraderie" (page 45), or even intimacy, until she meets Yan? How do you think each is changed through their relationship with the other?

9. Why is gaining power over men so important to Yan, while Ming prefers to lose herself in books? What does each hope to gain? In what ways are the two women similar?

10. At the end of the book, Ming writes, "I have never wanted to see the city as much as I do today—it's nothing close to perfect but it's where I'm most comfortable" (page 239). Compare this perception of the city to the perception that she has upon first arriving at the university. Using Ming's changing feelings toward the city, can you track her growth? What does her perception of the

city at the end of the story tell us about how she has changed?

11. Throughout the story, it seems that Ming believes that someone like Yan can teach her how to become a woman. She writes that she was looking for someone "to help me realize my womanhood and discover my sexuality" (page 228). Does Ming learn how to realize her womanhood and discover her sexuality from Yan?

12. Near the end of the book, Ming visits a bar where she meets a woman. The woman says to her, "A little innocence always makes a woman more alluring" (page 237). By the end of the book, what does Ming learn about what actually makes a woman alluring?

13. Why do you think Yan disappears without letting Ming know that she is leaving? Do you think her leaving had anything to do with her relationship with Ming?

14. Why do you think Fan Wu entitled her book *February Flowers*? For what might "February flowers" be a metaphor?

15. If the narrator did not tell the reader that the story was set in 1991 China, how would one surmise this? What details does Fan Wu use to let the reader know where the story is set and in what time period?

16. Ming makes many references to the fond time that as a child she spent "alone in the dark attic" (page 224). Why do you think this memory is so strong and lingering for Ming? What does the dark attic represent to her?

17. It seems that Ming could have easily searched for and perhaps even found Yan once she had disappeared. Ming tells

us that she had so many questions to ask Yan, yet further writes, "I was afraid to bring back the memories. Even if she had enclosed her contact information, I doubt I would have called or written back" (page 227). Why do you think Ming was afraid to bring back these memories? What does Yan and that time represent to Ming?

18. In the end, what do you think Ming has lost? What has she gained? Do you think Ming would agree that the trade-off was worth it? Has whatever Ming has lost been replaced with something of more value?

19. One might say that Ming represents the China of old while Yan represents the China of new. This struggle between old and new seems to be alluded to throughout *February Flowers*. Discuss and find examples of how we see this struggle reflected in the city itself, the lives of the students at the university, and within the characters of Yan and Ming.

Wu, Fan, 1973-
February flowers : a novel

MAY 2012

CPSIA information can be obtained at www.ICGtesting.com
Printed in the USA
LVOW131046220412

278633LV00002B/5/P

9 781416 549437